Spinifex

Geoffrey Morlet was born in Perth in the 1930s and went to school first in WA then later in Victoria. He studied medicine at Adelaide University, and went on to specialise in ophthalmology, following his father's footsteps. Prior to specialising, he worked with the Royal Flying Doctor Service for two years, and then spent a year in a rural general practice. He then furthered his studies in the UK, having worked his passage there and back as a ship's doctor. He practised ophthalmology in Melbourne for some years before returning to Western Australia.

He is married to Elisabeth, with three children and nine grandchildren. He is still in practice, together with his son Nigel.

Spinifex

Geoffrey Morlet

LYTHRUM PRESS
Adelaide

Lythrum Press
54 Currie Street
Adelaide SA 5000
Tel: (08) 8415 5150

www.lythrumpress.com.au

Published 2005

Cover design Stacey Zass, Colorperception
Cover photographs Chris Barry (main photograph)
and Geoffrey Morlet

National Library of Australia
Cataloguing-in-Publication

Morlet, Geoffrey
Spinifex

ISBN 1 921013 07 9

I. Title

A823.4

Foreword

There is no doubt the Pilbara region of Western Australia is a unique area. The landscape can be both harsh and yet beautiful, with colours that defy description. Development of the region's abundant resources, in particular iron ore and natural gas, has resulted in considerable growth for the region. Whilst pastoralists, indigenous people and a few townsfolk were the original providers of essential services, they have been joined by engineers, miners, truck and train drivers and many others as towns have grown and developed.

Rural and remote areas of the region have relied and will continue to rely on young professionals to provide health and education services. Technology may have changed but the need for essential services remains the same. The Royal Flying Doctor Service of Australia is part of this big picture.

To capture the spirit and culture of those original characters and the land in which they lived and played is not easy, but Geoffrey Morlet has done so with uncanny accuracy.

For those of you who have spent some time in this region, memories of the heat, the isolation, the race days and picnics will come flooding back. For those who haven't, Geoffrey's descriptions will provide an accurate insight into life at that time.

Dr Bernard Cresswell
Past President
Royal Flying Doctor Service of Australia

Author's royalties from sales of *Spinifex* will go to
the Royal Flying Doctor Service.

Also by Geoffrey Morlet

The Journey

PART ONE

LEAVING HOME

Chapter 1

'Hurry up darling, we want to arrive before dark!' she called up the staircase.

Out in the street, light snow had started to fall, and people bustled past, rugged up against the cold. It was colder than usual for this time of the year, and more bad weather was forecast.

Matthew appeared at the top of the stairs wearing only a bath towel.

'Where are my thick socks, Penny?'

'In the laundry basket. Hurry up, we are waiting!'

'Come on Daddy, we're waiting,' Chloe echoed, standing beside her mother.

'Down in a minute!' he answered.

Finally they were ready. Penny had the bags by the front door and a hamper of sandwiches and hot drinks for the journey. Out in the street it was freezing. 'The coldest December for years,' they said on the news.

Matt helped Chloe and Penny into the estate, and then loaded the bags into the back. He wiped the snow off the windscreen before getting in, then switched on the ignition. The starter motor whined and the engine coughed and spluttered. On the third try it started, and Matt gunned it to 'blow out the cobwebs.' By the time they cleared the suburbs of London the snow was falling steadily, and visibility was bad.

'Sorry darling, we just have to go slowly, so we'll be late arriving,' said Matt, peering through the windscreen as the wipers scraped the snow away.

Once on the motorway they made better progress. The snow had ceased, and visibility improved. They passed Reading, and stopped at Oxford for lunch. It was already two o'clock.

'Did you phone your folks?' Matt asked, as they pulled off the road to a 'comfort stop'.

'I spoke to Mummy, and said we would be there before dark if possible, and certainly in time for dinner.' Penelope's parents lived in a village near Stratford-on-Avon now that her father had retired from his busy dental practice.

It was warm in the car, and Chloe had curled up in the back seat with a pillow, but woke as soon as they stopped. Matt stayed in the car, and watched as they walked to the toilet block. Chloe looked so tiny as she reached up and took her mother's hand. She had just turned three.

'Time we had a boy to keep her in shape,' Penny had said as they sat together in front of the fire the previous evening. 'It's a good time to think about it, while you have your four weeks holidays.'

Matt had put his arm around her and kissed her cheek. 'I think about it all the time,' he said with a smile, and kissed her again.

He had met Penny at a hospital party when he was a house surgeon, and they went out together for the next year. They became engaged when Penny had finished her nursing training, and was working in the hospital as a staff nurse. They were married in the little church in her parents' village, and then Matt settled down to serious study for the Primary examination of the Royal College of Surgeons.

Matt sat the examination in the spring, but was not optimistic about the result in spite of his months of study. Not many passed first time. To his surprise and great delight he passed! He and Penny had celebrated with dinner at a restaurant and a good bottle of wine; a luxury they could rarely afford on his meagre salary.

He became a junior registrar in a surgical clinic as part of his training program to become a surgeon, and after several months, Penny became pregnant.

Three years had gone by and Matt was now studying for his next exam, the finals for his Fellowship. Penny had gone back to work in an outpatient clinic, as they needed the money. Little Chloe went to the hospital crèche, and Penny picked her up at the end of the day.

It was the day before Christmas Eve 1960, and they would be returning from Penny's parents before New Year. Matt planned to stay home and study for the next few weeks, and maybe have the evening meal ready when Chloe and Penny came home. The exams started in March.

Penny and Chloe came back to the car, their faces flushed with the cold. They ate the sandwiches and had a hot drink, then were on their way.

They drove on to Banbury, and then turned off to Stratford. The sky was black with low clouds, and by three thirty it was almost dark. It was still freezing cold, and snow covered the countryside. The road wound through wooded hills, and Matt concentrated on his driving. Chloe was asleep again, and Penny dozed. A light mist had descended, making visibility worse.

As they came around a curve in the Matt saw a truck approaching at speed. He took his foot off the accelerator, but suddenly the truck slewed across the road towards them! Black ice!

Desperately Matt hit the brakes, and swerved to the side of the road. The truck struck the back wheel of the car, and spun it on the icy road; it careered out of control, and rolled over and over down the embankment before slamming into a tree.

The truck driver managed to stop on the road, and rushed down the slope to the car. It was the right way up. He peered in through the broken window. There was no sound.

He struggled with the door and finally got it open. Three broken and bleeding bodies lay motionless and silent. Horrified, he ran up to the road and franticly flagged down an approaching car, telling the driver of the accident.

It took twenty minutes for the ambulance and police to arrive.

'This one is alive,' called the Ambulance man.

Painfully Matt opened his eyes. Everything was blurred and very bright.

'Where am I? What happened?' He struggled to sit up, and a gentle hand restrained him. A blurry figure spoke. 'Just lie back and rest now.' It was a woman.

'Where's Penny? Where's Chloe?' he cried out. There was no reply.

'What's going on?' he shouted. His voice reverberated painfully in his head, and he slumped back on the pillows.

'Please try to rest, the doctor will be along in a minute.'

'Who are you?' he asked.

'I'm your nurse,' the figure replied.

Gradually his eyes focused, and he looked around the room. It was an intensive care unit. He knew the scene well. With difficulty he moved his head, and saw the intravenous drip in his left arm. The right was in a plaster cast, and his left leg was in an extension frame. It hurt to breathe. A man came towards the bed. 'He's awake, Doctor,' she said quietly.

The doctor sat down on a chair beside the bed.

'How do you feel?' he asked, leaning towards him.

'What happened? Where's Penny and Chloe?'

'Dr Harrison, you've been in a terrible accident, and you are badly injured.'

'Penny and Chloe?' he croaked.

The doctor paused, then said softly, 'Matthew, they're dead.'

Chapter 2

Spring had come, and the garden was full of blossoms. The air was still and perfumed, and the sun shone brightly.

Matt sat in a wheelchair by the fishpond. He was still struggling to comprehend what had happened. In an instant his family had been destroyed, and his life was in tatters. Why had he survived? He had no desire to go on living.

He looked at his right hand. He could move his fingers normally, and the broken bones had knitted. So what? He would never go back to surgery. If only they had let him die too.

'Come along Matthew, time for your physiotherapy.' His nurse had arrived, and turned his chair round.

'For God's sake leave me alone,' he muttered. 'I don't want physiotherapy.'

He had been in the rehabilitation hospital for nearly two months now, and whilst his body was healing well, he remained emotionally shattered, and resisted any attempts by the staff to help him.

'Just leave me alone, I want to stay here,' he muttered angrily.

The nurse wheeled him inside in silence.

'What are we going to do with Matthew Harrison?'

It was the weekly clinical meeting of the medical staff, where they evaluated their patients' progress, and discussed their problems.

'He's making good progress physically, and can now walk with a stick. He seems to have not suffered any brain damage, in spite of his severe head injury, but he still can't cope emotionally.' His doctor summarised the situation.

The little group pondered over Matt's problem, and decided that more specialised psychiatric help was needed; perhaps some group therapy.

By mid-July the summer was at its glorious height. 'The best for years,' the gardener told Matt as they stood talking by a bed full of roses; the air was heavy with their perfume.

Matt had 'turned the corner', his doctor had told him that morning, and he was ready to face the outside world. Matt wasn't so sure but had said nothing.

'Matt! You have a visitor,' the nurse called to him from the door. Matt threw his cigarette in the flower garden and walked slowly inside.

'Hello Matt, you're looking well.' The tall greying man stepped forward and they shook hands. Sir James Watson FRCS was the head of the Department of Surgery at Matt's hospital. He had been in fairly constant contact with Matt's doctors over the months, and they had agreed that he should come and talk about work.

They sat in the lounge in comfortable chairs.

'About time you showed your face at the hospital, my boy, your job is still waiting for you.'

Matt looked at his hands and frowned. 'Well sir, I just don't know. Physically I've recovered well, but I don't know that I could cope with surgery again.'

His Chief offered a cigarette and lit both. 'Well, there's only one way to find out. Come and put your toe in the water. But first things first. Come up to London and get the feel of the outside world again.'

Matt's parents lived in a village in Devon, and had a small flat in London where he could stay. They had visited him over the months, as had Penny's parents. They had all been part of the rehabilitation program, and were important in helping him cope with the enormous burden of guilt he had felt.

Matt agreed to call on Sir James when he had moved in to the London flat, but gave no commitment to return to work. The thought of it terrified him.

They walked out to his Bentley in the car park, where they shook hands.

'It was good of you to come down to see me sir, I do appreciate it.' Matt held the car door for him.

'We'll be seeing you soon. Good-bye for now.' He drove off.

Matt watched him leave, and walked slowly back to the garden, deep in thought. The Chief was right. He would have to start sorting out his life – what was left of it. If he didn't go back to surgery, what else could he do? The first step was to get out of the rehab hospital, though it had become a home and a refuge to him, and he now felt comfortable and secure there.

Matt's mother and Penny's parents had gone through his apartment, and packed up for him. Matt had finally discussed it with his mother, and apart from photos, all belongings of Penny and Chloe went back to her parent's place. All his possessions went to his parent's flat to await his arrival. He could never have gone into their apartment again.

Chapter 3

It was noon on a Saturday in mid-August. London was hot and oppressive, and the little flat in Knightsbridge was airless and claustrophobic.

Matthew sat in a lounge chair still in his pyjamas, smoking. He had moved in five days ago, and already was regretting it. He missed the cocoon-like comfort of the rehab hospital, and felt lonely and vulnerable. Also, he was bored.

He had a shower, dressed, then picked up the telephone and dialled.

'Hello, Mrs Evans? It's Matthew Harrison, is … I'm fine now thank you. Yes, it was tragic, yes, yes, thank you. Is Tom at home? Yes I would, please.' He waited.

Tom had been his Best Man, and a lifelong friend. They went through Medicine together.

'Matt! Hello, good to hear from you! Are you still in hospital?'

'Hello Tom, I'm in London, at the folks' flat in Knightsbridge. Thought I'd just ring and make contact. … Yes thanks, I'm feeling fine now; well, no, actually I'm not. I'm bored stiff, and I want to talk to someone.'

'I've got nothing planned for the rest of the day, how about I come round?'

'That would be great, thanks.'

'See you in thirty minutes.' He hung up.

Tom had visited him on several occasions during his convalescence, and had been overwhelmed with sadness at the loss of Penny and little Chloe. In the early days he would just sit by Matt's bed in silence, as there were no words to be said. When he rose to leave Matt would take his hand and whisper, 'Thanks.' Tom watched Matt slowly return to life over time.

The doorbell rang. Matt let Tom in and they shook hands.

'Matt! You're looking great!' They walked to the sitting room.

'I've just boiled the kettle. Care for a cuppa?'

'That would be nice thanks.'

'Make yourself comfy.'

Matt disappeared into the kitchen, and came back with a tea tray. He sat down and poured two cups, offered milk and sugar, then a biscuit.

They sat in silence for a moment, sipping their tea.

'Well Matt. What next? Are you feeling up to work?'

'The Chief came down to see me last week, and wants me back.'

'What did you say?'

'Didn't commit myself, said I'd drop by one day.'

'So when are you going?'

'Haven't decided – maybe next week.'

Tom worked in the Department of Medicine in the same hospital, and was studying for his Membership of the Royal College of Physicians. He had sat once and failed, but that was the norm. He was still unmarried, and to save money, was living with his folks, at least until he had passed his exams.

'You know Tom, I don't think I can cope with the hospital now. All those well-meaning people who are just going to make my life miserable with their sympathy and kindness; the looks, the whispers when I go past. D'you know what I mean? I think I should go somewhere where I'm unknown.'

'Come on Matt, let's get some fresh air.' Tom said, standing and stretching.

They walked to Hyde Park, and sat on a bench by the Serpentine. There was a cool breeze blowing, and the model yachts cruised over the smooth water.

'Well Matt, what are the options now? You are nearly finished your surgical training, with only the final exam to get through. Why not settle down to study and have a crack at it?'

'Don't think I haven't thought about it. I just don't think I could apply myself to the study just now. I don't think I could concentrate. No, I need a change in direction, at least for the time being. Something entirely different.'

'Okay then, let's look at some possibilities. How about a trip to Antarctica as medical officer? No? Well, there is always 'darkest Africa', or some other outpost of the Empire. Perhaps New Zealand, or maybe Australia. You could get a job with the Flying Doctors or whatever they call themselves. Now that would be a change of direction. And very different,' Tom said with a smile and offered Matt a cigarette.

They sat smoking in silence and watched the children playing by the water.

'You know Tom you may have hit the nail on the head! Flying Doctors sound very exciting ... it may be perfect for me.' His face clouded. 'But it's on the other side of the world, and how would I get there? I couldn't afford the fare.'

'Matt, at least you've made a start. You've found something that interests you.' He stood up. 'Come on, let's go and have a pint.'

The warm atmosphere of the pub, heavy with smoke and beer, welcomed them as they entered, and they moved to a corner seat with their pints.

'If you are seriously interested in the Flying Doctor thing, why don't you discuss it with your Chief at the hospital?'

'Are you kidding? He wants me back in the system. I can't see him helping me to leave the country.'

They walked slowly back to Matt's flat, chatting. It was nearly seven o'clock, and still broad daylight. 'Why don't we have a bite in the Italian restaurant? It's not far from your place,' said Tom.

'Good idea, I'm sick of my own cooking.'

They ordered scaloppini and spaghetti, and a glass of house red.

'Why don't you go to the hospital on Monday, and talk it over with your boss?' said Tom, looking over his glass. 'The longer you sit in that flat on your own the worse you'll feel.'

Chapter 4

'Department of Surgery, can I help you?'

'Hello, it's Dr Harrison speaking ...'

'Oh hello Dr Harrison, this is Miss Browning. It's nice to hear your voice, are you feeling well again? What an awful ...'

'Yes indeed, thank you. I would like to make an appointment to see Sir James if I may, as soon as possible.'

'Just a moment Doctor, I shall just look at his appointments. Yes, here's a space, he could see you this afternoon at three if that suits you?'

'Thank you Miss Browning, that would suit me well. I shall see you then. Goodbye.'

Matt arrived five minutes early, and sat reading a magazine, after reporting at the desk. Mercifully, Miss Browning was out of the office.

The buzzer sounded, and the receptionist looked up at Matt. 'Sir James will see you now Dr Harrison.'

Matt stood up and walked to the green baize-covered door, which opened as he approached.

Sir James stood up from his desk, and held out his hand. 'Glad you came Matthew,' he said beaming at him. 'Do sit down.' He gestured to a couple of leather chairs by a small table. He sat down in the other one.

'Well my boy, what about some work? We must get you back to study too.' He looked expectantly at Matt. 'We could start you off with a light outpatient clinic, and a couple of operating lists to see how you feel.'

Matt sat looking at his hands. 'This is going to be difficult,' he thought.

'Sir, I have spent a good deal of time thinking about my future, and I have made a decision.' He paused. 'I am not ready to pick up my life where I left off, I need more time, and I need a change. I would like to go to Australia, and join the Flying Doctor Service for a while, and then perhaps come back to London.'

There was a long silence.

'Matthew, do you know anything about it? Have you spoken to anyone?' the Chief asked. He stood up, and walked over to his desk, hands clasped behind his back.

Matt had to confess that he knew nothing about Australia, or the Flying Doctors, and that it had got no further than his thoughts.

'Well Matt, I think the best thing I can do is help you sort it out. There's no doubt it would be a marvellous experience, and you would get a lot of basic surgery. But I think you should not wander too far from the pathway of academic surgery, as you still have the final of your exam to do, and without it, frankly, you cannot call yourself a surgeon.

'It so happens that the Australian High Commissioner is a friend of mine, and I'm sure he would be most helpful. If you like I'll have a chat with him, and see what I can set up.'

Matt thanked him as they walked to the door. 'Ring me at home on Wednesday evening, about seven,' he said, and gave Matt his card.

Matt walked to the lift, and as the doors closed Miss Browning stepped out of the other lift. 'That was close,' he thought.

He caught a bus back to Knightsbridge and walked to his flat. He made a cup of tea, and sat down in a comfy chair. 'Well, I've made a start,' he said aloud.

For the next two days, Matt busied himself going through his possessions, and sorting out his clothes. He pressed his suits, and took his shirts to the laundry. The flat was now quite organised, and he had a supply of basic food in store.

He had phoned Tom and filled him on events, and felt quite excited about the prospect of going to Australia.

At seven o'clock on Wednesday evening, he dialled Sir James at his home. A woman's voice answered.

'Hello, may I speak with Sir James please, it's Matthew Harrison calling.'

'Oh yes, he's expecting you. One moment please.'

Matt could hear her voice in the background; 'It's your young registrar, dear.'

'Good evening Matthew, have you changed your mind about the Colonies?'

Matt was a little taken aback. 'Er, good evening sir, actually, no, I'm still rather keen on the idea.'

'Splendid. I have spoken to the High Commissioner, and he is delighted to be of assistance. I thought it would break the ice a bit if we all had lunch together at my Club. He's free on Friday and if it's alright with you, we could meet at twelve thirty.'

'Thank you sir, that sounds marvellous, I'm most grateful.'

'Good, that's fixed then. Twelve thirty at the Naval and Military Club in Piccadilly. Just tell the porter that you are my guest. I'll see you then. Good-bye.'

'Good-bye sir, and thanks again.' He hung up.

A moment later, the phone rang. 'Hello darling, how are things going?'

'Mother! Great to hear your voice! How are you? How's Father?'

'We're both well, and coming up to London tomorrow; we hoped you would be able to meet us for lunch. Your father has an appointment with the accountant at two thirty, so we will have time for a good lunch.'

They arranged to meet at a quiet restaurant at twelve the next day.

Matt was waiting in the restaurant when his parents arrived, and stood up as they approached the table. He kissed mother on the cheek, and shook his father's hand. They sat down.

'You are looking tired dearest,' his mother said, searching his face with concern. 'Are you looking after yourself and getting regular meals and enough sleep?'

'Yes Mother dear,' he replied, patting her hand. 'I'm feeling very well now, thank you.'

They ordered 'Pimm's No 1s' all round, and studied the menu.

They settled for Dover Sole, and followed with fruit salad and ice cream, then coffee.

'I've got something to tell you,' said Matt, having waited for the right moment.

They put down their cups and looked at Matt expectantly.

'I have decided to go to Australia, and work with the Royal Flying Doctor Service.' He paused and looked at his parents. Father had not altered his expression, but his mother put her hand to her mouth and gasped, 'But dear, that is on the other side of the earth! What made you think of going there?'

'I've discussed it with Sir James, and he has invited me to lunch at his Club, to meet the Australian High Commissioner tomorrow.'

'Well, my boy,' said his father. 'You are getting the right connections, you must tell us all about it tomorrow night.'

Matt looked at his hands, 'I'm not ready to go back to my hospital, it's too soon, and I couldn't possibly study for my exam at this stage. Sir James agreed that the experience would stand me in good stead, and broaden my outlook on medicine in general. Don't worry, I'm not planning to emigrate. I'll be back to do my exam in a year or so. Who knows? It might be dreadful, and I'll be back on the next ship!'

His mother still looked dubious, but his father nodded as he listened. 'Matt, I'm sure you've made the right decision. A complete change will do you good.' He glanced at his watch. 'Good heavens! I mustn't keep the accountant waiting,' and stood up. He walked over to the counter and paid the bill, as Matt and his mother got up and made for the door.

'Cheerio Matt, ring us tomorrow evening.'

'Goodbye Dad, and thanks for lunch. I'll ring tomorrow.' They shook hands.

His father hailed a cab and disappeared in the traffic.

Matt and his mother walked a little way, and stopped at a small park. 'Let's sit for a moment,' Matt said. 'I want to talk to you.'

They sat on a bench in a shady spot.

'Mother, I miss Penny and Chloe terribly, and I still dream about them, then wake and realise that they are gone. Sometimes I dream of that dreadful moment in the car and hear Penny's scream. I can't talk to Dad like this, and I want you to understand why I must go.' His mother took his hand and said nothing. Her eyes were full of tears.

'A strange country with all new people to meet, and where nobody knows me; I just can't face the hospital and everyone being kind and sympathetic. I … I still feel so guilty.'

'My dearest boy, I do understand, and I'm sure it will be a new start in life for you. Who knows what is around the corner for you.' His mother smiled at him through her tears and dabbed her cheeks with her handkerchief.

They walked back to the roadside and Matt hailed a cab, and helped his mother in.

'Goodbye darling, ring us tomorrow.'

'Goodbye Mother.' He shut the door and the cab pulled away.

The next day, Matt arrived five minutes early at his Chief's club. He had never been inside a London club, and felt slightly apprehensive as he reached the door. He announced himself to the hall porter, and was ushered into an anteroom while the porter went off to find Sir James. It was a warm day, and Matt felt his hands sweating as he clasped them behind his back and studied the old paintings on the walls.

'Ah! There you are Matthew, come along.' Sir James stood at the door.

'The High Commissioner is running a little late, so we'll have a drink while we're waiting.' He steered Matt towards the bar.

'What will you have?' he asked, the steward waiting for the order.

'May I have a lemon squash?'

'Good choice, I'll have the same.' Sir James nodded to the steward.

They sipped their drinks and talked about work at the hospital, and had almost emptied their glasses when a tall, distinguished gentleman approached.

'Ah, John,' said the surgeon, rising from his chair with his hand outstretched.

'Hello Jim, good to see you.' They shook hands.

'Matthew, I would like you to meet Sir John Anderson.'

'How do you do, sir,' said Matt, shaking the offered hand.

'So you're the young man who wants to come to our great country?' he said with a smile.

'Do you want a drink, John?' asked the host.

'No thanks, let's go in to lunch,' he replied.

They followed the surgeon into the great dining room with its Adam frescos and Wedgwood designed ceiling.

At the table, Matt quietly 'took in' the Australian. He was about sixty he guessed, with thinning grey hair and a grey moustache, clipped short in military fashion. His face was sun-tanned, and he had a military air about him, Matt thought. He spoke with only a trace of an Australian accent.

'Your Chief has told me all about your circumstances, and I'm sure this will prove the right answer for you.' He did not make direct mention of the tragedy, which relieved Matt.

'Firstly you had better tell me what you had in mind. Australia is a big country, and you need to have your plans well laid before you set out.'

'Well sir, I know very little of your country except what I've heard from some of the Aussie doctors at our hospital, and what I've read, but I rather thought I'd like to work with the Royal Flying Doctor Service in some remote part.'

Sir John paused a moment. 'Probably the best place for you then, would be the north of Western Australia. Now *that* really is remote!' he said with a grin. 'Why don't you let me make some enquiries, and I'll get back to you. Also you'll need to think about how to get there, it's a darn long way from here, you know.'

'Any suggestions?' asked the old surgeon, putting down his knife and fork.

'Why not try to get a passage as a ship's doctor?' he replied. 'Good practice for your next job,' he laughed. Matt took an instant liking to his breezy manner.

They finished lunch and retired to the smoking room for coffee, sitting in comfy leather chairs around a table.

'Matt, if you could write down your telephone number, I will get back to you as soon as possible. What's a good time to ring you?' He handed Matt one of his cards and he wrote down the telephone number.

'Mornings are always good, but I really don't go out much right now.'

'Fine, then leave it to me, and I'll be in touch.' He looked at his watch. 'Must be getting along now. Thanks for lunch Jim … No don't get up. Good-bye for now Matthew.' He left the other two sitting at the table.

'Well my boy, the wheels are turning. Are you still quite sure you want to go ahead with this?'

'Yes sir, I'm sure, and I'd like to thank you for your help; and for an excellent lunch.'

They parted company at the door, and Matt promised to keep his Chief informed on his progress.

Chapter 5

Back in his flat, Matt flopped on his bed. He felt tired. He was excited at the possibility of being a ship's doctor, having read about the 'on-board activities' in novels. Would he wear a uniform?

He had bought a map and a traveller's guide about Australia at a bookshop, but there was very little about the remote country except the Aborigines, and the wildlife.

The map wasn't much help either, except to confirm what Sir John had said. It was a very big country!

The phone rang. It was Tom.

'Hello Matt, how are you getting on?'

Matt filled him in on his activities.

'Do you remember Willie Hudson? That's right, our Aussie House Surgeon at the hospital. Well, he and I are at the pub having a pint, and thought you might like to join us.'

'Certainly would, which pub? – Okay, I'll be there in ten minutes.' He hung up and put his shoes on. What a great opportunity to find out about Australia!

There was a buzz of conversation and a friendly smell of beer and cigarettes as he entered. He spotted Tom at a side table with Willie and walked over to them.

'Get yourself a beer and join us,' Tom said.

'Well,' said Willie as Matt sat down with his pint. 'So you want to go to Australia, eh?' His accent was very recognisable. 'Damn good idea I reckon,' he added, and took a swig of beer.

'Where do you live, Willie?' Matt asked.

'In Sydney, mate, and I can't wait to get back there.'

'Is that a big town?' Matt asked naïvely.

Willie looked at him over the top of his glass. 'You might say that,' he drawled. 'Most people speak English, except for some of the natives. The peaceful ones do, mind you, but the others are a bit wild.

Sometimes they chuck spears at the cars going past.' Matt looked apprehensive, and Willie winked at Tom unnoticed.

'Then there's the crocodiles. They're pretty bad at times, but mostly they eat dingoes and kangaroos that come to close to the edge of the billabong. Not many humans get eaten.'

'For God's sake Willie, stop your nonsense!' said Tom laughing.

Matt looked from one to the other. He had been away from hospital humour for too long.

Willie grinned. 'Matt, Sydney has more than a million people, and there is not a kangaroo for a hundred miles. In fact, I've never seen one outside the zoo. Same goes for crocodiles and dingoes. But you get all sorts of wildlife in the outback. But then you won't be going there will you?'

'Well that's just the point Willie, I want to work with the Flying Doctors in the north.'

Willie looked blankly at him. 'What the hell for? Are you a missionary type?'

'No nothing like that, I just want to get away from here and do something different for a while.'

Tom gave Willie a gentle kick under the table.

'Yair, well fair enough, but I don't really know anything about that part of Australia,' he said, returning to his beer.

'I'm thinking of going to the north of Western Australia to work,' he said.

'Christ! Now that really is "getting away" from civilisation! Why there?'

Matt told him about his luncheon.

'Must say you've got friends in the right places,' he said enviously.

The following Monday morning, Matt's phone rang. It was the Office of the High Commissioner. 'Dr Harrison? One moment please, the High Commissioner will speak to you.'

'Matt? Good. I've spoken to a few people about you, and if you go along to Australia House in the Strand on Monday and ask for Mr Greg Abbott, he will have some information for you.' Matt thanked him for his trouble. 'Not at all, I'm delighted to be able to help, and I wish you luck.'

On Monday morning Matt walked into Australia House, and asked for Mr Abbott. He sat thumbing through an Australian magazine while he waited.

'Dr Harrison?' A fresh faced man in his mid thirties with sandy hair stood at the door smiling at him. They shook hands, and he led the way to his office.

'Well, I've got some information that will be helpful to you.' He pushed a big manila envelope over the desk. 'Take this home with you. It contains information about the RFDS and how it works, and also a lot about the north-west of Australia.'

Matt reached forward and took the envelope. 'Mr Abbott ...'

He was interrupted, 'Call me Greg.'

'Greg, how do I go about organising a job?'

'I was coming to that, you see, each State has different rules. In Western Australia the RFDS own the aircraft and employ the pilots. The State Health Department employs the doctors, whereas in Queensland the RFDS employ the doctors and charter the planes and pilots from TAA, the national airline.

'I've spoken to our WA people, and they've contacted Perth regarding vacancies. It turns out that there will be a job in the north-west coming up at the end of the year; the present doctor is leaving. Surprisingly they never have much trouble filling the posts, so don't ponder over it for too long.

'On the question of how to get there, firstly if you wish to migrate we can provide an assisted passage. No? Well, we have contacts with shipping companies, who are often looking for doctors for their voyages, which is probably more in your line.'

An hour later they parted company with a handshake. Matt had applied for the north-west job and had his name down for a passage as a ship's doctor to Australia.

He had an appointment to see the Chief Medical Officer the next day for the obligatory medical examination for government employment, and as Greg put it, for a chat about the job. The CMO had worked with the Flying Doctors.

The CMO was middle-aged, tall, lean and athletic looking. He held his hand out as Matt entered. 'Welcome Matt, come and sit down. I'm

John Langdon.' They shook hands, and he sat down in front of the large paper-strewn desk.

'Let's get the formalities over first. We need to know all about you, so I'll get you to fill in the first page of this form, the personal details.' He pushed it over to Matt who took out his fountain pen. 'Cigarette?' He offered a gold cigarette case.

'Thanks,' Matt took one and settled down to the task as the CMO walked to the window and watched the traffic snaking past. It was a cool day, and light rain was falling.

'Now, I know that you had a pretty bad accident. How badly injured were you?' He made no allusion to his tragic loss.

He made notes as Matt told him of his multiple injuries and his long sojourn in the rehabilitation hospital. 'So I've made an almost complete recovery.' The older man looked over his gold-rimmed specs.

'Almost?' he repeated.

'Physically I'm fine. I'm fit for work, but I'm still too emotionally fragile to work in my old environment where everyone has known us … me that is, for years. I need a fresh start.'

'Well, let's give you the once over … Just a formality you know. Go behind the screen, strip to your undies, and hop up on the couch. Let me know when you are ready.'

When he had finished, Matt dressed and resumed his seat in front of the desk.

'Yes, there's not much wrong physically. You have healed well.' He finished off the form and pushed it over again. 'Would you sign there?' he indicated.

'Right. How about some lunch and I can tell you a bit about the job you are taking on.'

'Thanks, that would be very nice,' Matt replied, and they both stood up.

In a small café nearby, they ordered a plate of sandwiches, and a pot of tea.

'You have made a decision that you will never regret,' said John, munching a sandwich. 'The Northwest is God's own country, you know. After a year there you won't want to leave. It grows on you and gets into your blood. I still dream about it.' He had a far away expression.

'What are the medical facilities like?' Matt asked.

'The Northwest Medical Service look after the hospitals pretty well, and they are well equipped. The real problem is keeping the nursing staff. They blow in then move off, usually on a working tour of the country. In some places the senior nurses are married to men in the town, which gives some stability. The towns are all along the coast, and supplies come mostly by the State ships. The outback stations are self-sufficient, except for sugar, salt, tea, butter and flour. They mostly run sheep, with the best merino wool you will ever see. Some run cattle, and of course the outback is teeming with wild life.'

Matt sipped his tea, fascinated with the tales of the New World.

John went on. 'You know the station women are the salt of the earth. Conditions are harsh for them, isolated with little contact with the outside world except by radio. They used to have "pedal" radios, invented by a chap called Traeger in the early days. Now of course, they are all battery-powered.

'You know they will drive fifty miles to have afternoon tea with a neighbour? The distances are enormous. All red dust and spinifex.'

'Spinifex?' Matt interrupted.

'Yes, spinifex. It's a stunted, prickly little grass bush, grows to about two feet tall, and they're everywhere, miles and miles of nothing else. The distant hills always look a sort of powdery blue, especially early in the morning and at sundown, and the white cockatoos turn an old dead gum into a Christmas Tree then all fly off shrieking as you approach.' He paused. 'I spent nearly five years in the Northwest, and they were some of the best years of my life.' He seemed to be almost talking to himself.

'Back to business!' he said briskly. 'There is no dentist, and no vet in that part of the world, so you need to know a little about animals. Have you ever pulled a tooth out?'

Matt had to admit that he had not.

'You give your own anaesthetics, and deliver babies. There is a blood bank, in as much as a lot of locals are potential donors, and you have to round them up when you need blood. You take your own X-rays and develop the films, and a hundred other jobs that you've never imagined.' He stopped and took out a cigarette, and offered the case to Matt, who declined. 'Any queries?' he asked, blowing a plume of smoke in the air.

'I'm starting to wonder if I can cope with this job,' he said in an anxious tone.

'Don't worry, you will,' John replied. 'You are on your own, and you cope. Everybody does, you know.' He smiled at Matt then looked at his wristwatch. 'Well, I had better be getting back to work. My advice is to get around and visit the dental hospital, and the maternity wards to brush up. Go to the medical bookshop and get a copy of *Dental Surgery for Ships' Doctors*. You'll find it most helpful. Oh, and ask about a book on animal health. I'm sure they'd have a veterinary section.'

They shook hands, and Matt thanked him for his help. 'No doubt I'll see you before you go. Australia House has a good reading room, and lots of good books and magazines. You're always welcome to drop in, and we'll help you as much as we can.'

As instructed, Matt went to the medical bookshop and browsed around. He found the dentistry book; a slim paperback, full of illustrations. He also found a book on common illnesses in domestic animals.

By the end of the week, he was feeling edgy and bored. He was sick of reading about impacted wisdom teeth, and cat's diarrhoea. Now that he had made his decision he wanted to get on with it. He lay on the couch in his flat idly thumbing through the *British Medical Journal*. Suddenly, his attention was drawn to a column in the advertisements. 'Locum Positions Vacant.' A women's hospital was looking for a house surgeon locum for one month. What a perfect opportunity to catch up on his 'middy'!

He picked up the phone and dialled the number. The receptionist put him through to the Medical Superintendent, who on hearing Matt's reason for applying, thought the job would suit him well. He needed to visit the hospital first to see the Superintendent in person, and could take up the position in two weeks' time. The hospital was in the outer suburbs of London.

Chapter 6

The following week, he caught the tube and walked from the station to the hospital, an old Edwardian building, with a rather grand entrance, and a more modern wing with a large 'Admissions' sign over the glass sliding doors.

The Medical Superintendent was a short thin man with a rather nervous manner, who asked Matt about his background. He was curious about his departure from the surgical mainstream, but accepted Matt's explanation that it was all part of a broad-based medical education, and that there was a wealth of experience to be gained by going to a remote part of Australia. He took Matt on a tour of the hospital for the next hour, and introduced him to staff members they met. The place had a nice friendly atmosphere, and everyone seemed happy with their work. As he rode home in the tube he felt that he had made a good decision. That evening he rang his parents and told them what he had arranged.

For the next month Matt 'lived in' at the hospital, and when not delivering babies and doing rounds, he revised his textbooks of obstetrics. Also, he chummed up with the anaesthetic registrar, and spent as much time as he could learning modern anaesthetic techniques. They discussed practical ways of giving safe anaesthetics in remote areas.

The time went by quickly, and he returned to his flat for a good rest after more late nights on duty than he had done for years! The pay packet helped too, as his funds were running low. He felt confident about obstetrics and anaesthesia now.

Towards the end of September he received a letter in a brown manila envelope marked 'On Her Majesty's Service', from the Health Department of Western Australia.

The Commissioner of Health of Western Australia advised him that his application for the Northwest Medical Service had been successful, and he was to take up his duties as soon as possible in the New Year. Would he please acknowledge this letter and advise of his travel arrangements.

He rang Greg at Australia House and told him the news.

'Where have you been? I tried to ring you a couple of times.'

Matt told him about his locum job.

'Well there are a few possibilities for travel, so you had better come in so we can discuss them.'

Matt caught the bus to the city next morning. The days were getting shorter, and there was a chill in the air. With a bit of luck he might miss the winter he thought, turning up his overcoat collar.

Greg greeted him warmly. 'Congratulations on the job,' he said, shaking his hand. He led the way to his office and they sat by the coffee table. There were some papers on the table, and Greg picked them up. 'These are from shipping companies regarding ship's doctor jobs.' He sorted through them.

'The passenger ships nearly all want a doctor for the round trip, which wouldn't suit you, but the small general cargo ships carry a few passengers, and that's your best bet.

'There's one here from Green Star Line, a British company running general cargo from Europe to Australia. There's a ship called *Griffin* with twelve passengers and mixed cargo leaving Hull at the end of November to load cargo in Bremerhaven, then sailing to Antwerp and Australia via the Mediterranean. Passengers will be boarding at Bremerhaven and at Antwerp. The ship calls at Fremantle, in Western Australia, so what do you think? You should reach Australia in January.'

Matt felt a tingle of excitement. 'That sounds perfect! The timing could not be better!'

'Excellent. I'll ring the shipping company right away.' He picked up the phone. 'Get me "Green Star Line" please.' He waited.

'Hello this is Australia House calling about a ship's doctor position. My name is Abbott, Gregory Abbott. Yes, thank you, who? Yes, the Manager, thank you, I'll wait.

'Hello? Yes, Abbott from Australia House. I have a doctor who wants a passage to Australia, and the *Griffin* would suit him very well if the position were still vacant. … It is? Excellent! When would you like to see him? Just a moment,' he put his hand over the phone. 'This afternoon?' Matt nodded. … 'Yes that would be fine. Two o'clock? His name is Matthew Harrison. That's right. Thank you. Good-bye.' He hung up.

'Time for a quick bite,' Greg said, glancing at his watch. 'Care to join me?'

'Thanks, but no, I've got a few things to do before my appointment.'

He stood up, and they shook hands. 'You'll need the address,' Greg said, and held out a piece of notepaper.

'Thanks.' Matt took it and grinned. 'G'bye.'

The shipping office was only a short walk, but Matt wanted a little time to think before the appointment. He stopped at a newsagent and purchased a small leather-bound notebook, then went in to a café and ordered a sandwich and a cup of tea. He opened the notebook and wrote at the top of the first page, 'Australia'. Then 'Australia House' with the address and the names of those that he had met. He might need to contact them later.

At two o'clock he was standing in the waiting area of the shipping office. The room had two fine model ships in glass cases. The detail fascinated him.

'Superb craftsmanship don't you agree?' Matt turned to find a smiling middle-aged man standing at an open door. 'You must be Dr Harrison?' He held out his hand. 'My name is Frank Butler.'

'How do you do, sir?' said Matthew as they shook hands. He ushered Matt into his office, and directed him to a chair.

'Well, do you think you could cope with shipboard life?' the Manager asked with a smile.

'I hope so, I've never been to sea before,' Matt replied.

'Tell me about your medical experience.'

Matt detailed his training, and added that he had brushed up on anaesthetics and dentistry then added, 'also obstetrics.'

'Good Lord! You won't be having any babies at sea! We don't carry pregnant women.' They both laughed.

Frank asked Matt about his plans for Australia, and seemed genuinely interested. 'My daughter married an Australian mining engineer, and they have gone to live in a place called Kalgoorlie. Have you heard of it?'

Matt confessed that he had not.

'Sounds as though you are well trained for this job. There's a bit of paperwork to do, I'll get my secretary to go through it with you in a while. Cigarette?' He offered a packet.

'Thank you.'

'The ship sails from Hull on the twenty-eighth of November for Bremerhaven to load farm machinery and general cargo, and will be there for a few days. So far there are nine passengers registered, and two are embarking there. The rest join the ship at Antwerp. I suggest you join there too. Bremerhaven is not the nicest port in Europe.' He paused and drew on his cigarette. 'We will fly you over to join the ship with the other passengers about the sixth of December. What do you think?'

'Sounds marvellous! Whatever you say.' Matt was starting to feel the excitement of travel already.

'The next thing is for you to meet the Captain of the *Griffin*, who happens to be in the office today. The ship is undergoing a minor refit in Hull before the next voyage.' He stood up and they walked to the door. Frank paused. 'The Captain is rather gruff, but his bark is worse than his bite. His name is McKenzie, Andrew McKenzie.'

They came to an unmarked door, and Frank knocked.

'Enter!' boomed a voice with a Scottish accent.

The Captain was seated at a desk smothered with papers, and put down his pen as they entered. He stood up. 'Ah Frank, what can I do for you?' The accent was broad.

'Andrew, I would like you to meet Dr Matthew Harrison. He is your doctor on the outward voyage.'

The Captain would have been about fifty, and was short and stocky with a grey beard and grey thick hair. His eyes were blue and piercing. He looked hard at Matt over his horn rim specs. 'Is he now?' he growled. He walked towards Matt and held out his hand.

Matt winced at the crushing grip. 'How do you do, sir,' Matt said, retrieving his hand.

'Have you been to sea before?' he said with a steely glare.

'No sir. Apart from the channel ferry that is.'

The Captain snorted.

Frank came to the rescue. 'He is an experienced surgeon, Andrew, and came to us on the recommendation of the Australian High Commissioner.'

The Captain seemed unimpressed. 'Well I hope he's better than the last one.' He looked Matt up and down. 'How old are you, lad?'

Matt felt his colour rising. 'I'm twenty-nine sir,' he answered.

He returned to his desk and sat down, while the other two remained standing. He put his pipe in his mouth and went through the ritual of lighting it using several matches. Finally it belched a cloud of smoke.

'Are you joining in Hull?' he asked; his tone was softer.

'We thought it best to fly him to Antwerp with the passengers,' Frank replied.

The Captain nodded, and puffed smoke.

'Well I'd better be getting back to my work,' he said looking at the spread of paperwork. 'Good to meet you,' he nodded to Matt. 'Cheerio,' he said, dismissing them.

Back in his office, Frank said. 'Don't let his gruff manner upset you, he has a heart of gold – so they say.'

Matt looked at him with raised eyebrows.

Frank handed him over to his secretary who spent the next ten minutes filling out forms. She gave him a booklet with the 'Green Star' logo on the cover, entitled 'The Ship's Doctor – Protocol and Guide Lines.'

'You will find this helpful,' she said smiling at Matt's concerned expression.

'I'll be in touch with you in a couple of weeks to let you know the latest plans,' she said as she showed Matt out the door.

Chapter 7

By the end of October all plans were made. Matt had acknowledged his appointment with a confirming letter to the Western Australian Health Department, and the shipping company wrote to him with details of his position with them.

He was to receive one shilling as payment for his services as ship's doctor on the voyage, and he would have free board and passage to Australia. This, he was told, was the standard arrangement with medicos, who were entitled to charge passengers a fee for services. His duty statement, however, pointed out that members of the crew, as company employees, were to be treated free of charge. He was to report to the Captain on joining the ship, who would thereafter advise him of his duties.

The letter went on to enclose suggested dress for the voyage, ranging from winter attire to the southern hemisphere summer, including transit through the tropics. He would not wear a uniform.

The Purser's Office would be his source of onboard information, and the currency on board was English pounds. Once in international waters, cigarettes and alcohol were duty free. There was no shop on board, but some basic items could be purchased at the Office. He was to report to the shipping office one week before his departure date with his passport, for final details.

Matt read the letter several times, with a feeling of excitement. It was really happening! He spent the next weekend with his parents talking excitedly about his prospects, and seemed happier than they had seen him since the accident.

The following week, Matt took the train to Stratford, where he stayed with Penny's folks, and told them of his plans.

He visited the graves of Penny and Chloe, in the little churchyard where they had been married. He stood beside them and wept as the painful memories flooded back, and the awful finality overwhelmed him. He returned to London feeling miserable and depressed.

With only two weeks to go, he packed his textbooks in a tin trunk, leaving out a few that he might need on the voyage. In another trunk, he packed most of his winter clothes that he was unlikely to need in Australia. He put in mothballs and closed the lid. It would await his return!

He bought a large strong suitcase, and armed with the company list, went about London buying suitable clothing both for the voyage and for his arrival in Australia.

Tom accompanied him on some of his shopping trips, and at one 'Gentleman's Safari Outfitters', stood and watched with an amused expression as Matt tried on a variety of clothes suitable 'not only for the plains of Africa, but also for the Antipodes,' the salesman told him. Matt settled for some comfy boots and a safari hat with a plaited leather band.

At last all was ready. He had packed his suitcase for the voyage, and also a smaller suitcase with a few changes of socks and undies, and toiletry requirements to tide him over while in transit to the ship. His trunk and large case were sent to the shipping company for transport to the ship in Hull.

A few days before the ship sailed from Hull, Matt presented himself at the office, with his passport. The secretary gave him an update on the schedule. The ship would be in Antwerp on the fifth of December. On the same day, they would travel by train to Southend, then fly to Ostend. A bus would then take them to the ship in Antwerp.

The Manager came into the office. 'Hello Doctor Harrison, all set for the voyage?'

'Yes sir, all ready to go,' Matt replied with enthusiasm.

'I hope you have a pleasant voyage,' he said as they shook hands. 'If you want a passage home again, write to me and I will try to arrange it.'

'That's kind of you sir, and thanks for all your help.'

'Ring me the day before you go, in case there are any alterations to the itinerary,' the secretary said. 'If not, catch the eleven-ten from Victoria Station to Southend-on-Sea. One of our agents will meet you when you arrive to take you to the airport.'

On the fourth of December, Matt rang the secretary, and was informed that he would be travelling with seven passengers, and they were to proceed the next day as planned. The ship, however, may be delayed, as it was snowing in Germany, and this had slowed down the loading. If necessary the company would arrange hotel accommodation for them.

That evening Tom and Matt went out to a restaurant in Soho for dinner. Tom had been there before, and assured Matt that the rather sleazy exterior in no way reflected the high quality of the establishment. As it was Matt's last night in town, he was Tom's guest.

Inside, the subdued lighting and the rich drapes and décor suggested middle European origin. Hungarian, Matt thought, as they were shown to a table. A trio of musicians dressed as gypsies played soulful music, and moved around between the tables with a violin and two guitars.

Tom ordered a bottle of champagne and they sat back enjoying the continental atmosphere. 'Here's to the future,' said Tom raising his glass.

'The future,' Matt repeated as they clinked glasses and drank.

The food was delicious, and they chatted as they ate, drifting back over their school and university days, and things they had done together. It was a happy, nostalgic evening, and inevitably, thoughts of Penny and Chloe flooded Matt's mind, and crept into the conversation.

Matt's face clouded as he thought of his lost loved ones, and Tom leant forward, looking him in the face. 'Matt, you will always love them, and never forget them, but you must let them go now, and keep only the happy memories with you. When you leave tomorrow, it will be like starting again in a new life, and you mustn't carry sadness and regret with you.'

'You're quite right,' said Matt, slurring a little as the second bottle of champagne was taking effect. 'No regrets. Here's to the New World.' They raised their glasses to the toast.

It was raining out in the street, and they hailed a cab with their overcoat collars turned up against the cold.

They stopped at Matt's flat. 'Do you want to come in for a cup of coffee?' he asked.

'No thanks Matt, I must get home.' He held out his hand and they shook. 'Goodbye dear old friend. Write to me when you get settled.'

Matt promised to write, and thanked Tom for the great evening. He watched as the cab drove off, with a feeling loneliness and loss. He was now completely alone.

Chapter 8

Next morning Matt woke to the sound of rain beating against the window. He made a mug of coffee and sat in front of the heater. He had slept badly and woke with a headache from the champagne. He sipped his coffee, having his first misgivings about the coming events of the day. 'Too late now,' he thought. 'The die is cast.'

After a shower he felt revived, and he dressed in the only winter clothes that he was taking with him. After tidying up, he rang his mother to say goodbye, and to tell her about the things he was leaving in the flat.

The rain had stopped when he reached the street, carrying only the one suitcase. He hailed a cab and told the driver, 'Victoria Station.'

He arrived at the station with fifteen minutes to spare, and found the platform, where the train was waiting. There were groups of people standing around, but nothing to identify them as ship's passengers. Matt put his case down and lit a cigarette, surveying the travellers.

At ten past eleven, a whistle blew, and a shout came: 'All aboard!'

Matt found himself in a cabin with an elderly couple, and a young woman with two children. Another whistle and the train moved smoothly away from the station. He was on his way!

He sat looking out the window at the flat uninteresting countryside as they headed east. The children, a boy of about eight, and a little girl with blonde hair aged about five, sat one each side of their mother and chattered endlessly, whilst the old couple dozed.

The trip took just over an hour, and as they disembarked from the train, Matt saw a man standing with a notice. 'Green Star Line Passengers.'

Matt walked over and introduced himself. 'Very good sir. When we have all the passengers, we'll drive to a café for a quick lunch.' He had a northerner's accent.

Within a few minutes the passengers had gathered, all seven. The agent led them out to a small bus, and stowed their bags in the luggage hold. When they were all seated, he introduced himself, and said that they would stop for a quick bite on the way to the airport.

The café was expecting them and had a table set for nine.

'Well,' the agent said when they were all seated. 'Do you all know each other?'

There was a mumbled 'No.'

'In that case, I will read out your names, and if you want, you can say a few words to introduce yourselves.

'Mr and Mrs Booth.'

The elderly couple nodded and smiled. The old man said, 'We come from Melbourne and we've spent the last year tripping around England and Europe. We've had a marvellous time, but we're glad to be going home.'

The next was Mrs Hughes, a middle-aged woman, who said that she was travelling with her cousin Mrs Jones, and that they too were going home to Melbourne.

The young woman with the two children was introduced as 'Mrs Tapley and her two children.'

'I'm Joan Tapley, and this is Peter, and this is Jillian.' She was obviously English.

'We are going to Sydney to join my husband who is working there.'

'Last of all, this is Dr Harrison, who will be ship's doctor for the voyage.'

Matt smiled at the group. 'Nice to meet you all,' he said.

They had sandwiches and tea, and talked among themselves until the agent looked at his watch. 'Must be getting along now,' he said and stood up. 'Bus leaves in five minutes.'

At the airport, they went through Customs, and Passport Control, and then sat in the waiting area, looking out on to the tarmac and the grey sky. The plane was a twin-engined freighter, carrying several motorcars and a few passengers; it bore the insignia 'Channel Airways' on its fuselage. With the loading completed, the passengers were called.

Matt had never flown before, and felt a shiver of excitement as he climbed up the metal stairway. As he entered, he was greeted by a smiling airhostess, who showed him to his seat. There was only a small passenger cabin, and it seemed that there were no other passengers apart from his group.

One after the other, the engines whined and spluttered, then roared into life, until the cabin vibrated with the thunderous sound. The plane lurched forward, and taxied to the end of the tarmac, where it turned and halted. The pilot revved each engine to the maximum then returned it to idle. The hostess quickly checked that all seat belts were fastened then took her seat.

Matt looked out the window as the pilot opened the throttle and the plane charged forward, faster and faster, with the tarmac whizzing past in a blur and everything in the aircraft shaking and rattling. Suddenly the nose lifted and they were off the ground. Matt could feel his pulse racing, as he wondered to himself whether he could cope with flying in the outback of Australia.

They flew just above the clouds, so there was no view of the Channel as they crossed, and after about thirty minutes the plane started to descend, bumping its way through the clouds again.

The airport at Ostend was unimpressive, and it started to rain once they were inside the airport building. The agent who had travelled with them spoke to the customs officers, and they were waved through.

Another small bus was waiting for them outside, and once the bags were stowed, they boarded.

As they drove inland the temperature dropped, and although the bus heater was turned on, they still felt the cold. On and on they travelled, with the dusk gathering and snow lying on the ground.

It took three hours to reach Antwerp, and by then it was pitch black. As they drove through the dimly lit streets, it started to snow again. They reached the wharf, and the bus stopped at a building. The agent got out, turning up his overcoat collar in the cold. He disappeared in to the building, then after a few minutes he emerged and got back into the bus accompanied by a rush of icy cold air and a flurry of snow.

'Ladies and gentlemen, I'm sorry to tell you that the ship has been delayed, and will not berth until tomorrow morning. The Company has booked you all in at the Excelsior Hotel, and will pay for your board and lodging. Are there any questions?' He paused. 'None? Well we'd best be getting along then.'

The Excelsior Hotel was old, with an air of decaying elegance. The agent had told them that it had been the headquarters of the Gestapo during the occupation. The floor of the entrance hall was made of marble, with dark wood furniture and a crystal chandelier. An elegant marble staircase led to the upper floors, with an ancient wire cage lift beside it.

As Matt stood in the foyer he could imagine the red swastika banners and the black uniformed and jackbooted Nazis of the war days. He shivered. The taint of the dreaded Gestapo seemed to still linger there.

There were no formalities at the desk, as the Company had arranged everything, and he was given the key to his room.

The other passengers had all gone up to their rooms, and the lobby was empty. Matt walked over to the Concierge.

'Do you speak English?' he asked.

'Of course,' he replied with a pained expression.

Matt smiled. 'Sorry. Is the dining room still open?' he asked.

The Concierge softened. 'No sir, we were not expecting any guests, but there is a beer hall just around the corner, and you can get a meal there.'

Matt thanked him, changed five pounds into Belgian francs, and then picked up his case.

'Oh, and there will be breakfast served in the morning sir,' he added.

Matt went up in the lift, and found his room. He opened the door and was slightly taken aback by the elegance. There was period furniture, and a large double bed, with enormous pillows and an eider down bed cover. The window drapes were heavy and looked new, and the carpet was thick.

He put his case on the bed, and went in to the bathroom. There was a large bath, with a modern shower added at one end and a bidet beside the toilet. The taps and fittings were all gold-plated and the floor was white marble.

He freshened up then looked at his watch. Seven thirty. He was hungry.

As he walked through the lobby the Concierge signalled 'to the left.' Matt gave him a wave and walked out to the street. The air was freezing, and he turned up his collar as he walked to the corner. About fifty yards away he saw the beer hall's neon sign.

Inside the atmosphere was warm and smelled of cigarettes and beer, with a whiff of cooking cabbage. He sat at an empty table and was immediately attended by a pretty waitress. 'Beer please,' he asked.

'Eenglish?' she asked with a smile.

'Yes, do you speak English?'

'Not speek Eenglish, sorree.'

'Beer' she understood, and brought back a large glass with a foam collar.

'Food?' Matt asked, pointing at his mouth and patting his stomach. She looked puzzled, then brightened and hurried off, returning with a menu. It was written in Flemish.

He looked helplessly at the waitress, who realised his problem, and pointed at an item. 'Good,' she said, and patted her stomach. Matt nodded to her, and she headed for the kitchen.

Matt sat and sipped his beer, taking in the scene. There were about twenty tables and a dozen or so people sitting at them, eating and drinking. There was some background music, and a row of men sitting at the counter with pots of beer.

The Belgian beer was as good as it's reputation, and when the waitress returned with a large steaming dish of food, he ordered another beer, and started to eat. It was a brown stew-like dish, with boiled potatoes and cabbage, and it tasted marvellous.

He finished his meal, and sat back with a cup of coffee and a cigarette. 'Well,' he said to himself. 'Here you are in a strange land, on your own, and nobody knows you. I hope you've made the right decision.' He got up and paid the bill, then walked back to the hotel.

Weary after a long and eventful day, Matt climbed into bed, and slept heavily.

Chapter 9

The loud jangle of the telephone woke him, and he sat up in the darkened room uncertain of his whereabouts. He picked up the phone. 'Hello?'

'Doctor Harrison? This is the agent, Fred Bolton speaking.'

For a moment Matt was lost. 'Oh, yes, good morning Mr Bolton.' He squinted at his watch: seven thirty.

'I'm sorry to trouble you so early sir, but the *Griffin* has berthed, and I have a message for you from the Captain.' The northern accent seemed broader on the phone. 'He would like you aboard at ten this morning, to report to the Purser's Office. Would it suit you if I pick you up at nine thirty?' Matt thanked him and hung up. He still felt half-asleep. He walked to the windows and drew back the drapes. It was a clear grey dawn, with snow still piled on the windowsill.

At eight thirty, Matt walked down the great staircase carrying his bag. He felt refreshed after a shower and shave. He left his case with the concierge, and said to call him if the agent arrived. He would be at breakfast.

To Matthew's disgust, breakfast consisted of coffee, and a tray of cold sliced sausage and cheese. Sliced rye bread, pastries, croissants and strawberry jam completed the buffet. An elderly waiter creaked past. 'Excuse me,' said Matt. 'May I see the breakfast menu?' The waiter looked nonplussed.

'I would like bacon and eggs, please.'

'Sorry,' said the waiter with a polite smile. 'No Englees.'

'No eggs and bacon either,' said a voice behind him. It was old Mr Booth. 'I've already tried that on them. Just have to make the best of what's there,' he said grinning.

At nine thirty sharp, Fred arrived and found Matt waiting in the lobby.

'Had a good breakfast then?' he asked.

'Excellent thank you,' he lied.

Out in the street the air was freezing, but the sky had cleared and the sun shone weakly.

'We've got a few minutes to have a bit of a look at the city if you like,' said Fred, holding open the door of a black Mercedes.

They drove to the City Square where there was a statue of a man poised to throw a severed hand. 'That's where the name of the city came from,' said Fred. '"Ant werpen" – means "hand thrown". The legend says that a terrible giant called Antigoon lived on the banks of the river Scheldt in ancient times, and when sailors refused to pay his toll, he punished them by cutting off their hands. Finally a Roman soldier named Sylvius Brabo killed the giant, then cut off his hand and threw it into the river. Actually it is only a legend, but even so, the hand is the symbol of Antwerp, and features on its flag.'

Matt was impressed with Fred's knowledge of the city.

They drove on past the great Cathedral of Our Lady. 'You can still see the damage done in the war.' Fred pointed. It was a fine Gothic structure, which had miraculously not been destroyed by the severe shelling and bombing of two wars. It had been started in the thirteenth century, Fred told him, and the foundations were laid on a bed of goatskins, as the soil was wet and marshy, so the legend said.

They arrived at the port at ten minutes to ten and parked the car. The ship was sparkling with its new paintwork, and the dockworkers were busy swinging nets of cargo from the wharf to the hold. They climbed the gangway, where a sun-tanned good-looking young officer stood at the top. Fred greeted him by name, and then introduced Matt. 'This is Colin Smith, the third mate.'

They shook hands. 'So you're the new doc?' he said. Matt nodded. 'Welcome on board, I hope you enjoy the voyage,' he said with a pleasant smile that showed his white teeth.

'We're off to get him settled,' Fred said, steering Matt towards a doorway.

Matt felt a thrill of excitement as they walked along a passageway to the Purser's Office.

The Purser was aged about fifty, with balding fair hair, and a little overweight. He had bright blue eyes, but one was slightly turned out and had a white pupil. It was obviously sightless. He greeted Matt warmly, and introduced himself as Victor Bentley.

'Just call me Vic. You will be pleased to hear that your steward assistant was a field ambulance man in the war. I will get him to show you the sick bay presently. First let's get you settled in your cabin.'

'I'll see you before you sail,' said Fred. 'I've got a bit of work to do with the Captain.'

He went off to the Bridge, leaving the Purser to show Matt to his quarters.

'We've given you a passenger cabin, as we don't have a full complement of passengers. I'm sure you will find it comfortable,' Vic told him as they walked forward along a passageway. 'Also you will be accessible to the passengers, if any need your services.'

They reached the panelled cabin door, and Vic opened it with a key, letting Matt walk in first.

Matt was surprised at the size, and commented on it. 'Well actually it's a double cabin, so you can use the second bunk as a day bed.' Vic said. 'Your suitcase is there,' he pointed. 'Your tin trunk has been stowed below, but you can get to it if you need.'

'Thanks, it's full of books and things that I won't need on the voyage,' he replied.

'Right, well I'll leave you to get settled, and when you're through, come back to my office.'

Matt unpacked his cases and stowed his clothing in the drawers under the two bunks, and in the hanging wardrobe. The drawers all had to be lifted upward before they could be pulled out, so that they would not fly open in a rough sea. The cabin had polished wood panel walls and a thick maroon carpet. A door opened to the bathroom that had a toilet (referred to, Matt learned, as a 'head', though he never found out why). There was a large bath with a shower fitting, and a hand basin with a mirror above. Again, all the drawers featured 'lift up' security. Once everything was unpacked and put away, Matt walked back to the Purser's Office. There was a man in steward's uniform standing talking to Vic. 'Ah just at the right time,' he said. 'Matt, this is Charlie Hopkins, your sick bay assistant.' Charlie was in his mid thirties, Matt guessed, with a tough face and brown eyes. He had a scar down his left cheek. He held out his hand. 'Pleased to meet you Doctor,' he said with an easy smile. They shook hands.

'I hear you were in the Medical Corps during the war,' said Matt.

'Well yes I was, but only the last part of it. By the time I was old enough it was nearly over. I trained as a Medic, and served in a Field

Ambulance in France and in the advance in to Germany. Had quite a bit of action in the last few months. After the war I stayed on in the occupation forces and worked in a hospital.'

'With you on board, I doubt if a doctor is necessary!' Matt joked.

'He certainly is,' he replied. 'What would happen if I got sick?' They all laughed.

Matt took an immediate liking to him. He had a quick wit.

'Would you like to see the sick bay, sir?' Charlie asked.

'Yes please, and call me Matt.' He replied.

'No sir, you are a ship's officer, and I'd land in the brig if I did that, but I'll call you 'Doc' if that's okay.'

'Okay with me,' Matt replied. 'Let's go.'

'When you've done that, show him around the ship, Charlie,' Vic called after them.

'Right-o, sir,' he called back.

Two decks down, the sick bay consisted of a long narrow cabin with four bunks, which could be screened off, and room on each side of them to attend the occupant. At the end there was a bathroom with shower and toilet. It was all freshly painted white, and looked immaculate.

The next cabin was the doctor's consulting room and dispensary. There was a small desk, an examination couch, and a lot of cupboards. A deep hand basin for 'scrubbing up' was located under the porthole.

'What's in all the cupboards?' asked Matt.

'Drugs, dressings and everything needed for the voyage,' Charlie said, opening one to demonstrate.

'What about surgical instruments?' he asked.

'We have minor surgery instruments here for stitching up and pulling teeth, etc., but the full operating kit is kept by the Captain. I've never seen it.'

'Why on earth would he do that?' asked Matt with a puzzled expression.

'Board of Trade regulations,' he replied. 'Anyhow, if you want to check through them, you'll have to ask the Captain.'

Recalling his meeting with the Captain, Matt decided to change the subject.

'Once we are on our way you had better take me through the stock, so I know what we've got.' Matt closed the cupboard.

'We'll start when you want, Doc,' Charlie replied.

'Tell me about the day to day duties,' Matt asked.

'Well, it depends on the Captain, and they all have different rules,' Charlie said. 'Now this Skipper is fairly tough, and mostly goes by the book. He has a daily inspection of the ship, and usually wants the doctor to accompany him. He didn't get on well with the last doctor, so he might be a bit hard on you at first.'

'Thanks for the warning, I'll be on my best behaviour,' he said with a grin.

'We usually hold sick parade before the ship's inspection. My job is to assist you when required, and to do steward's duties for the rest of the time,' Charlie said as they walked out of the office.

'For starters, I'd like you to help me with sick parade, at least until I've got the hang of it and find out where everything is.'

'Taken for granted,' said Charlie. 'Now let's show you the ship.'

The *Griffin* was an old ship, built just before the second war, and had plied the Atlantic in convoys. She was slow, and could only make about twelve knots at the best.

She had been lucky not to be sunk, for in one U-boat attack, a torpedo had skimmed across her bows, but had not been followed by another, as a destroyer was hot in its pursuit. Some of the present crew had served on her and told stories of the war days.

She was eight thousand ton, and a typical 'general cargo' ship with a black hull and a raised forecastle. The forward cargo deck had a boom crane aft of its main hold, and was a scene of activity as men worked the crane to swing pallets of cargo up to the ship, and then lowered them down into the hold.

The superstructure was sparkling white with two rows of oblong windows below the bridge deck. From the bridge, the boat deck ran aft with four lifeboats sitting between davits ready for an emergency.

The funnel was painted white with a black boot top. On each side was a large green star.

They walked aft to a companionway that led down to the aft deck. Here too was a hold with a boom crane, but the hatch was secured and covered with canvas. The deck was deserted.

'The Bosun is in charge of loading cargo; he and the watch Officer, and they don't let passengers on the deck then as it's dangerous.

We're okay here though,' Charlie said as he led the way down on to the deck.

'We will be loading more cargo as we go through the Mediterranean,' he said as they walked past the hatch cover. 'When we reach the Indian Ocean and warm weather we put up a canvas swimming pool on this deck.' Charlie shivered at the thought.

They walked to the stern rail and leaned on it looking around the busy port.

This is one of the biggest ports in Europe,' Charlie said as they gazed over the wide span of water. 'This is actually the estuary of a huge river – the Scheldt, and we have to sail about fifty kilometres to reach the North Sea.

'When do you think we'll sail?' asked Matt.

'Well, the Captain didn't discuss it with me,' he said with a grin. 'I guess they will finish loading by mid afternoon, and the passengers are coming aboard after lunch, so we may sail late afternoon.'

Charlie looked at his watch. 'Nearly lunchtime, we best get back to see Vic.'

Back at the Purser's Office, Charlie headed off to do his other job, and Vic lead Matt to the dining saloon that was located two decks below the bridge, and looked forward through oblong windows to the busy scene on the deck below. Two uniformed men sat at a table eating; otherwise the saloon was empty. Vic took Matt over to them. 'Gentlemen, may I introduce our doctor, Matthew Harrison.'

The two stood up. 'Matt, this is Martin Black, our first Officer, and Jack Dunne, Second Officer.' They shook hands.

'Will you join us?' Martin asked.

'Thanks,' Vic replied, indicating a chair for Matt. They sat down.

'Care for a drink, Doc?' asked Martin. Matt noted that they were drinking water, and declined.

Through lunch they made light conversation. The First Officer, or 'Mate' as he was generally called, was a man about Matt's age, and had a wife and daughter living in London. He was friendly and affable, and Matt took a liking to him. Jack didn't have much to say, except that that he was not married, and was only happy when he couldn't see land.

'Does the Captain eat in the Saloon?' Matt asked.

'Yes, as a rule,' Martin replied, 'but as we will be sailing tonight, he will eat on the bridge with the pilot.' Matt took out a packet of cigarettes and offered them.

Martin held up his hand. 'Sorry, but smoking is not allowed in the dining saloon, Company rules. We'll move next door and have some coffee and a smoke.' He patted Matt on the shoulder as they got up. 'Don't worry, you'll soon catch on to the system.'

Next to the saloon was a smaller room with a notice on the door, 'Officers' Lounge'. They sat in leather chairs as coffee was served, and smoked cigarettes.

'What are you going to do in Australia?' asked Jack, blowing smoke in the air.

'I've got a job with the Royal Flying Doctor Service in the north-west of Western Australia,' Matt replied. Jack looked blankly at him.

'I've heard about them,' said Martin. 'Sounds exciting.'

Matt told them what he knew about it as they sipped their coffee.

The officers excused themselves and went back to their work, so Matt retired to his cabin as everyone seemed busy, and he did not want to get in the way. He sat down at his little desk that doubled as a dressing table with a mirror on the wall above it, and wrote a letter to his parents, telling them all the news. He promised to write from each port on the way. He finished the letter and dropped it in the box at the Purser's Office then went back to his cabin and stretched out on the bunk.

He woke with a start and looked at his watch, four thirty, he had slept for more than an hour. Outside it was dark.

There was a new sound, the throb of the engine. It was the sixth day of December 1961, and they were under way!

He put his shoes on and pulled on a thick jumper, then headed for the deck. As he opened the metal door, the cold air hit him. It was a clear night, and sea was quiet. Phosphorescent waves broke from the ship's side as it ploughed along. There was no moon. He walked around the boat deck, and went down on to the main deck aft to the stern rail, and stood watching the churning water in their wake. In the distance he could see the twinkling lights of the port they had left behind.

It was too cold to stay on deck, so he walked to the passenger's lounge, situated above the dining saloon, and under the bridge.

There was a strange couple sitting when he entered. The man stood and held out his hand. 'I am Dr Gerhard Schultze, and this is my wife Christa.'

Matt introduced himself, and shook his hand. He nodded politely and smiled at his wife.

'Well I'm very pleased to have another doctor on board,' Matt said when they were seated.

'Ah, let me explain,' said the German. 'I am not a medical doctor; I am an electrical engineer. We are going to visit our married daughter and family, who live in Sydney.'

Gerhard was about fifty, Matt guessed, and obviously well educated and cultured. He wore a cream raw silk jacket, with a red bow tie and dark trousers. He was olive skinned, with black hair, greying at the temples, and wore glittering rimless glasses. As he spoke, his piercing brown eyes fixed Matt without blinking. He looked extremely fit.

Matt wondered what he had done during the war and tried to visualise him in a Nazi uniform.

He'd not met Germans before. Christa was blonde and well groomed, and looked somewhat younger than her husband. She had cold pale blue eyes, but a pleasant smile that showed her white teeth. Her English was perfect, though like her husband, she spoke with an accent.

The Booths came in, likewise dressed for dinner, and Matt introduced them. He then excused himself and returned to his cabin to dress. When he returned, wearing a blue blazer and tie, the lounge was filled with passengers.

The children were well scrubbed up, and standing politely beside their mother who was talking to the German couple.

A steward in a white jacket served drinks, and another carried a tray of canapés. Martin came in dressed in a blue uniform with three gold stripes on his sleeves. He walked around the room introducing himself to all, and said that the Captain sent his apologies. He was obliged to stay on the bridge until the pilot left the ship.

They sipped their drinks and nibbled canapés, all a little restrained in the new environment and their first night at sea.

In the passageway, a gong was sounded. 'Ah, dinner. May I lead the way?' the Mate said putting down his glass.

The dining saloon was brightly lit, and the tables were laid with white tablecloths and shining silver. Martin stood at the door and said as they entered, 'Just sit at any table. Once we are settled, you will be allocated tables, changing every few days.'

The meal was simple and excellent, with coffee served at the table. After dinner Matt excused himself and returned to his cabin. He felt tired and a little depressed. He climbed into his bunk and read a book.

Next morning after a good breakfast, Matt walked out on deck. It was still cold, though the sun was shining, and there was no wind. The ocean was like glass, and a light mist lay on the water. Matt leaned on the rail looking at the water. As he stood, his mind far away, he was startled by the sudden blast of the ship's klaxon, followed by a voice on the loud hailer. 'Boat drill! Boat drill! All passengers to bring their life jackets and report to the boat deck.' Matt guessed that he was probably included, and dutifully fetched his life jacket and hurried to the deck. There the passengers were allotted to lifeboats, and were told the rules. After they were dispersed, Matt stayed on deck, watching the sea birds hovering.

'Good morning Matt.' He turned.

'Good morning Martin, lovely morning.'

'The Captain would like to see you on the bridge. Follow me.'

Matt felt a flutter of anxiety, as though he was a schoolboy summoned by the headmaster.

They reached the bridge where the Captain stood beside the helmsman. Through a glass window at the back of the bridge, Matt could see Second Officer Jack poring over a large chart on the table, with a pair of dividers in his hand. In front of the wheel was the binnacle housing the ship's compass. The Helmsman's eyes were glued to it.

The Captain turned as they stepped onto the bridge. 'Ah, Doctor, welcome aboard. I hope everything has gone smoothly up to now.' He was surprisingly affable compared with their last meeting.

'Yes thank you, sir, and I'm very pleased to be here.'

'Come into my cabin, I want to have a talk with you.' He led Matt back past the chart room to a little office-like cabin with a couple of comfy chairs. A door led to another cabin. 'That's my day cabin,' he said as if reading Matt's mind. They sat down, and the Captain went through the ritual of lighting his pipe.

'Now then,' he said through a pall of pleasantly scented tobacco smoke. 'What kind of a doctor are you?'

Matt was taken aback. 'I beg your pardon sir?'

'Are you handy with a knife?' he asked, smiling at Matt.

'I've been in surgical training for the past four years, and have only to sit the final exam to become a specialist surgeon,' Matt told him.

'Why haven't you done that?' He was uncomfortably direct.

'Well sir, that's a long story, and in any case, I want to have the experience of outback Australia before I become too specialised.'

'We don't usually have any serious problems at sea, but we get injuries in rough weather sometimes. A lot of routine stuff, a few malingerers, an occasional tooth to pull.'

He leant over and pressed a button.

'Starting tomorrow, I want you to hold sick parade at O-eight hundred each morning, then report to me at O`-nine thirty for ship's inspection. You can give me the health report before we start.'

A young lad in steward's uniform knocked and entered. 'Ah Jacob, get the doctor and me a mug of coffee, and some digestive biscuits.'

'Yes sir,' he said with a smile and disappeared.

'He's my cabin boy. Cheeky little devil, but he does his job well.'

Jacob returned as if by magic bearing a tray with steaming mugs and biscuits.

'That didn't take you long,' the Captain said.

'I knew you would ask for it, so I had it all ready sir,' he replied with a cheeky smile.

'Be off with you!' the Captain growled as he disappeared out the door.

'See what I mean?' he said with a chuckle.

They finished their coffee, and the Captain stood up. 'Come along, I'll show you 'round the bridge.'

When they returned to the bridge, Martin was standing by the Helmsman. 'Ship on the radar sir,' he said. The Captain put his face in to the soft rubber viewing-funnel.

'Have a look,' he beckoned Matt.

On the screen Matt saw a blob light up as the radar beam rotated.

'Just over the horizon,' Martin said, picking up some binoculars.

Fifteen minutes later it was close. It was a passenger liner of about twenty thousand tons, he was told, and they passed each other with only a few hundred yards between. There was much tooting of horns and waving, and then she was gone.

Matt spent the rest of the day familiarising himself with the contents of the dispensary cupboards. Charlie showed him how the paperwork was done, and the sterilising techniques for minor surgery.

That afternoon a notice went up on the dining saloon door with table allocations. Each table had one or two ship's officers at it, however Matt was treated as a passenger, to do the rotations with the others. He would start at the Chief Engineer's table.

Chapter 10

Next morning, Matt arose early, and was on deck at dawn. They were crossing the Bay of Biscay, and the sea was rough with a strong south-west wind in their teeth. It was too cold for comfort, and the ship's movement made it difficult to walk the deck, so he went in to breakfast. The saloon was empty.

As he sat down a steward brought a menu.

'Care for a cooked breakfast sir?' he asked, bracing himself against the roll of the ship.

'Yes thank you, I'm starving,' Matt replied, taking the menu. 'I'll have bacon, fried eggs, sausage, and tomato. And toast and coffee.'

The steward smiled in approval. 'Won't be many passengers in this morning sir, a bit too rough for them.'

'Let's hope they don't need the doctor,' he said with a grin.

The steward went off to the galley.

He arrived at the sick bay before eight, and found Charlie already sitting at the desk writing.

'Morning Doc,' he said looking up. 'Just writing up the daybook for our first sick parade. No starters so far.'

'What have we got for sea sickness?' asked Matt. 'I'm sure to have some sick passengers.'

'To be honest, I don't think anything helps much, but they usually get their "sea legs" in a few days,' Charlie replied. 'The last Doc used hyoscine mixture – that sometimes worked.'

'Why didn't the Captain like him?' Matt asked.

'Well it's like this. All sea captains are taught how to cope with simple medical problems, as some don't carry doctors. Our last Doc was silly enough to argue with the Captain about some medical problem, and of course he was right, but he made his points in front of other officers, causing him to lose face, and the Captain never forgave him.'

'Well, I'm not likely to repeat that. As far as I'm concerned, he's right even when he's not,' said Matt with a grin.

By nine fifteen, there had been no sick to deal with, so Matt headed off to the Purser's Office, where he was to meet the Captain.

Martin, carrying a large flashlight, and Vic were talking when he arrived. Both were in uniform with caps on.

Third Officer Colin joined them, followed by the Captain, in full regalia.

'Good morning gentlemen,' he said beaming at them. 'Let's get started.'

One by one, the Captain and entourage inspected the crew's cabins, followed by the main kitchen. The cook was standing to attention, and answered various questions about his department. The cold rooms were next, followed by the storerooms. Colin made notes of the Captain's comments, favourable or otherwise.

They came to the sick bay, and found Charlie busy on some task. He stood to attention as the Captain entered. 'Well Charlie, everything shipshape?'

'Aye aye sir, the Doctor has it all under control,' he replied.

Captain McKenzie looked at Matt with eyebrows raised.

'Yes sir,' Matt said pre-empting the question. 'We have it all sorted out.'

'Any sick passengers?' the Captain asked Matt.

'Not yet sir, but if the weather holds, it won' be long I reckon,' Matt replied.

'How are you holding up?' he asked.

'Just fine sir, started with a good breakfast.'

The Captain smiled and nodded approvingly.

As they left Matt winked at Charlie, who grinned.

The next day they entered the Mediterranean through the straits of Gibraltar. In the early morning light Matt could see the snow-capped Sierra Leone to the north, and the looming mass of the Atlas Mountains to the south. It promised to be a fine day.

By the end of the day they were steaming towards Marseilles, their first port of call. The weather was quite balmy, and as the sun sank to the horizon, Matt stood leaning on the stern rail, looking at the churned wake disappearing into the golden pathway.

All day he had thought of Penny. It was the tenth of December, her birthday.

Matt watched the sunset feeling depressed and miserable. If only he had been taken too. How lonely his life had become. It was bad enough in London, but here there was no one to talk to. How easy it would be to just slide over the rail and disappear. He would not be missed for some time. He was not afraid to die.

'Good evening Matt.'

He started.

'Sorry, I didn't mean to creep up on you.' It was Martin.

'Hello Martin, no problem, I was far away. Lovely evening.' The great mountains of cloud astern were edged with gold, and the sea was quiet.

'You must be feeling a bit lonely,' he said, seeming to read Matt's mind.

'Yes, you're right. I guess it's the first time in my life that I've been totally alone.'

'Matt, on a ship, we are one big family, and we are all friends. We all help each other.'

Matt turned and smiled at Martin. 'Thanks, that's nice of you.'

'Come and have a drink before dinner.' He led the way to the saloon.

The next morning when he woke, they were anchored off Marseilles and due to dock later in the day.

Matt stood on the deck looking at the port. The ocean sparkled in the morning sunshine, and towering over the city was a great white rock with a church on the top. Above it stood the golden statue of the Madonna, glittering in the sunshine. It was a wonderful sight.

After a good breakfast, he arrived at the sick bay and was astonished to find a queue of sailors waiting for him. He walked in and shut the door behind him. Charlie was busy unpacking a parcel from the cupboard.

'Mornin' Doc,' he said looking up with a cheery smile.

'Charlie, what the hell is going on? Are they all sick?'

'No way, Doc. All as fit as fiddles. They have come for their ration.'

'Ration?' Matt looked at him perplexed. 'Ration of what?'

'Frenchies.'

'Frenchies?'

'Yair Frenchies.' Charlie held up a little packet.

'Good Lord! That's a condom!' Charlie spluttered.

That's right Doc, Board of Trade regulations. Three each.'

'I'll be damned!' said Matt, astonished. 'Well, you better get on with it.'

Charlie put the cardboard box on the table and opened the door. The first sailor shuffled in and took his 'ration' without comment. The others followed, mostly silent, with an occasional 'Ta.'

To Matt's surprise, the last in the queue was Jacob, the Captain's steward.

'G'morning Doc,' he greeted Matt with a broad smile.

'Jacob, how old are you?' Matt asked sternly.

'I'm eighteen, and old enough,' he replied with his cheeky grin.

Charlie dished out his ration and he disappeared. 'No other problems: we'll get those when we sail,' he said.

'Oh? Like what?' asked Matt.

'Always the odd cut lip, black eye and bruises, not to mention those who think they got a dose of the pox. Sailors are like that Doc.'

They berthed at ten o'clock in the busy harbour, close to the old port, and in no time the covers came off the hatches, and the boom cranes were manned.

It was a bright sunny day with no wind as Matt stood looking down at the scene of activity. The wharf labourers sweated and shouted to each other in rough French, while the clanking boom crane swung the palates of cargo in to the hold, supervised by the Bosun, with his whistle.

Matt went to the Purser's office, and was greeted by Vic. 'Hello Doc. Are you going ashore?'

'That's what I was going to ask you. Am I allowed to?'

'Certainly, but you must have a pass to get by the Customs and Immigration fellers.' He held out a pass. 'All the passengers have gone ashore.'

'When do we sail?' Matt asked.

'Dawn tomorrow, for Genoa. Must be on board by midnight,' he said. 'You'll need a few bob in the local currency too,' he said offering him a few bank notes. 'Five quid in francs, you can fix me up later. Do you speak any French?'

'Just school boy level, but it will get me lunch.'

Matt thanked him and went down the gangway. He walked along the cobbled streets around the old port, and up to the city. It was good to stretch his legs on dry land. He stopped at a street café and bought a bread roll with ham and mustard, and a cup of coffee, and sat at a table as he ate and watched the passers-by.

He wandered around the city for a couple of hours, and then strolled back to the old port, where he saw Mrs Tapley and her children. They had just bought balloons from a street vendor, and they floated above them on strings.

'Hello Doctor, we've just been out to the Chateau d'If on a launch,' she said as he approached.

'Yes and we saw the gaol where they kept the Count of Monte Cristo,' said Peter. 'He dug a tunnel and escaped.' He was keen to air his knowledge.

As they walked together back to the ship, little Jillian held his hand. Matt felt a pang as he thought of Chloe. 'Are you married Doctor?' her mother asked.

He paused, and then said. 'No, no I'm not married, and please call me Matt.'

Jillian tugged his hand and he looked down. 'Can I call you Matt, too?' She looked up at him with wide blue eyes. Matt felt a lump rising in his throat.

'Of course you can Jillian, and you too, Peter. I hope we will all be good friends.'

When they reached the ship, they found the work still going on, with pallet after pallet of cargo disappearing into the holds.

Jack was at the head of the gangway. 'Hello Mrs Tapley. Had a good afternoon?'

'Thank you, yes, we went out to the Chateau D'If.'

'Yes and we saw the Count of Monte Cristo,' said Peter, his imagination running away.

Matt excused himself and went to his cabin. He lay on his bunk. 'Let them go,' Tom had said, but how could he? They were always with him.

At sunset the next day they anchored off Genoa. There was an air of excitement in the dining saloon that evening. He was still at 'Scotty' the Chief Engineer's table, and by now had learned not to pace him with drinks! He had a weakness for Scotch whisky, but drank water with his meals. The danger time was after dinner.

Next morning the port was a hive of activity, with the winches clanking and the whistles and shouts; this time in Italian. Matt watched for a while then went to breakfast.

He arrived at sick parade to find Charlie dishing out condoms to the queue of sailors. So far there had been no casualties, and the passengers seemed to have their sea legs.

He went ashore and walked around the wharf, and up into the old city through narrow streets with worn cobbles. The sky was grey and there was a cold wind. By lunchtime he'd had enough, and when it started to rain he took a taxi back to the boat.

They sailed at midnight, as Matt lay asleep in his bunk.

Their final Mediterranean port was Livorno, or 'Leghorn' as the English called it, where they were to load marble chips. It had been the principal port of the Italian navy in the war, and was heavily bombed by the allies. It was now an important army and air force base.

The Green Star ships had never called there before, so this visit was special, and at the Company's suggestion, there was to be a party on board.

They berthed at dawn, and after breakfast with nothing better to do, Matt joined the Booths and Joan Tetley and children on a day trip to Pisa.

It was a clear winter's day and the little bus made good time on the motorway. They pulled in to the town, and parked by the green lawn near the cathedral and the famous 'Leaning Tower'. The Booths took photos, and Matt, with the Tapley family, climbed the circular stairway up the top of the tower with their guide. Matt was alarmed at the feeling of insecurity as they climbed higher and higher. The angle of lean seemed to increase! At last they reached the top, where, as the guide pointed out, about five hundred years before, Galileo had dropped two cannon balls – one large and one small to prove his theory on falling bodies. Matt peered over the edge, with the nasty feeling that he too was about to fall. Little Jillian held on tightly to his hand.

They wandered through the cathedral, which also seemed to be on a lean, and then entered the circular baptistry where the guide demonstrated its famous echo with his fine tenor voice.

'They all sing,' Mr Booth commented.

They sat in the sun eating pizza, and drank red Chianti poured from a raffia-covered bottle, while the Tapley children played on the swings in the park.

Back at the ship, preparations were well under way for the evening. Invitations had gone out to all the city dignitaries and the deck was festooned with coloured lights. Matt changed into a blue jacket and tie, and strolled into the saloon where he found a couple of the ships junior officers chatting. They were talking about the agent – whose name was Fanfani – the subject of some coarse comments.

At seven the guests arrived in breath-taking splendour! The first on board was Signor Fanfani with his wife. As they stepped on to the deck, the assembled officers gazed at Signora Fanfani with astonishment. She looked like Gina Lolobrigida, with shoulder length Titian hair, lustrous eyes, and a beautiful suntanned figure that set off her emerald green silk gown, casually covered with a mink fur stole.

As Signor Fanfani introduced his wife to the drooling officers, a procession of portly middle aged men in glittering uniforms, accompanied by their elegant wives, climbed the gangway.

Among them were the Mayor of the city, the Chief of Police, the Chief of Customs, an Army General from the local garrison, the Air Force Commanding Officer and a number of other important officials. All were resplendent in uniforms glittering with gold braid and rows of medals. Each had a partner in fine costume and furs, festooned with jewellery.

Matt had never seen such a line up of dignitaries!

In the saloon the guest and passengers all mixed, whilst the Captain and officers circulated.

The first major setback was that very few of the guests spoke English! Stewards brought around drink trays, offering glasses of sherry or beer, but there were few takers from the guests. Likewise the trays of canapés seemed not to the Italian taste.

As Ship's Doctor, Matt had been given a table for the occasion, with the Booths, the Customs Chief and his wife, and another younger Italian couple, the husband in Air Force uniform with lots of gold braid and medals, and his comely wife in a beautiful gown with a pearl necklace. None of his guests spoke English!

When they were seated, Matt produced from his pocket a tourists' phrase book in Italian/English, and attempted to introduce himself and the Booths to their guests, much to their amusement.

The Customs Chief was a large bald man with heavy features and a booming voice. His swarthy complexion suggested a southern origin. Dressed in a sky-blue uniform covered with shiny buttons, medals and gold braid, he reminded Matt of the pictures he had seen of Mussolini during the war.

The Chief joined in the spirit of the occasion as they passed the little book around the table with much hilarity. By contrast, his wife was thin, with a sharp plain humourless face, and made no attempt to join in the halting conversation.

Glasses of water were poured, and the first course – vegetable soup – was placed on the table. The next course was a hot Madras curry, served with rice and poppadums.

The Customs Chief at that moment was holding up the tourist book in one hand and gesticulating with the other as he attempted to converse with Mrs Booth. While he waited for her response, he scooped a large fork-full of curry into his mouth. The effect was dramatic! His face suffused, and he stood up with his hand on his mouth, tipping his chair over backwards!

'Vino!' he bellowed, between choking noises. 'Vino!'

The room fell silent and all eyes were on him, as he stood with bulging eyes, looking as though he would explode!

Matt came to the rescue and offered a glass of water. 'I'm terribly sorry we have no wine. You see, this is an English ship. Perhaps you would like a glass of beer?' At this, Mr Booth convulsed with laughter, and received hostile glares from the startled guests.

The hapless Chief gulped water and then sat down, sweating and puce in the face, with his eyes streaming as he fanned his mouth with his hand. His wife looked absolutely appalled, and pushed her plate away.

Within ten minutes the party had broken up, and the guests were making their farewells. Matt noted that the plates of curry at other tables were hardly touched! It was indeed an unfortunate choice!

Later, in the Officers' Lounge the Captain summed up the situation.

'Och weel, we should've given them spaghetti I suppose.'

They agreed to put it down to experience – or lack of it – and do better next time!

'Not for a few years – if we're lucky,' the Skipper growled over his whisky.

Next morning, the loading continued until midday, then the

hatches were closed and covered, and the ship prepared for sea. Nothing was said about the previous night's fiasco!

It had been a still afternoon, and the ocean looked grey and oily smooth as they sailed into the gathering dusk.

After dinner, as they approached the straits of Messina, they were treated to a fireworks display from Stromboli, a volcano in the little group of Aeolian Islands north-east of Sicily. The volcano, one of the world's most active, stood ten thousand feet above the sea, and belched a great red spout of fire that reached up to the black sky, ending in a glowing cloud that spread above the mountain. Matt stood with the Tapley children who watched in awe.

The next day when they woke, they were steaming across the Mediterranean, with a cold head wind, and a choppy sea. As the sun went down they were approaching Port Said, and docked at seven. They would stop overnight, take on more fuel oil, and then set sail with the Canal Pilot.

After dinner that night the 'gully-gully man' came on board and amused the passengers with his sleight of hand tricks. Little Peter sat cross-legged in front of him as he squatted on the deck, and was mortified, blushing to the roots when, after intoning 'gully-gully' a few times, the man produced a live chicken from inside Peter's short trouser leg!

He then took a five shilling piece from Mrs Booth, and after having her write her name on a piece of paper, he folded up the coin and threw it over the side. The old lady snorted with indignation, but was appeased next day when a steward returned it to her, still wrapped, and quite dry.

The weather had become warm and the officers turned out in white shorts during the day, as the ship sailed slowly through the Suez Canal. At one point where the canal was quite narrow, a row of Arabs stood urinating towards the ship and making obscene gestures. The ladies hurried in doors.

They watched a beautiful sunset at the Bitter Lakes, then continued on, through the Red Sea, to reach Aden next day.

They could not dock, as the city was rioting – gunfire could be heard from the ship. But it could not stop the hoard of bumboats paddling out to greet them. Some merchants were allowed on board to set up their wares on the aft deck. The passengers gathered around and eagerly haggled for 'bargains.' Aden watches had a reputation for working for about a week, and rolls of film ran out after two or three exposures. The rolls of silk and printed cotton were popular with the women, however, and were snapped up.

Matt watched the scene from the boat deck above with interest, but resisted the temptation to go down and bargain with the traders.

Chapter 11

Next morning they headed out into the Indian Ocean.

Outside the Purser's Office was a great chart on the wall, and each day the First Mate ruled a red line showing the ship's progress over the previous twenty-four hours, from their start in Hull, through the ports of call. Now there was only ocean before them for the next two weeks.

It was the day before Christmas Eve and Matt woke early. He lay on his back thinking back on the terrible events a year ago. Somehow they seemed like a bad dream, and now his pain was less intense.

Perhaps he really was starting to let them go.

Sick parade that morning produced the first minor casualties. A cook with a nasty cut hand and two sailors who probably had gonorrhoea, picked up in Genoa at the same brothel.

Matt stitched up the hand, whilst Charlie started the others on a course of penicillin injections.

The ocean was now a sparkling blue, and dolphins played around the bows as they ploughed along, heading south-east towards Western Australia. That night, he saw for the first time the Southern Cross shining brightly in the velvety black sky.

Christmas Day was celebrated in traditional style with a banquet luncheon. Roast turkey, ham, plum pudding with brandy sauce, and lots of champagne. Apart from those on watch, all the officers were present, and the Captain made a speech. Matt retired to his cabin and spent the rest of the afternoon dozing.

On Boxing Day, the crew, supervised by Sam Doust, the Bosun, set about building the swimming pool on the aft deck beside the hatch cover. It was made from long planks of wood, set up to form an oblong box about fifteen feet wide and twenty feet long. When it was all secure, a heavy canvas liner was dragged into position and lashed to the timber. The fire hose was then connected and the pump turned on. Seawater gushed in, and soon the pool was two-thirds full, with over six feet of water in it.

It took a couple more days before the weather was really warm enough to swim, but the German couple had spent each day lying in their bathers, covered with coconut oil, sun baking. They were both well tanned, and spent all morning splashing in the pool or sun bathing.

As they approached the Equator, the weather became progressively hotter, with little or no wind. Great monsoon clouds loomed on the horizon, and the humidity increased each day.

New Year's Eve came and went without a great deal of celebration, though after dinner, Matt unwisely joined the Chief Engineer for a few celebratory drinks. He produced a bottle of Black Label Johnny Walker Scotch and threw the cork out the porthole. At midnight, the ship's horn let out a blast to welcome the New Year, and with three-quarters of the whisky gone, Matt excused himself and walked unsteadily to his cabin, leaving Scotty to finish the bottle.

The wall chart recording their progress indicated that they would be crossing the Equator the next day, and after dinner that evening, a notice to that effect was posted on the notice board. All passengers were requested to group on the aft deck at eleven o'clock next day, as King Neptune would be boarding the ship to interview all those who had not crossed the equator before.

Next morning after the sick parade and ship's inspection, Matt went on deck to find that an awning had been rigged over the end of the aft deck to give protection from the fierce sunshine, and on the canvassed hatch cover a 'throne' was placed, awaiting King Neptune. A gangplank had been erected between the hatch top and the pool, extending across to the other side. Flags and bunting were strung around the whole area.

At eleven all the passengers and a lot of crew had assembled under the awning. Those who had not crossed the Equator before were advised to wear their bathers.

At eleven thirty, the ship's horn sent out a blast, and a voice on the loudspeaker announced that the ship was now crossing the Equator, and that King Neptune would be boarding the ship.

At the sound of a trumpet, everyone turned to see a green apparition carrying a three-pronged spear with seaweed draped over it climb over the ship's rail, accompanied by two similar creatures. The King was helped up onto the hatch cover, where they settled him on his throne. The uninitiated were called for: some crewmembers,

Mrs Tapley and children, the German couple, and Matt.

From a scroll of paper, the King called the names, and thumped his trident spear on the deck. 'The Tapley family!' he roared. They came forward, little Jillian clutching her mother's hand. The King stood, and draped a necklace of seaweed around mother's neck, then gave each child a green lollipop on a stick. They were then told that it was customary to now jump in to the pool, but optional. Little Jillian shrank back, and was sat on the canvas as Joan walked to the middle of the 'gangplank' accompanied by the assistant monsters, then held her nose, and jumped. Peter followed and splashed about, then climbed out with his mother to applause.

Next came the Germans. Christa received a necklace, but for Gerhard there was more in store. Three large pots were produced from behind the throne and the two assistants proceeded to dollop him with coloured gooey stuff, made, it turned out, by the assistant cook. At first Gerhard looked outraged, and drew back, but quickly surrendered and smiled reluctantly. The assistants led him to the pool and amongst cheers, pushed him in.

Matt was next, and got red, green and yellow stripes, then followed Gerhard into the pool. Fortunately the coloured goo washed off easily. The crewmembers were treated a little more roughly, and one wrestled with the assistants, causing them all to fall in the water. But no one was hurt, and it was taken in good spirits. When all were done the King made a brief speech, welcoming newcomers to his domain, and each was presented with a certificate.

The Captain shouted drinks for the passengers, and chatted with them under the awning as the ship surged on through the sparkling blue ocean.

The fine weather held for the next two days, but then there was a dramatic change. After dinner that night the Captain announced that they were heading straight towards a tropical cyclone, and although they had altered course to avoid the worst of it, cyclones could change their direction quickly and they must be prepared. They all returned to their cabins to secure their belongings.

Matt secured his drawers and cleared the bench top of objects. Once in his bunk, he raised the leeboard as instructed, and clicked the locks. Hopefully this would prevent him from rolling out.

Through the night the weather deteriorated, and the ship started to pitch and roll.

Matt lay in his bunk in the dark as the noise level increased, and the ship lurched violently in the huge seas. He drifted off and slept fitfully, woken from time to time by the ship's violent movement, and from the crashing sounds that came from the ship's bowels. At first light someone pounded on his door. 'Doc! Wake up Doc!' Matt struggled out of the bunk, climbing over the leeboard. He crashed across the room as the ship rolled steeply, and fell on the carpet. 'Coming!' he shouted, then opened the door. It was Charlie.

Charlie was hanging on to the passage rail. 'Get some clothes on quick, we've got work to do!' He panted, still out of breath from battling the elements.

As they made for the sick bay, hand over hand along the rail, Charlie filled him in. One of the crew had slipped on the deck and struck his head on a steel stanchion. He was found unconscious and bleeding in the scuppers, but as two men tried to drag him to safety, a wave washed the three of them along the length of the deck. They were rescued and carted below.

The sick bay looked like a war zone, with three injured men in various states of consciousness, lying on blood-soaked sheets.

The first victim had a bad laceration on his scalp, and was bleeding profusely. He was out cold. Of his rescuers, one had an obvious broken wrist, while the other had a badly swollen and bleeding nose.

Matt shot some morphine into both, then turned his attention to the unconscious man.

He stitched up the jagged wound in his scalp, and checked him over. He had lost a fair bit of blood, but his vital signs were stable.

Next came the fracture. The bone was displaced and before it could be set, it had to be straightened. In spite of the morphine the man groaned in pain as Matt tried to manipulate the bones. Finally, in seemingly good position, he encased the arm in plaster of Paris and settled him in a bunk with leeboards on both sides, next to the unconscious man.

The nose was difficult. The morphine had deadened the pain, but blood still poured out.

Matt sat the injured sailor in a chair with Charlie behind holding his head steady. Matt sat in front, and using a head mirror, he focused the light up the bleeding nostrils, then slowly and carefully, packed the nose with ribbon gauze, using a long pair of forceps. Finally he too was tucked into bed, with an ice pack over his nose.

Matt and Charlie peeled off their blood-soaked gowns, washed, and sat down. It was nearly noon, and they had worked non-stop since seven. Being two decks down, the ship was more stable, but still it was difficult to stand and keep balance. Charlie made coffee and they drank and smoked cigarettes in silence.

There was a knock on the open door. The Captain entered accompanied by the Martin.

'Well Doctor, I see you are earning your keep,' the Captain said looking around at the bloody mess. 'How are the men?'

'One unconscious, but stable, the other two are recovering. One has a broken wrist, and is out of action. The other, a broken nose, but will probably be okay in a couple of days, at least for light duties,' Matt replied.

'Good. We've gone through the worst of the weather now, and the barometer is starting to rise.'

By four that afternoon the wind had moderated, and the ship's movement was less. The unconscious man was stirring, and the other two, having slept off the morphine, were ready for more. Charlie had cleaned the place up, and order was restored. He then went off and arranged for food to be brought to the sick bay for the injured and also for him and Matt.

By eight in the evening the sailor with the head injury had regained consciousness, and could take fluid.

Charlie elected to sleep the night in the sick bay, and to call Matt if there were problems.

Matt walked wearily back to his cabin and collapsed on his bunk.

Next morning the sun was shining and the sea was at its sparkling best again. Matt dressed and went to the sick bay.

'Well Charlie, how was the night?' he asked.

'The boys were a bit restless, but they all settled eventually,' he replied.

'You go and clean up, and have breakfast, while I stay here,' he told Charlie.

They left the Tropic of Capricorn, and were on the last leg of their journey. The wounded had recovered, but were all scheduled for X-rays when they reached Australia.

As the days went by Matt started to become more and more excited about his future. He lay for hours re-reading the information he had on the north-west of Western Australia until he knew it almost by heart.

At dinner a few days before landfall, now sitting at the First Officer's table, Martin asked him where he would be staying in Perth. Matt really hadn't considered this, so next day he sent a telegram to the Health Department, advising them of his imminent arrival, and asked them to arrange accommodation, and advise him on arrival.

Life on board had been easy and comfortable. Fortunately he had had no medical nightmares, and he had enjoyed the company of the officers who had treated him as one of them. It was like living in a cocoon, and in a few days, he would emerge back into the real world.

On the last night at sea, the Captain held a cocktail party, with all the passengers and off-duty officers. It was held on the aft deck, which was strung with lights. The night was warm and pleasant, with no breeze except that created by the ship's steady forward motion.

The stewards circulated with drinks and canapés, and all the passengers had dressed for the occasion. The officers were smartly turned out in their whites. The Captain called attention and thanked the passengers for travelling in his ship and for their friendly co-operation and adaptation to ship board life.

Mr Booth stood up and thanked the Captain on behalf of the passengers for their comfortable and safe passage, then called for three cheers for the Captain and his crew. They responded loudly.

Matt packed his belongings before bed, and slept soundly.

Next morning he was up before sunrise, and out on deck, but there was no sign of land. After breakfast he went to the sick bay and found Charlie packing the cupboards, and checking the stores. Matt signed the letters requesting X-ray and medical attention for the injured crewmen while they were in the port of Fremantle.

At the Purser's Office, Vic told him that there would be no inspection this morning, so he strolled out on the boat deck, meeting Martin on the way to the bridge.

'Come on up to the bridge, we'll see land soon,' he said, and led the way. It was a sparkling brilliant morning, with the bluest of blue water. Already there were sea birds in the sky, following the ship, and a light breeze blew from the east. The Captain was not on the bridge, and Colin stood by the helmsman.

'How far off now, Colin?' asked Martin.

'Should see land in about fifteen minutes,' he replied, squinting through his binoculars.

Martin took Matt into the chart room, and showed him their position on the chart spread out on the table.

'Land ho!' called the starboard lookout, looking through his binoculars. Matt could see nothing. Martin lent him a pair and he searched the horizon ahead. Finally he saw it. A dark line on the horizon.

'That is Rottnest Island,' Colin said, 'about twelve miles off the coast.'

An hour later they were abeam of the island, heading for the channel to Gage Roads, the anchorage where they would pick up the pilot.

The coastline was low-lying and featureless, with a line of white beach at the water's edge and red dots of rooftops between the grey-green foliage. With binoculars it looked more interesting, but it was nothing like he had imagined.

There were several ships lying at anchor as they steamed slowly towards the port of Fremantle, and as Matt watched, the pilot boat approached at speed. Alongside, the pilot caught a rope ladder, and scrambled aboard.

He was escorted to the bridge, where the Captain greeted him, and handed over command.

Slowly they crept into the harbour, escorted now by two tugs that fussed and tooted as they shepherded their charge in towards the wharf. Light lines with a 'monkey's fist' on the end were thrown and caught, then the heavy mooring ropes were hauled from the ship to the great bollards where they were secured.

It was mid January 1962, and the voyage was over.

Chapter 12

Matt watched as the gangway was lowered, and when secure, the officials came aboard. First the Customs and Immigration officers, followed by the agent, and his assistant.

A Steward tapped Matt on the arm. 'Excuse me sir, but the Purser would like you to go to his Office.' Matt followed him down.

'Ah there you are Doc,' said Vic. 'This is Steve Harley, our agent.' They shook hands. 'Got some mail for you Doc,' he said and passed over a bundle of letters.

'Now what about your injured?' he asked.

'Just a formality at this stage, they need X-rays, and the broken wrist may need re-setting, as I had no X-ray on board. I've done letters for them addressed to your company's doctor.'

The agent spoke to his assistant, who arranged for the men to go ashore as soon as cleared by Customs.

Matt excused himself and went to his cabin. He sat at the desk and opened his mail. There was one from his mother, and one from Tom. A few bills that had been sent on, and one local, in a manila envelop with 'Department of Health WA' at the top. He opened it first.

It was signed by the Commissioner of Health, who welcomed him to Western Australia, then told him to take a taxi, using the enclosed authority to bill the Health Department. He was to stay at the Esplanade Hotel in Perth, and to come to the Department on Monday morning at nine.

Matt put the letter down, puzzled at the delay, until he realised that today was Friday. He read his mother's letter next, which told him local gossip, and hoped he was well and looking after himself.

Tom's letter told little more, but added some hospital gossip. He had seen Sir James Watson, Matt's old Chief, at a Christmas party and told him that he'd had a letter. The Chief sent his best wishes, and said that he looked forward to hearing from Matt in due course.

Matt had a last look around his cabin, then closed his suitcases, and carried them out to the Purser's Office. Steve, the agent, was standing talking to Vic and greeted him as he walked up to them. 'Well Doctor, have you got everything?'

'No, not really,' he replied, 'I've got a trunk of books somewhere.'

'Don't worry about that,' said Vic. 'I'll look after it and see that Steve has it in safe keeping for when you want it.'

Steve nodded and handed Matt a card. 'Give me a call at the office when you get settled and I'll have the luggage delivered.' Matt tucked it in his wallet.

The Customs officer appeared around the corner. 'Are you the Doctor?'

Matt nodded. 'Matthew Harrison,' he said holding out his hand.

'I'm told that you are leaving the ship here. Have you anything to declare?' he asked in a stern voice.

'Er, no, I don't think so.' Matt replied.

'Right, good-o,' he said and walked off.

Matt looked at Vic with a surprised expression. 'Don't worry, they're all like that,' he said with a grin.

For the next hour Matt wandered around the ship saying goodbye to his shipboard companions, who were all travelling on to the eastern ports. He found Charlie doing the final chores in the sick bay, and shook his hand warmly. 'If I ever need an able assistant in my future practice, I'll send for you Charlie,' he said giving him a slap on the back.

'Thanks Doc, but I won't hold you to it,' he replied with a grin.

Back at the Purser's Office Vic told him that the landline was connected, and he would call a taxi for him.

They walked out on deck together, and Matt made his farewells at the top of the gangway.

'Hope to see you again on the homeward voyage,' he said, shaking Matt's hand. 'We'd like a Doc like you every time,' he added. 'Oh, and I nearly forgot.' He put his hand into his pocket and produced a one-shilling coin. 'With the compliments of the Company,' he said with a grin, passing it to Matt.

'Thanks a lot,' said Matt, turning it over in his hand. Then added with a smile. 'Do you need a receipt?'

With a wave, he descended the gangway to start his next adventure.

Matt's cases were already on the dock at the foot of the gangway, and as he reached them, a taxi drew up. The driver called out the window. 'Are yer the Doc?' The broad accent took him by surprise.

'Yes, yes I am,' he replied picking up his cases.

'Ere, lemme fix 'em,' he said as he got out. He was dressed in shorts and a tee shirt, with rubber 'flip flop' thongs on his feet. He picked up the cases and stowed them in the boot.

'Where yer goin'?' he asked as Matt got in. Matt told him the hotel, and they drove off.

'First time in Perth?' the driver asked over his shoulder.

'Yes,' Matt replied, unaccustomed to chatty taxi drivers.

'Would yer like to see a bit of the place on the way?' he asked, looking up at Matt in the rear mirror. 'Won't cost yer much more.'

'Thanks, that would be nice.'

They passed through Fremantle, and crossed the bridge over the Swan River, which ran through the harbour to the ocean. They turned and drove down to the seaside, and followed the road along the coast for a few miles. The sparkling blue water and snow-white beach was a glorious sight, with the afternoon sea breeze just ruffling the water. 'God's own country,' the driver remarked. The sunlight was so intense that it made Matt's eyes water.

They left the ocean and drove back to the river, which had expanded into broad reaches, some miles across. A few riverboats carved up the smooth water. As they drove, the driver gave a running commentary on the scenery. They drove around a winding road beside the river, with a steep escarpment on the left side of the road. 'Up there's Kings Park,' he pointed. 'Yer get a great view of the city from there.'

They rounded a bend and the city of Perth lay in front on the edge of the river, sparkling like a jewel in the sunshine. The breeze had not yet reached the city and the water was like glass, reflecting the buildings in the clear air.

They pulled in at the Esplanade Hotel, a large two-storey colonial style building with wide verandas, situated near the river. A porter came out and took the bags, as Matt handed the driver the voucher, and a five-shilling piece as a tip, thanking him for the tour.

The day had become very hot, and Matt, dressed in a coat and tie, felt uncomfortable. The hotel by contrast was cool and quiet as he walked in. Ceiling fans turned slowly, stirring the air. There was an atmosphere of tranquillity about it.

His room was upstairs, and French windows opened out on to the balcony, looking out to the river. The cool sea breeze was now gently wafting in, and moved the curtains. It was a large room with a fan in the high ceiling. There was a large wardrobe, a chest of drawers, and a dressing table. The bed was large and soft, and in the corner there was a hand basin with hot and cold water and a towel. Above the basin was a cabinet for toiletries with a mirror on it. The bathroom was along the passage.

Matt unpacked, had a wash, and stripped to his underwear, then stretched out on the bed. The warm weather made him sleepy. He was just drifting off when the telephone rang, startling him.

'Dr Harrison? This is Reception. There's a call for you.' He waited, the phone clicked. 'Dr Harrison?' A man's voice.

'Speaking,' Matt replied.

'This is the Health Department, Dr Peter McLean speaking. The Commissioner asked me to call you to ask if you are settled in comfortably.'

'Thank you Dr McLean, I've just arrived, and am in my room. Everything is just fine thank you.'

'I don't suppose you have any plans for the weekend, so I thought you might like to spend the day with us tomorrow. We could have a swim and a barbecue.'

'That sounds marvellous, thank you,' Matt replied.

'Great, we'll pick you up at ten, okay?'

'Thanks, I'll be waiting for you.'

Matt lay back, hands behind his head, and looked at the ceiling. 'So far so good,' he thought.

The first part of the adventure went well, with no problems, and already he felt like a new person, wandering in a strange New World, full of exciting new things. He thought of Penny and little Chloe, but without pain now, just a loving memory of them. And now for the next real challenge, the Northwest! He drifted off to sleep.

It was six o'clock when he woke, and still warm. He put on his dressing gown, took his towel and toilet bag, and went down the passage to the men's bathroom. He took a long hot shower, followed by a cold one and, refreshed, walked back to his room to dress for dinner.

Downstairs in the cocktail bar there were a few couples, sitting with drinks, chatting. He ordered a dry martini, and took it to an empty table. There was a dish of mixed nuts on the table. He sat sipping his cocktail and nibbling nuts, listening vaguely to the chatter when a voice behind him said, 'May I join you, or are you expecting company?'

Matt turned. A sun-tanned man in his fifties stood smiling at him. 'Please join me, I'm alone,' he said half rising.

The older man held out his hand. 'My name is William Corbett – call me Bill.'

They shook hands, and Matt introduced himself. Bill signalled the waiter. 'I'll have a scotch, ice and water thanks,' and seeing Matt's near empty glass, 'and another one of those,' he pointed at Matt's glass.

Bill Corbett was a well-built man with strong hard hands. His grey hair was thinning, and his blue eyes twinkled from his weather-beaten brown face. His manner was warm and friendly.

'Are you a newcomer to Perth?' Bill asked as the drinks arrived.

'Just got off a ship from England.'

'Cheers, and welcome,' Bill raised his glass.

'What brings you to Perth?' the older man asked.

'I've come to do a job in the North,' he replied, deliberately vague.

'Really? What sort of work do you do?' he persisted.

'Actually, I'm a doctor, and I'm going to work with the Royal Flying Doctor Service in the Northwest.'

'Well now, that's just where I live!' His face lit up in a wide smile. 'I've got a sheep station called Spinifex Plains, up in the Pilbara district.' He paused and offered Matt a cigarette.

'Where are you going to work?' he asked.

'A town called Roebourne, I've been told, wherever that is,' Matt said with a shrug.

'It just happens to be where we live!' said Bill with a chuckle. 'That's marvellous!' Bill looked at his watch. 'Time for dinner. Are you eating here?'

They got up and Bill led the way to the dining room. They were shown to a table for two.

'I've been down for the sheep sales. Bought a stud ram. We breed merino sheep, and damn good ones at that,' he said. 'I'm driving back on Monday.' They sat and studied the menu then ordered their meal.

'When do you start your job?' Bill asked.

'I'm not sure what my plans are at this stage, I've got to report to the Health Commissioner on Monday,' Matt replied.

'Well, I'll give you our address, and postbox number, also our radio call sign so you can contact us when you get there. The station is only fifty miles out of town.' He took out a pen and wrote the information on a page he tore out from a notebook, and gave it to Matt.

They settled into their meal, which was just like home cooking, and quite delicious. While they ate, Bill told Matt a lot about the area where he lived, and the town he was going to. After the meal they ordered a cup of tea. 'What are you doing for the weekend?' Bill asked.

'One of the Health Department doctors is taking me out tomorrow,' he replied.

'Well if you're at a loose end on Sunday, let me know, I'd be happy to organise something.'

Matt thanked him. They left the table, and Matt excused himself, saying that he had letters to write. He went up to his room and flopped on the bed, feeling too tired to write.

Next morning Matt was up early, and ate a hearty breakfast. He was not sure what to wear for the occasion, being totally out of his normal sphere, so he settled on light slacks and an open-neck shirt, and to play safe, he put on a blue blazer. He wrapped up his swimming costume in a hotel towel, and went down to the foyer just before ten.

Just after ten, a car pulled up at the Hotel and a man got out. He walked over to Matt with a broad smile. 'You must be Matthew Harrison,' he said holding out his hand. He was tall, and well built, with a deep suntan, and dressed in shorts, cotton knit shirt and sandals. They shook hands and walked to the car. He opened the front door for Matt.

'These are the kids, David and Elizabeth,' he gestured to the children in the back seat.

They both smiled at Matt and shyly said, 'Hello.'

'We'll head home first,' he said, 'then go to the beach before the breeze comes in.'

They drove up to Kings Park, above the city. 'Thought you might like to see a bit of the place on the way,' Peter said, as they drove through the park gates. They drove past the War Memorial, and stopped to look at the splendid view of the city below, then drove along a winding road lined with stately gum trees. At the foot of each tree was a metal plaque in the ground. In answer to Matt's unasked question, Peter said. 'Each tree is a memorial to a serviceman killed in the last two wars. Their name is on the plaque.' They drove on in silence through the Park.

Peter turned into the driveway of a pleasant bungalow style house in Nedlands, a suburb between Perth and Fremantle. Peter's wife met them at the door. She was a pretty brunette.

'Darling, this is Matt Harrison from England,' then to Matt, 'My wife Jenny.'

'Hello Matt, and welcome to our country, I hope you like it here.' She had a pleasant speaking voice and an attractive smile.

'We thought we would go down to the beach before the sea breeze comes in, are you coming too Jenny?'

'No dear, I've still got some things to organise for lunch. You all go and don't hurry back, we'll have a late lunch.'

'Matt, I see you have your bathers with you, come and change before we go.' Peter led him to the bathroom.

The beach was magnificent! Matt had seen the French Riviera, but it was no comparison to this. The clean snow-white sand was scattered with colourful beach umbrellas, and bathers lay sunning themselves. The ocean was deep blue, changing to green over the sand nearer the shore.

There was a metal tower on the beach with a lifesaver at the top scanning the ocean with binoculars. 'On shark watch,' Peter told him.

A light offshore breeze was blowing from the east, and the sand was hot under foot. They dropped their towels, and with the children in the lead, ran to the water. Matt had learned to swim whilst at school, and plunged into the cool sparkling ocean.

Fortunately he had a bit of a suntan from the boat, but even so he could feel the bite of the sun. Peter told him that every summer the hospitals had bad cases of sunburn from people trying to get a tan too quickly.

Matt splashed and played with the children, and by the time they came out of the water they had accepted him as a friend.

Back at the McLean's place, Jenny had prepared salads and lit the fire under the barbecue. After a shower to get the salt off, Matt emerged dressed in his slacks and shirt.

'Let's have a beer,' said Peter bringing out a tray with a bottle of icy beer and three glasses. 'Jenny, are you having a beer?'

'No thanks, I'll go on getting lunch organised, and leave you both to talk.' Peter poured two glasses.

They sat on cane chairs on the veranda, looking over the neat back yard. On one side a brick hearth had smoke emerging from its little chimney. Peter pointed at it. 'That's the barbecue – made it myself,' he added with pride. 'We practically live outside in the summer, except when it's too damned hot. Cheers!'

Matt took a sip of his beer. It was icy cold and very gassy. He was careful not to change his expression, but inwardly shuddered. 'Nothing like our beer,' he thought.

'First thing we have to do is get you registered with the Medical Board. Did you bring your medical degree?' Matt nodded. 'The Commissioner thought you might like a bit of time to acclimatise, so he plans to put you in the Fremantle Hospital for a few weeks, to get the feel of the place. Anyhow, we can't turn you loose on the unsuspecting citizens of the North until you are fully registered. The Senior Surgical Registrar is going on holidays, so you will do his work. We can get you a provisional registration to work there until the Medical Board's next meeting.' Peter sensed Matt's disappointment.

'There are a few tasks you'll have to do in the North that you may not have thought about, and this is a great chance to sort it out. For example, blood transfusion. You have to keep a panel of donors whose blood will be checked by the Red Cross Blood Bank, and you have to cross-match them with your patient, then bleed them. That's just one thing. Then there's X-rays. You have to take them and develop them yourself. And teeth. You've probably not pulled any before. There is a State Health Department dental clinic in Fremantle, and they will get you to do a few.'

Matt warmed to the idea. He had never done X-rays nor had he cross-matched blood, except as a medical student.

'Darling, ready to start cooking?'

'Okay, coming.' Peter got up and went inside, then appeared with a tray of meat.

'Come and give me a hand. Bring your beer,' Peter said over his shoulder as he headed for the barbecue. There was a shade-house near the fireplace with a long table and chairs, set with a colourful tablecloth and utensils. Peter put the tray on the side of the barbecue, and carefully placed sausages, lamb chops and pieces of steak on the wire grill over the glowing embers. He topped up their drinks as they stood watching the sizzling meat.

'This is a whole new experience for me,' said Matt, watching with fascination. He had never seen so much meat at one time outside a butcher's shop. 'Will we eat all that meat?' he asked.

Peter looked at him with surprise. 'Struth, I was wondering if there was enough!' he replied, giving the meat a prod with a long handled fork. 'You'll find that Aussies are big meat eaters.'

He turned the meat over, and rearranged it on the grill. 'Nearly cooked!' he called to Jenny who came out the door with a tray of salad and jacket potatoes that she had cooked in the oven. The children were packed off to wash their hands for lunch.

Jenny had all the food laid out on the side table and Peter added the plate of cooked meat. 'Help yourself,' Peter said, handing him a fork. He put a chop and a sausage on his plate.

'You haven't much of an appetite,' said Jenny with a smile. 'Won't you have some steak, or more chops and sausages?'

Matt looked apologetic. 'Thanks Jenny, I'll eat this first. You see I grew up during the war, and food was rationed. Meat was very scarce and a luxury.'

'What did you eat then?' asked David across the table.

'Well, we had plenty of eggs and some bacon, and mostly we ate baked beans, and vegetables. Sometimes we had chicken, but that was a special treat. We didn't have steak at all for years, and I guess you just get out of the habit of eating meat.'

Peter leaned over and filled his glass with beer. 'Well you'll have to start practising for the Northwest,' he said with a grin.

They settled in to serious eating, and Matt surprised himself by eating another chop. 'Must have been the sea air,' Matt suggested cheerfully as he munched into it.

After lunch Peter led Matt to a couple of chairs under a tree, as his wife and the children cleared the table. 'Well, what do you think of

Australia so far?' he asked as Matt settled himself.

'I think it's fine,' he replied cautiously. 'A bit too hot though,' he added.

'Wait till you get to the Northwest mate, this is nothing!' he said with a grin. 'But you soon acclimatise.'

Jenny joined them, and they sat chatting for the next hour. After a cup of afternoon tea, Peter drove him back to the hotel, and said to ask for him on Monday morning when he arrived at the Department of Health, and he would take him to the Commissioner. They shook hands, and Peter drove away with a toot of the horn.

Matt felt tired and a bit sunburned, and was already full of food. He kicked off his shoes, and stretched out on the bed.

Next morning Matt went down to the dining room at eight thirty. A maid in uniform showed him to a table, and took his order. He opened the newspaper he had picked up on the way in and glanced through it.

'Can I join you?' Bill Corbett stood smiling at him.

'Of course,' said Matt, returning his smile.

'You look a bit sunburned,' he said as he pulled in his chair. 'Did you have a good day yesterday?' He gave his order to the maid.

Whilst they waited for their bacon and eggs, Matt told his older friend about his activities of the day before.

'What are your plans for the day?' Bill asked as they ate.

'I've got some paperwork to get through, and I think that will occupy most of it I'm afraid,' he replied, not wanting to get involved in another day's outing.

'Well, if you have no plans for this evening, you might care to join me for a little supper at a restaurant by the river.'

'Sounds great, thanks, I'd love to,' he replied.

Matt spent the morning writing letters, and getting things sorted out for Monday. He finally located his medical degree at the bottom of the suitcase. He would need it tomorrow. He sorted through his clothes, and put out what he wanted to wear next day. He'd need a lot more summer clothes, he realised.

Instead of lunch, Matt took a walk along the river's edge. A limestone retaining wall had been built along the shoreline, and the river water lapped against it. There was no breeze, and the sun stung his skin. He could feel the sweat running down the middle of his back. 'Christ! This is just the start. How will I cope with the heat in the north?' he mused.

An hour later and back in his room, he took a cold shower, and lay on the bed under the ceiling fan. As he drifted off, he wondered how long it took to acclimatise to this fierce climate.

He was awake when the phone rang. It was Bill.

'Still feel like going out?' he asked. 'Good, well I suggest we meet in the bar at six thirty, and take it from there.' Matt agreed, and hung up. He glanced at his watch. Five thirty.

He dressed slowly, wearing an open neck shirt and slacks, then took the Sunday newspaper with him, and sat on the balcony, where a cool sea breeze was ruffling the surface of the river.

At six twenty five he went down to meet Bill. They climbed into his Holden utility, its upholstery stained with red dust in spite of a recent clean. 'It gets into everything,' Bill replied to Matt's comment.

They drove to a restaurant by the river where Bill had booked a table, and sat down.

'Like a beer?' Bill asked. 'Just the weather for beer,' he added. 'We drink little else in the north you know.'

Matt accepted out of politeness. He really didn't care much for Australian beer. He was hungry though, and ordered fish and chips with salad. Bill had steak.

Bill asked about the war days in England, and Matt talked freely, and for the first time since he left his homeland. He felt comfortable with Bill.

Inevitably the subject came up. 'No girlfriend left behind?' he asked with an inquisitive smile.

Matt looked at his plate, as the memories suddenly flooded in.

'Sorry, that was a tactless question,' Bill added hastily.

'No,' Matt replied, looking up. 'I'm glad you asked. You see, I had a wife and a little daughter, and they were killed in a road accident. We were driving to her parents' for Christmas, and we skidded on the ice. I was in hospital for a long time, and I didn't want to go back to my old job, so I came to Australia.' He spoke quietly, with no emotion.

'I'm so sorry,' Bill said earnestly.

As they ate in silence for a while, and Matt realised that for the first time that he could speak about his lost loved ones without feeling choked up. It seemed that only happy memories remained now.

Back at the hotel, Matt said goodbye to Bill, who was leaving at dawn to drive north. He promised to let him know when he arrived to start his new job.

Chapter 13

Next morning, Matt was on the doorstep of the Health Department at nine sharp. At the reception desk he gave his name, then asked for Dr McLean. The girl picked up the phone and spoke.

'He will be here presently,' she said.

Matt sat and picked up a *Time* magazine.

A few minutes later Peter appeared at the door. 'Ah! Hello Matt. Come along.'

As they walked, Matt thanked him for their hospitality on the weekend.

They reached a door with a sign 'Commissioner of Health.'

Peter knocked, and opened the door. 'Good morning Steve, this is Dr Matt Harrison from England.'

The man behind the desk stood, and came around to greet them.

'Dr Harrison! It is a pleasure to meet you.' He beamed as they shook hands. 'Won't you sit down?' He gestured to a chair. Peter excused himself and departed.

The Commissioner was about fifty, short and suntanned. He had gingery hair and a carefully trimmed beard, showing a few grey streaks. He offered a packet of cigarettes, then a lighter as Matt thanked him and took one.

'Well, you have come a long way to be with us,' he said gesturing with his cigarette, now in a holder. 'What are your first impressions of our country?' He tapped his cigarette over an ash-tray.

'Very favourable sir, but I'm still adjusting to the climate.'

The Commissioner nodded. 'Yes, it will take a little while, which is one of the reasons why I thought a few weeks here would be good for you. Also, you will be helping us out by filling in while one of the surgical registrars is on vacation. Oh and you had better call me Steve. We are fairly informal here.'

They chatted a while, then he picked up the phone and asked his secretary to find the Chief Clerk and send him in.

When the clerk arrived, they got down to business. A temporary registration had already been arranged for him, and his medical degree and certificate of training were passed over to the clerk. He was formally appointed to his position in the North West Medical Service, and signed the contract as required. He was commenced on his salary from the Health Department, retrospective two weeks, which meant that he would get a cheque immediately! When Matt looked surprised, Steve said that he guessed he would be running short of cash by this time, and this was a small concession they could make.

'Amen to that,' Matt thought, and thanked Steve for the gesture.

'Your salary is better than the surgical registrar's, so it's better that we pay you rather than the Hospital for the next few weeks,' Steve added with a grin.

The clerk advised him to open a bank account immediately so that future salary could be paid in directly, and suggested that Peter take him under his wing for the day to get things organised. For the rest of the day, Peter guided Matt about, first to the bank, where he opened a cheque account, depositing the small amount of money he had left after the trip.

Next, Peter drove him down to Fremantle Hospital, and parked the car. There was a strong sea breeze blowing, and it was several degrees cooler than in Perth.

The Superintendent opened his door and ushered them in. He was a solidly built man with a round red jovial face, and sandy hair.

'G'day,' he said pumping Matt's hand. 'Welcome to Freo.'

He pointed to the corner where there was a coffee table and four chairs. When they were seated, he turned to Matt and said with a smile, 'So what made you want to come to this outpost of the Empire?'

Matt was taken aback by the bluntness of the question, and what he perceived to be a hint of sarcasm in his tone.

'Well sir, from England it seemed like a good idea.'

'Do you still think so?'

Matt felt his colour rising, was he being deliberately rude?

'I'm sure I'll like it very much, once I get acclimatised.'

The 'Super' went to the phone and ordered afternoon tea. He sat down again, and his manner became friendlier. 'It'll take a while. Up there the summer is hotter than hell, but you actually do get used to it. Now, let's talk about work. Tell me about your surgical experience.'

For the next five minutes over a cup of tea, Matt told him about his surgical training, and passed over the table a letter that Sir James Watson had given him, should he need a reference.

The Superintendent sat back in his chair, and carefully read it through.

'Well,' he said, looking up from the page. 'You seem to have a good background training, but just remember, up there you are on your own. You do the anaesthetic, and the surgery, the X-rays, and the film processing – everything. There's no back up. So, if there are any gaps in your knowledge, now is the time to fill them. Next week the Surgical Registrar goes on two weeks' leave, and I want you to do his job. Meanwhile this week will give you time to tie up a few loose ends.'

For the next half hour they worked out a program, which included time in the X-ray department, the Dental Clinic, and the Blood Bank.

'Well, that takes care of the rest of this week, and if there is any spare time you better get in to theatre to get into the swing for the next two weeks. He reached over and picked up the phone. 'Yes, page Dr Johnson please.'

He put the phone down. 'Bob Johnson should be finished in theatre, I'll get him in so you can meet him.'

The phone rang. 'Bob? Have you finished? Well come round to my office anyhow, I want you to meet your locum.'

A few minutes later there was a knock on the door, and the Surgical Registrar entered. He was a stocky, dark-haired man dressed in a white boiler suit and a white coat with a stethoscope protruding from the pocket.

'Bob,' said the Super, 'meet Matthew Harrison. He's doing your job whilst you are on vacation.'

Matt rose and they shook hands.

'Have you finished in theatre?' asked the Super.

'Just one more case Boss, an emergency appendix,' Bob replied, as he lit a cigarette.

'Why don't you take Matt in with you? He may be able to teach you a thing or two,' the Super said with a grin.

Matt looked sharply from one to the other. 'More tricks?' he wondered.

'If you've got the time, you're welcome,' said Bob affably.

'Well,' said Matt hesitating.

'Don't worry, I can drop you back in Perth when we've finished, I've got to go to the city later,' Bob added.

'I'll catch up with you later in the week,' said Peter.

Later, as they were leaving the Hospital, the Super called Bob aside. 'How did you get on?' he asked quietly.

'Don't worry, he's good – very good,' he replied.

By the end of the week, Matt had covered all the unknown subjects and had performed well in the operating theatre. He felt happy and confident. He had moved in to the Resident Medical Officer's quarters, which were both convenient and comfortable.

He spent the next two weeks working hard in theatre during the day, and doing his share of Casualty Department work in the evenings.

In his spare time, he had sorted out all his belongings for the next adventure, and had purchased clothing more appropriate for the Northwest.

The Commissioner had rung him on Thursday of his second week as locum Surgical Registrar to say that they had booked his flight to the North West the following Wednesday morning, and that the flight departed at six thirty in the morning. He would be picked up at the Hospital at four thirty. 'Make sure you set your alarm,' Steve had cautioned him.

On his last Saturday night, the Super had invited some of the Hospital staff to his home for a barbecue.

Bob Johnson, a bachelor, was back from vacation, and picked up Matt from the 'Quarters' at seven thirty, and they arrived to find about 30 people standing with drinks in their hands, all talking loudly.

'Looks like the party's been going for a while,' said Bob as they walked in.

The Super, approached. 'G'day,' he beamed, holding out his hand to Matt, 'Thought you must have got a better offer.' He winked at Bob, who moved off with a grin.

'Sorry Sir,' Matt started to apologise.

'Don't worry; only kidding, and as we're not on duty, call me Dave. Come over to the keg and have a beer,' he said over his shoulder as he walked off.

Matt followed. Dave handed him a glass of beer. He sipped it and shuddered. It was icy cold, full of gas and very much stronger than English beer.

'I'll never get used to this stuff,' he thought.

With a glass in his hand he moved around, talking to his colleagues from work, and meeting their wives and female friends. Only a few of them were married, and on the whole, were some years younger than him.

By nine thirty, they had barbecued and eaten steak, chops and sausages with bread rolls and tomato sauce, and consumed a good deal of beer. There didn't seem to be much else to drink, apart from a large jug of fruit punch.

Matt was fascinated, he had never been to a party like this. The men had congregated around the keg talking, telling jokes and laughing loudly, while the girls had found chairs and sat in a group, chattering and seemingly enjoying themselves.

Dave came up to him and gave him a pat on the shoulder. 'Hope you're having a good time,' he said, slurring a little.

'Yes, thank you, I'm having a great time,' he replied. 'I guess this is a typical Aussie barbecue,' he added, trying to think of something to say.

'Where you're going, you'll look back on this as a very civilised occasion,' he said with a wide grin. 'Things get pretty rough up the North.' He then said more seriously, 'Here's a bit of advice. When you get there, never drink at the bar in the pub.' Matt looked puzzled.

'You'll appreciate why when you've been there for a while,' he said enigmatically.

The party broke up when the keg was finished and the guests departed, mostly with the girls driving their inebriated partners' cars. Fortunately, Bob was sober, and dropped an even more sober Matt back at the Quarters.

By Tuesday night, Matt had completed his packing, and had arranged for his books and some of his heavy gear to be sent north by the State Shipping Line that ran a regular service as far as Wyndham, and all ports along the way.

He turned out the light, having set the alarm clock, and lay back in the dark, wondering about the next adventure – the Northwest!!

PART TWO

THE NOR'WESTERS

Chapter 14

Matt stood on the tarmac at the aerodrome, dressed in shorts, shirt, long socks and shoes. The sun had not yet risen and the morning breeze made him shiver. The fuel tanker had just driven off, after filling the tanks, and the last of the luggage was being stowed on board the aircraft, an old twin engine DC3 – or 'Dakota' as they were known in the war days.

There were about twenty passengers waiting to board the plane. 'An odd assortment,' Matt thought as he looked around the group standing near the plane. A couple of businessmen he guessed, dressed in tropical suits, and carrying brief cases, some couples with children, workmen dressed in shorts and four dark-skinned men in dirty clothes, he took to be Aboriginal men, standing with a man dressed in khaki slacks and shirt with an army style hat. He looked like a policeman.

A smart hostess stood by the steps and checked boarding passes as they filed on board, and found their seats. The hostess walked up the sloping aisle and back, checking that the seat belts were fastened, then took her seat at the rear.

The rising sun caught the silver wing as the left engine whined, coughed and spluttered, then roared into life, with a blast of flame and smoke from the exhaust. The right engine followed, and the noise in the cabin became deafening. They taxied to the end of the tarmac, and the ritual of revving each engine was performed. Then the plane thundered down the airstrip and lifted in to the sky.

Matt looked out the window as the plane banked and climbed in to the clear morning air. Below, the earth looked parched and brown. There had been no rain for two months he'd been told. The city of Perth passed below them, sparkling in the morning sunshine. It seemed smaller from the air.

Levelled out at about four thousand feet, the engines quietened as the plane settled in to cruising speed.

Matt felt no apprehension on this occasion as he did crossing the

English Channel, and presently the hostess leant over the empty seat beside him and handed him a small tray with a cup of tea and some biscuits. He thanked her with a smile. Conversation really was not possible with the engine noise.

Their first stop was Geraldton, where they were told to stay seated, while some freight was unloaded. The air became uncomfortably hot in the fifteen minutes on the ground, and they were glad to get airborne again.

As the day wore on, the plane stopped at three more remote towns. Each felt hotter, and looked more primitive than the one before, Matt thought gloomily, wondering what his destination would be like.

The hostess had told Matt that this flight was the 'milk run', and that normal flights made only one stop. Lunch consisted of a tray with sandwiches, and a cup of tea, and more biscuits.

Finally, at about four in the afternoon, the plane descended to Roebourne, Matt's destination.

Looking out the window, Matt saw only a few houses and buildings. Perhaps the town was on the other side of the plane, he thought. As the plane banked, he could see the ground through the window on the other side. There were only a few more buildings to be seen.

The plane bumped on the gravel airstrip, and came to a stop beside a corrugated iron shed, where a man stood leaning on a post in the shade.

Matt said goodbye to the hostess, then stepped out of the plane. He was met by a blast of scorching hot air, and immediately set upon by a swarm of flies that seemed intent on getting in to his mouth and nose. He stumbled down the steps and walked to the shed, trying unsuccessfully to brush away the flies.

The waiting man straightened up as he approached and held out his hand.

'G'day, you must be the new Doc,' he said with a grin, ignoring the flies that settled on his face. He was short, muscular and deeply suntanned, wearing a khaki shirt with the sleeves cut off, black shorts and army boots. About forty, Matt guessed.

They shook hands.

'Me name's Bert, I'm with the PWD,' he informed Matt, who was none the wiser, and still doing battle with the flies.

'Matt Harrison,' he managed to splutter, spitting out a fly.

At that moment the plane's engines thundered into life, and a storm of red dust engulfed them.

'Grab yer bags,' Bert shouted over the din, 'and chuck 'em in the back.' He pointed to a Holden utility, like the one Bill Corbett had driven in Perth, but covered in red dust.

Matt picked up his cases and put them in the back, avoiding a pile of greasy metal junk.

He climbed in to the cabin, which was like an oven, noting that his clothes were already covered in red dust, and his whole body was running with sweat.

Bert swung in behind the wheel. 'Matron was coming over to meet yer, but she's busy delivering a baby, so she rang me.'

The Holden bumped along the road, followed by a plume of red dust. 'I hear yer just got off a ship from England,' he said, glancing at Matt. 'Reckon you'd find it a bit different 'ere,' he went on. Matt opened his mouth to speak, but no noise came. His mouth and throat were parched and his tongue felt coated with red dust. He managed a croaking sound.

'That's the Aboriginal reserve over there.' He pointed to a collection of tin sheds, with a few stunted trees. 'And this is the river,' his guided tour continued. As they approached a line of gum trees, the road changed to a bituminised surface.

The river was like an oasis, and Bert slowed down as they approached the water. Matt could see no bridge. An ancient Aboriginal man sitting on a log beside the water waved at them. Bert waved back. The road disappeared into the water, and in low gear, Bert drove in.

'The crossing is OK in good weather,' Bert said as they slowly drove on a concrete track with water up to the wheel hubs. 'When we get a big rainstorm, the river comes down real quick, and can sweep yer off the crossing. After a cyclone, it can run twenty feet deep.'

They reached the other side to Matt's relief, leaving the coolness of the shady place and relative absence of flies. He felt some envy for the old man sitting on the log.

As they drove, Matt learned that 'PWD' stood for Public Works Department, and Bert Harris was the local 'boss'.

They passed a group of stone buildings with a sign that read 'Police', outside which four Aboriginal men worked with pick and shovel digging a drain. They were stripped to the waist wearing only shorts, and their muscular black bodies shone with sweat. Matt was impressed with their physique, and said so to Bert.

'Yair,' he said. 'Round these parts the "full bloods" are big boys. They vary from place to place, though. This lot are doing a bit of time. Probably got on the plonk.'

Matt looked puzzled. 'Plonk?'

'Yair, booze. Yer see, the abos are not allowed to drink alcohol in this country. They're not like us; they just drink until they're pissed.' Matt's vocabulary was expanding by the minute.

He said nothing, but thought back on the Super's barbecue. He wondered if there was so much difference in their attitude to drink.

They pulled into a driveway that led to a group of stone buildings similar to the Police station. A large sign read 'Roebourne District Hospital'.

On each side of the drive was a grass lawn, watered by slow turning sprinklers. Around the lawn were shady trees with bunches of red flowers amongst the green leaves. If Matt hadn't felt so overwhelmed by the heat he might have appreciated their beauty.

They left the car in the drive and walked to the veranda. Matt noticed a thermometer by the doorway. It registered 105° Fahrenheit.

'Cooled down a bit,' Bert commented, seeing Matt's interest. 'It got up to a hundred and twelve at lunch time.' He thumped on the door.

Presently a woman dressed in a theatre gown, with rolled up sleeves, and a mask hanging from her neck opened the door. 'Hello and welcome,' she said with a bright smile. 'Come in,' she stood back and ushered them in, brushing back a strand of black hair from her face. 'Sorry I couldn't meet you myself, we just had a baby.'

She held out her hand to Matt. 'My name is Mary Summers, I'm the Matron.' Matt shook her hand and introduced himself.

The room had a linoleum floor, a wall of glass louvres, all open to the shady side of the building, with chrome-legged table and chairs in the centre. Above, a ceiling fan turned slowly. A side table was laden with teacups, plates and a large cake under a glass cover.

'I'll bet you could do with a nice cuppa,' she said. 'Just the thing to cool you down.'

'I gotta get back to work Matron, if yer don't mind, but thanks all the same,' said Bert.

Matt was impressed with his respectful manner.

'OK Bert, and thanks for your help.'

Bert turned to the door. 'See yer later Doc, I'll drop yer cases at the 'ouse,' he said over his shoulder, as he left the room.

'Sit down Doctor; I'll get you some tea.'

She left the room then returned, followed by a middle-aged woman carrying a tea tray.

'This is Polly Button, our cook,' Mary said as the tray was set down. 'Dr Harrison is taking over from Dr Frank,' she explained. Polly gave a shy smile and nodded at Matt, then left the room before he could speak.

The Matron looked about Matt's age, and was a handsome suntanned woman, with a strong face and arched black eyebrows. Her eyes were dark brown, and she wore her black hair tied back in a ponytail. She spoke softly, with an Australian accent that seemed to suit her.

'Well,' Mary said as she served tea and a slice of orange cake. 'You look as though you've had a long day. You're probably wanting to settle in to your quarters, and have a shower.'

She looked at him with sweat running down his face. 'Don't worry, you'll be acclimatised in a week or so.'

'If I live that long,' Matt replied ruefully, mopping his face with a dust-stained handkerchief.

Mary laughed.

'Frank will be back soon; he's been down to Onslow doing the weekly clinic.'

Frank Wolinski was a migrant doctor, and had served in the district for the past three years. He was now going to a country practice in the south. He was to fly south the following Saturday, after 'handing over' to Matt.

As they spoke, a plane flew over the hospital. 'Here they are now,' she said.

'Do you want to come over to the air strip with me?'

Remembering the dust and flies, he answered. 'No thanks; if it's OK I'll wait here.'

Mary went off to retrieve the doctor, and Matt stretched out his legs. The ceiling fan certainly made life bearable.

Matt heard the car return, and the doors close. A moment later the Matron came in accompanied by the doctor. He looked about forty, was thick set, with a broad suntanned face and receding sandy hair.

'Hello and welcome, I am very glad to see you,' said Dr Wolinski, pumping Matt's hand and beaming.

Matt introduced himself, though it was hardly necessary, for, as it turned out, everybody in town knew about the new doctor.

He declined the Matron's offer of tea. 'No thank you Mary, I must get Matt settled in the house.'

'Come Matt, we will walk over to the house – and please call me Frank.' He had a mid-European accent. 'Cigarette?' he offered a packet. Matt took one and Frank held up a match, then lit his own.

'You will like it here,' he said as they walked out of the Hospital. 'It is a small community, and everyone knows each other. They walked towards an old house a few hundred yards away.

'This is your house,' he said. 'My wife has gone south already, and I am all packed up, and fly out on Saturday.'

The sun was low and the day had cooled noticeably, though the flies still plagued them as they walked. Frank laughed as Matt swatted at the flies on his face. 'You know, after a while, you don't notice them,' he said.

Frank had an engaging manner and Matt felt at ease with him.

The house was old and made of crumbling mudbrick, with a rusting corrugated iron roof. It was built for the first Magistrate of the Pilbara District about a hundred years ago. It was now due for demolition, Frank told him.

They entered through the kitchen door. The kitchen had a kerosene stove and a kerosene refrigerator, and whilst they were both efficient, they took a little getting accustomed to, Frank said.

For the next half hour Frank showed Matt around the house and surrounds. It had obviously been a fine establishment in its day, though was now in a state of decay, with white ants in the floor of some of the bedrooms, and cracks in the walls.

It was a great house in the old days, Frank told him, and it had been surrounded by a fine terraced garden. At one time there had been a tennis court, now lost in the surrounding low scrub and red dust. Only a small lawn beside the house, and some colourful oleander trees, remained.

A wide veranda surrounded the house, two corners of which had been turned into rooms, with fly wire mesh walls. One of the corner rooms contained two beds, and the other had a table and cane chairs.

Inside, the sitting room was impressive, with a polished wooden floor of wide planks and a ceiling fan. The wood came from sailing ships Frank told him, and the electricity from the hospital generator. There were comfortable looking cane chairs and a lounge, with cushions covered with bright floral material. French windows with fly wire screens opened on to the verandas, and a warm breeze was wafting in.

Over the next two days, Matt followed Frank around the hospital, attending ward patients, and conducting the morning clinics.

He learned how to use the radio, and watched as Frank spoke with people on remote stations about their health problems.

Mary had organised a party on the Friday night to farewell Frank, and welcome Matt. It was to be held in the Masonic Hall, and it seemed that most of the town had been invited.

There was to be a reception first, starting at seven thirty, and then a barbecue out the back.

The hall was located just up the road from the pub, and at seven thirty people drifted out from the bar, and wandered up to the reception. Matt and Frank arrived punctually, and found the hall to be full of people, mostly sitting on chairs all around the walls. The atmosphere was stifling. Mary walked up on the stage and made a short speech. She thanked Frank for his service to the community over the past few years, and said how much he would be missed.

Frank was obviously well liked by the locals, who not only applauded loudly, but also had contributed money towards a gift. When the applause died down, Mary presented him with a large box. Frank was almost overcome emotion, and hesitantly thanked them all. He told them that the last three years had been his happiest, and that he would always remember them.

'And now I want you to meet the new doctor, Matthew Harrison, from England.' There was a small wave of polite applause.

'Come with me,' Mary said, taking Matt's elbow. 'You're going to meet the town folk.'

They walked slowly around the room shaking hands as Mary introduced them one after another.

'I'd like you to meet Fred Walters, he's the Town Clerk.'

'G'day Doc,' they shook hands. 'We've dug a few new graves for yer,' he said, grinning at Matt.

'Er, thanks very much,' Matt replied, 'I'll try not to fill them.'

They moved on slowly around the room, making polite conversation and shaking hands. Finally they finished the roundabout, having heard nothing but praise for Frank.

'Thank God that's over,' Matt thought, mopping the sweat from his face. 'This man will be a hard act to follow.'

'Come on everyone!' Mary called out. 'Time to eat.'

She led Matt outside, where there were a couple of 44-gallon drums cut length ways and standing on legs. Each was covered with a thick metal mesh, and was full of red-hot coals, ready for cooking. There were trays of meat on the table; baskets of buttered bread rolls and dishes of salad. A large tub full of ice was stacked with bottles of beer.

'Well what d'yer reckon, Doc?' Matt turned. It was Bert Harris, with two glasses of beer in his hands. He offered one to Matt. 'Reckon yer'll get on OK here?' He took a swig of beer. 'Bloody big change from your country, I'll bet.' He wiped the froth from his mouth with the back of his hand and grinned.

Matt took a long pull at his beer. He was coming to terms with the sharp bitterness of the icy drink. It seemed to suit the harshness and heat of the rugged country.

'Yes Bert, it is a big change, and that is just what I wanted. I think I am going to like living here.'

'Yair, well, when the Doc's gone,' he said, nodding towards Frank, 'you let me know if yer want any help. I live in the house just down from yours. It's a new one,' he added.

Matt gave him a friendly pat on the shoulder. 'Thanks Bert, I'll do that.'

The next day, Matt drove the Holden utility to the airstrip with Frank and his suitcases.

'This is a good bus,' said Frank. 'It was new last year, and I've had no trouble with it.

'There's a canvas awning that fits on the back, and a stretcher to slide in. You are the ambulance man too, you know,' he said with a laugh. 'If you want to put it on, ask Bert.'

They reached the airstrip, and pulled up by the tin shed, next to the airline agent's car. Matt went to open the door, but was stopped by Frank's sharp 'Wait!' As he spoke a cloud or red dust that had been trailing behind caught up and enveloped them. 'Don't worry, you'll soon get used to it,' he said, opening the door when the dust had dispersed.

They waited only a few minutes before they heard the engines of the approaching plane, and watched as it gracefully touched down on the gravel airstrip, stirring up a plume of red dust as it taxied towards them. The waiting agent wheeled the steps to the plane as the door opened.

'Hello Johnnie,' called a pretty hostess. 'Here's the mail.' She handed him a bag.

'Only one customer for you,' said Johnnie.

Frank and Matt walked to the plane. 'Why it's Doctor Frank!' exclaimed the hostess. 'I heard you were leaving.'

The agent stowed Frank's bags in the hold as he turned to Matt and said, 'Goodbye, my new friend, I hope your time here will be happy and rewarding.' They shook hands.

Frank turned and walked up the steps. With a smile and a wave, he disappeared into the plane. The door was shut and the engines spluttered into life.

Matt got into the ute, and watched as the plane taxied to the end of the strip, then thundered past him and climbed in to the bright blue sky.

He sat for a few minutes taking stock of the situation. He was now completely alone, and as far from England as he could possibly get, both physically and culturally.

'Well,' he said to himself, 'that's what I wanted.'

He wiped the sweat and dust from his face and drove back to the town.

Chapter 15

Matt parked the ute at the back of the house where there was a shed that doubled as a garage. He noticed the canvas covered metal frame in the back corner and the stretcher beside it.

One entered the house at its rear, either by the kitchen, or the bathroom, as the front of the house with the grand old front door, looked out over the river flats at the foot of the hill. A path across the little lawn led to stone steps down through the oleander trees, to the remains of a gravel driveway, where coaches would have drawn up in the early days. Now there remained only a parched wilderness.

Matt walked to the kitchen past the out-door toilet and laundry, and opened the door. To his surprise, Mary was standing at the open refrigerator, stacking in parcels of food. She turned as he entered, and smiled at his surprised expression.

'Thought I'd better give you a bit of a start with the catering,' she said. 'Also you may need a lesson on the vagaries of kerosene stoves and fridges.'

Matt was a little lost for words, but managed, 'Thanks awfully Mary, that is most kind of you.'

She produced a jug from the fridge.

'Some lemonade – I just made it. Would you like a glass?'

For the next half hour he and Mary sat at the kitchen table with the jug of lemonade between them. Matt with pencil and paper made notes as Mary told him about where to buy this and that.

It seemed that Dalgety's store supplied most things, supplemented by two Chinese shops and another general store. One of the Chinese shops doubled as the town baker, but the pub provided the most sort-after amenity, and was never without customers, Mary said.

For the rest of the weekend, Matt drove around the town getting his bearings, and at home experimented with the kerosene stove. On Monday morning, he started work.

His 'Surgery' was a fairly large room with a concrete floor. The furnishing was sparse, and consisted of a large desk and bookshelves, and a few plain wooden chairs. An examination couch with an adjustable lamp occupied one wall, and an X-ray machine on wheels stood in the corner. A small adjoining room was set up as a dark-room for processing X-rays.

Outside his surgery a row of Aboriginal people sat waiting, and one by one he attended to their mostly minor ailments, providing medicine from the Dispensary when necessary. Then with the matron, he did a ward round, examining the few inpatients.

There were two wards; male and female, and a 'native ward' out the back. The indoor wards were roomy and fresh, with ceiling fans, and polished wood floors. The native ward on the other hand was a Nissen hut made of corrugated iron, and shaped like a big water tank cut in half length-ways with a door each end and a few windows along the side. The floor was concrete, and it was partitioned half way into male and female areas. The whole place looked dark and dirty.

Sitting on a 'cyclone' bed with only a mattress and a soiled blanket was a young Aboriginal woman nursing a new-born baby. 'Good morning Margaret, how's the baby today? Feeding OK?'

The girl looked at Matron briefly then lowered her eyes and spoke in a whisper.

'She's a bit shy,' said Mary, 'Comes from out of town, just came in to have her baby.'

'Margaret, this is our new doctor, he's going to have a look at you, and the baby.'

The girl gave Matt a frightened look. Matt smiled at her and sat down on the edge of the bed.

'May I hold your baby for a moment Margaret?'

She looked at Matron who nodded, then reluctantly passed the baby to Matt, who cuddled it for a moment then lay it on it's back and unwrapped it. 'Well, I see he's a fine boy,' he said, as he checked the healing umbilical cord site.

He listened to his heart and chest, and had a gentle feel of his abdomen, and his limbs.

'He's a fine healthy boy Margaret,' he said passing him back to his mother.

'You haven't met Mibbin yet,' said Mary. 'He is our Orderly, and a damn useful man. He has a workshop around the corner.'

Mibbin was in the shed, working with a file on a piece of metal held in the bench vice. He looked up as they entered and smiled widely. 'G'day Matron. D'you want me?'

He was a tall, well built man, probably half-caste, Matt guessed, as his skin was a light colour.

'Mibbin, this is our new doctor.' She did not introduce Matt by name.

Mibbin nodded at Matt and smiled.

Matt held out his hand. 'Hello Mibbin. Glad to know you.'

Mibbin looked at Matt's outstretched hand, then at his face. After a moment's hesitation he took Matt's hand and shook it.

'G'day doctor,' he said. His face was wreathed in smiles.

'Mibbin, you haven't started the engine yet.'

'No Matron, I jus' bin fixin' 'im up a bit. 'E's ready to start now,' he replied, his voice quiet and husky.

'Good, you can show Doctor how it works.'

They walked to a tin shed behind the hospital, with wires stretching from a pole across to the main building.

'This is our power house,' Mary said.

'There is no town electricity, and we all have our own generators. This is a real vintage piece, and turns out 110 volts direct current – when it works properly,' she added with a laugh.

'We start it each morning and turn it off about ten o'clock. If we need power for the X-ray machine at other times, we start it up.

'The line runs to your house too, and works the lights and fan. Oh, and when the X-ray is being used, we have to turn everything else off to get enough power to run it.'

Mibbin opened the door, and he and Matt entered.

There was an old Lister diesel engine with a generator connected, and a large fuel tank.

Mibbin picked up a crank handle, and connected it to the flywheel. He opened a valve, then started turning the handle. He cranked faster and faster, then shut the valve and deftly removed the crank handle as the engine chugged into life and picked up speed. Mibbin stood back admiring it. 'Not bad eh, doc?' He smiled widely.

Matt looked around the shed. On both sides there were holes in the walls and large dents.

'How did *they* get there?' he asked with a puzzled expression.

Mibbin held up the crank handle. 'Dis fella done it. If you don't get 'im off quick, 'e gets stuck on and go round fast. Den you wanna get out quick, becos then dat 'andle 'e come off an' go bang through dat wall.'

Matt thanked Mibbin for the lesson, and they walked back to the hospital veranda.

Susan, a half-caste nursing aide, called out, 'Matron, Harry Dobbs is waiting for the Doc at the clinic.'

Matron introduced Susan to Matt. She added enigmatically, 'Harry's the Postmaster.'

Mary said, 'I'll leave you to it. I've got a few jobs to do. Oh, and by the way, Wednesday's Onslow trip is off. RFDS radioed to say the plane was out of action with a major service, so you don't have to go till next week.' She turned and went inside.

Matt walked to the surgery, where a lean wiry suntanned middle-aged man was waiting. He wore khaki shorts and shirt, and rubber flip-flop thongs. He had a dog with him.

As Matt approached, he held out his hand. 'G'day, Doc, I'm Harry Dobbs, and this is Bessie.' His handshake made Matt wince.

'Well!' he said jokingly. 'Which one is the patient?'

'She is,' he said.

Matt's smile wilted. 'Yes, well, come in.'

The dog looked at Matt and bared her teeth with a low growl. 'Don't worry, she won't bite yer,' he said leaning down to give her a pat.

'Well what's the problem?' Matt asked when they were both seated.

'It's like this, Doc, we didn't want 'er to have any pups, and so we asked the Doc to fix 'er.'

'And?'

'Well, 'e done an operation, and now she's got a nasty sore on her belly.'

'I see, well you'd better put her on the couch,' said Matt, first putting a rubber sheet over.

'And that's not all,' Harry went on. 'Then she 'ad a litter of pups.'

Matt struggled to suppress a laugh.

'Well Harry, why on earth didn't you go back to Dr Frank with the problem?'

Harry looked uncomfortable. 'Well Doc, yer see, we paid ten quid for the operation, and me missus got flamin' mad when Bess got pregnant, and wanted 'er money back, so I calmed 'er down and told 'er we'd best wait for the next Doc. So that's it yer see.'

Harry held the dog still whilst Matt cautiously examined the wound. 'Few buried stitches in there causing the trouble,' he said washing his hands. 'They will have to come out, and also, she will need an anaesthetic.' He came back and sat at the desk.

'Now listen Harry, I'm not a vet, and I certainly won't charge for doing the job. So if you want me to try to fix her up, come back tomorrow afternoon at two o'clock, and don't give her anything to eat all day.'

After they left, Matt got out his animal book. There was no mention of anaesthetics!

At lunchtime, Matt asked Mary what sort of anaesthetic one should give a dog. She put down her fork and after a moment's thought replied, 'Haven't a clue, why?'

Matt told her the sad story. 'Struth, I wonder what he took out?' she said laughing.

'Well, I guess he took one kidney and one ovary. He certainly didn't take two of either,' Matt replied grinning.

He asked Mary about Frank's veterinary activities, but she said that he never discussed them. However she was surprised about the fee.

That night Matt lay awake pondering the question of the dog's anaesthetic. Suddenly it struck him. Paraldehyde! Yes that was it! Back in his undergraduate days, they had done physiology experiments on anaesthetised rabbits that stank of paraldehyde. But how much, and how would he administer it?

In his half asleep state he remembered that he had on a couple of occasions given an injection of paraldehyde to obstreperous drunks – once through the seat of the pants while the victim was held down by a couple of burly policemen. About 10cc was the dose he recalled, so a dog would need a good deal less. With that sorted out, he drifted off.

Next day Matt hunted round in the dispensary, and found a glass vial of paraldehyde.

'Who's that for?' Mary asked, looking up from her record book.

'Bessie.'

'Who?'

'The postmaster's dog.' Mary rolled her eyes and went back to her work.

At two o'clock sharp, Harry appeared at the door with Bessie on a lead. 'Come in Harry,' Matt called, busy filling a glass syringe with paraldehyde. 'Put Bessie up on the couch, and hold her firmly while I give her an injection,' he said over his shoulder.

Suddenly the thought struck him. Where would he give the injection? Dogs don't have a bottom like people. He felt the thigh muscle. It would have to do.

'Hold on now Harry,' he said as he jabbed in the needle and pressed the plunger.

The effect was instantaneous! With a scream of pain the dog leapt off the couch, and galloped round and round the room yelping and barking, whilst Matt and Harry hurriedly stood up on chairs to be out of danger! Gradually the dog slowed down, and finally collapsed on the floor with its tongue hanging out. They both watched in horrified silence.

'Cripes, Doc,' said Harry, bug-eyed. 'I think yer've done 'er in!'

Matt stepped down and cautiously felt the neck for a pulse, keeping clear of the chain-saw teeth.

'It's OK Harry, she's asleep. Put her up on the couch.' He avoided lifting her himself in case she suddenly 'came to life'.

Matt quickly explored the wound and removed several stitches. He cleaned out the debris and pus, then filled the wound with penicillin powder and put on a firm dressing.

He gave Harry a bottle of penicillin tablets instructing him to put them in her food for the next week.

'Right then Harry, you'd best take her home. She will sleep for a while yet.'

Harry, visibly shaken by the experience, picked up the dog and made for the door.

He turned and said. 'Yer know what, Doc? I reckon that injection must 'ave 'urt like buggery.'

'Yes Harry, I think you're right.' Matt replied, recalling from years ago that a drunk had made a similar comment before he passed out.

'I'll call round and see her in a few days,' he said.

'Thanks a lot, Doc, I know yer did yer best.'

Harry left Matt pondering on the last remark.

On his way home Matt passed by Mary's office.

'How did you get on?' she called.

'Oh just fine,' he replied nonchalantly.

'Lucky you didn't get bitten. She's a vicious beast that dog.'

Matt went home and poured himself a stiff whisky.

The next morning, he went to the post office for his mail.

Harry greeted him as he entered. 'G'day, Doc. Bessie's OK. 'Ave a look.' He pointed to the corner of the room where Bessie lay on an old blanket. As Matt walked towards her she stood up unsteadily and with hackles raised, she growled and bared her teeth. Matt retreated.

'Just keep her inside for a few days, and don't forget the penicillin,' he said over his shoulder as he left.

Chapter 16

The following Wednesday Matt was to fly down to Onslow, the next town on the coast. He had briefly stopped there on his journey north, and out the plane window, had seen a few houses and a big jetty with a ship alongside.

The RFDS base was further up the coast at Port Hedland, and made the plane available to the Roebourne doctor every Wednesday for the regular Onslow clinic. On other occasions, a radio call would summon the plane to cope with emergencies.

Matt was up and dressed as the sun came up, and had finished his breakfast when he heard the drone of an aeroplane approaching. He watched as the little plane did a circle around the hospital, and then turned towards the airstrip. A car horn sounded. It was his transport.

Mary was waiting with the engine running. 'Good morning Matt,' she greeted him.

As they drove Mary said, 'Slight change in plans this-morning. Bullaroo Station radioed in, and wants you to stop on the way and pull out a tooth. I've packed the dental bag for you. Frank used to do them on the airstrip under the wing.'

Matt opened his mouth, then shut it, unable to find appropriate words.

'On the airstrip,' he managed. 'Under the wing. Yes, right. No problem.'

The plane landed as they arrived, and taxied towards them, putting up a plume of red dust in the slipstream. The engine died, and the pilot climbed out.

'Hello Mary,' he said. Then turned to Matt holding out his hand. 'G'day Doctor, I'm Jim Dickson.' They shook hands.

'Call me Matt,' he replied.

'Jim do you know about the stop on the way down?' Mary asked.

'Yes, the station radioed the base to make sure we knew,' he replied, then looked at his watch. 'We'd best be on our way. Bye Mary, see you at about five,' he said with a cheery smile, and turned towards the plane with Matt in pursuit.

The plane was a four-seat Cessna 180 with dual control, and the sign VH-FDZ painted on the fuselage and under-surface of the wings.

Matt climbed in to the passenger seat beside the pilot, feeling a surge of excitement as he looked at the controls, and the bewildering array of instruments on the panel in front of him.

'Right!' said Jim, 'lets go.'

He moved the control console back and forward, and then turned it from side to side. It was like a steering wheel with the top and bottom segments missing. The dual control in front of Matt followed his movements. 'Mind you don't obstruct the control,' Jim said, 'and keep your feet off the pedals.' He clicked a switch on the panel and pressed the starter. The engine spluttered into life. The noise was deafening and the whole cockpit shuddered and shook! Dials on the panel leapt into life, and needles flickered information. Matt could feel his heart pounding!

Jim taxied the little plane to the end of the airstrip, and then turned.

He pulled on the hand brake and revved the engine, at the same time clicking a control panel switch off and on.

'You OK?' Jim shouted. Matt nodded, and as he did, Jim opened the throttle and the plane leapt forward. Within seconds they were airborne and climbing like an elevator. Matt watched the altimeter needle race around to five hundred feet. Jim throttled back a little and raised the flaps. The plane went on climbing, but at a slower rate until they reached four thousand feet, when Jim levelled out and adjusted the trim and engine revolutions for level cruising.

He looked at Matt and grinned. 'Easy isn't it?' he shouted. 'Feeling OK?'

Matt nodded with a grin and gave a 'thumbs up'.

Jim picked up the microphone. 'Hedland Base, this is Foxtrot Delta Zulu, do you read? Over.'

The speaker above his head crackled into life. 'Foxtrot Delta Zulu, this is Hedland Base. We read you loud and clear. Over.'

Jim gave the flight details, and signed off.

It was too noisy for conversation, so Matt leaned against the window and watched the ground below slowly passing beneath. The ocean was off to the right, as they flew over great saltpans, and miles of red earth, spotted with spinifex and small trees. Tidal creeks edged with mangroves wound sinuously like glittering green snakes across the empty land.

After about twenty minutes Jim nudged Matt and pointed down. Far below was a homestead surrounded with green gardens. 'Bullaroo.' He shouted. As they came in to land a utility approached the airstrip trailing a plume of red dust.

With the flaps down, Jim throttled back, and eased back on the console. The plane dropped lower and lower. Suddenly a klaxon sounded – the 'stall indicator' Matt learned later – and the plane touched down with hardly a bump.

Jim taxied to the waiting ute then cut the engine.

As they climbed out, a middle-aged woman approached. 'Good-morning. You must be the new doctor; I'm Peggy Saunders.' She held out a suntanned hand and shook firmly as Matt introduced himself.

Standing a few yards behind Peggy was a well-built elderly Aboriginal man. She turned to him. 'Willy, bring that chair from the ute.' Willy sat himself on the chair in the shade of the wing, and brushed off the flies that had suddenly found them. 'He's had tooth ache for a few days,' Peggy said as Matt opened his dental instrument bag on the ground.

'OK Willy, which one?' Matt said as he opened his mouth. Willy pointed.

Matt peered into the cavernous mouth. He put his finger in to feel the gum, and removed it immediately with a dark blob of gooey stuff stuck to it.

'Erk!' he said in disgust, flicking the revolting muck from his finger. 'What the hell was that?'

Peggy laughed. 'Oh that's "bulgai" – a mixture of tobacco and ash. They all chew it, and store in their cheek.'

Throughout this pantomime, Jim had been leaning against the wing strut watching with amusement. He called out. 'Matt, I've got some water and a dish in the plane if you want to wash.' Looking somewhat shaken, Matt gratefully washed his hands, and as he did, Jim whispered to him.

With renewed enthusiasm, Matt re-examined Willie's mouth – keeping his fingers out, then turned back to Peggy and said. 'Look, this is going to be a difficult tooth, and might bleed a bit. Why don't we take him on with us to Onslow, and we can drop him off on the way home?'

Peggy looked unimpressed, but had to agree, and with no further ado, they bundled Willy in to the back seat of the plane, and strapped him in.

They got in and shut the doors, waving to Peggy.

'Jim you saved my reputation with that suggestion,' Matt said with a grateful smile, then wrinkled his nose and looked back at Willy. 'Pfew! A bit fruity!'

'Let's get the show on the road,' Jim replied without further comment, and hit the starter button.

Thirty minutes later they were over Onslow, and circled the hospital. The ocean was the deepest blue, with a snow-white beach curving around the bay to the big jetty on the point. There was no ship there today.

They taxied in to the shed with its adjacent fuel depot, and got out. Jim locked the plane and they walked over to the shade. The heat was intense and the flies aggressive.

A white Ford sedan pulled up, and a suntanned young man dressed in shorts and shirt got out.

'G'day Jim,' he said as he approached. 'I see we 'ave a customer.' He glanced at Willy.

'Matt, this is Tom Atkins, he runs the hospital.' They shook hands.

'That's quite true, but you'd better not say it to Matron,' he said with a broad grin. 'My other job is hospital orderly.'

'Right,' he said. 'Jim and Willy in the back, and you in with me, Doc.'

As they drove into the town, Matt commented on the twisted metal telephone poles lying on the ground. 'That was the cyclone last year,' Tom answered. 'Fair wrecked the place, I tell you.'

A little further on he pointed out some demolished houses. 'The hospital took it OK,' he said, just rattled the roof a bit. 'Course everyone goes to the pub when the big blow comes. Solid as a rock it is – that's it over there.' They drove past a stone two-storey building near the beach with a sign 'Beadon Hotel' and a little further on, a similar vintage building with the sign 'Police Station' painted on the wall.

The hospital was located almost on the beach. Originally it had been well back, but over the years, the cyclones washed away the sand, and eroded the low sand dunes. The building looked decrepit, with corrugated iron walls and roof, and wooden shutters that could be battened down over the windows.

They drove up to the front veranda, which had a few wooden steps down to the drive.

A black dog covered in flies lay asleep under the steps and ignored their arrival.

At the top of the steps the Matron stood waiting.

She was a short stout woman in her sixties, Matt guessed, and was dressed in a white uniform, spotted with purple dye. Her petticoat hung down some three inches below, and she wore sandshoes on her otherwise bare feet. Her face was suntanned and wrinkled.

Over her short grey hair she wore a tennis shield, pulled down over her spectacles, and in the corner of her mouth a hand-rolled cigarette hung between her scarlet painted lips.

'Morning Matron,' Jim said cheerily as they climbed the steps. 'This is our new doctor …'

'Who's he?' she interrupted, jabbing a finger at Willy, the fag still in her mouth.

Jim explained, and returned to his introduction of Matt.

'Well, Doctor. Pleased to meet you. Come along and we'll have morning tea before starting work.'

She led the way in to the kitchen, where a great iron wood-fired stove radiated enormous heat. A large woman was bent over it, stirring something in a big pot.

'Hey Maggie!' Matron bellowed. 'She's deaf,' she added for Matt's benefit. Maggie turned, her beefy red face running with sweat.

'This is the new doctor,' she shouted. 'We'll have morning tea now.'

Maggie's face creased in a great smile showing her spaced square teeth. 'Nice to meet yer, Doc,' she said in a loud deaf voice, waving her dripping wooden spoon in Matt's direction.

Matron led them in to the dining room that was marginally cooler than the kitchen, and Maggie followed them in with a teapot. The table was set with cups and plates of cake and biscuits.

Over tea, Matt asked if there were any problems.

'No,' Matron replied, as she rolled a cigarette. 'All going OK. One of the native girls had her baby yesterday – she 'ad a few fits, but she's OK.' Matt choked on his tea. 'Fits?' His eyes bulged. 'How was her blood pressure?'

Matron ignored the question. 'Well come along, we'd better get going.'

There was a group of people waiting on the veranda, but Matt brought Willy in first. 'I think we should do an X-ray first,' said Matt.

'Yer can't. It's broke.' Matron replied.

'Ah, well. I'll just stick in the anaesthetic, then see a couple of people while it is working.'

He handed Willy a glass with antiseptic in it. 'Here Willy, have a good rinse and spit it in that bowl.' Matt watched and shuddered.

'Right then Willy, open up wide.' Matt felt the 'landmarks' at the back of the mouth with his finger, and then slid the needle in as he had been taught.

'OK Willy sit outside, and I'll call you later.'

Matt saw a couple of patients, then called Willy back.

Willy sat on the plain wooden chair, and matron shone the spotlight in to his mouth.

Matt located the carious tooth and applied the dental forceps. 'Right now Willy this won't hurt.'

Matt said as he rocked the tooth.

Willy let out a bleat and rose up from the chair following the forceps. 'Arrgh! Aaah! Doc!'

Matt recoiled. 'What's up Willy?' he asked, having perfect faith in his anaesthetic technique.

'Aw Doc! 'im plurry hurt!' Willy said reproachfully.

'Right then,' Matt said. 'More anaesthetic.'

Once again he shot in some anaesthetic, and Willy returned to the veranda.

The second attempt was met with a similar response from Willy, so again Matt injected the anaesthetic. 'Don't worry, "three times lucky" Willy,' Matt said with a pat on the shoulder as he sent him out.

It was approaching lunchtime when Willy was summoned again. He sat despondently on the chair and opened his mouth.

'You won't feel a thing this time, Willy,' Matt said, applying the tongs.

'Arrrgh! Jesus Doc!' Willy squawked, his eyes bulging.

Matt was visibly shaken. What was wrong? He looked at the anaesthetic vial. Yes, it was the right stuff. Maybe Aboriginals are more resistant to it, he wondered.

At this point Matron intervened.

'I think we'll all knock off for lunch. The stuff should have worked by the time we finish.'

She led the way out of the clinic, and detailed Tom to lay Willy down on a bed.

'Poor old bugger's havin' a rough time,' she said out of the corner of her mouth.

Lunch was a major event. In spite of the heat of the day, they started with soup, and then went on to a large plate of baked meat and vegetables, with thick gravy. Following this, Maggie proudly presented her speciality. A large baked apple pie, served with tinned cream.

With creaking belly and sweaty face, Matt returned for the afternoon's clinic. Willy was all ready in the chair, watching Matt carefully.

'We might just put in a bit more anaesthetic Willy, just to make sure. Open wide.'

Willy opened his mouth, showing the whites of his eyes as Matt injected.

'Right! Off you go.'

Willy lurched out the door and flopped on the veranda bench.

Ten minutes later, he was back in the chair, but now Matt had some reinforcements.

Tom stood behind the chair and took a firm grip on Willy's head while Matron pointed the light.

Matt braced himself, and carefully applied the forceps. With a sudden twisting heave, he staggered back, brandishing the bloodstained molar in his tongs. Willy gave a long groan, and slumped in the chair.

'There we are! All over!' Matt said with a mixture of relief and triumph.

Willy groaned again and rolled his eyes.

'Tom, put 'im on a bed till they're ready to go.' Matron said, as Willy was helped through the door. Hands on hips, she watched, shaking her head.

The rest of the clinic ran smoothly, and as Matt packed up his instruments, Matron said quietly. 'About that blood pressure.' She looked a little embarrassed. 'That came in after me training, and I never got round to learning 'ow it worked.'

Matt smiled at her. 'Well, how about I teach you how to do it next time? Oh, and how about you call me on the morning schedule through the week and let me know how things are going.'

'Can't do that,' she replied. 'The radio's broke. Got full of water in the last cyclone.'

'Ah, well never mind then. See you next week.'

They bundled Willy in to the car, with Jim beside him, and headed for the airstrip.

As Tom helped Willy in to the plane's back seat, and strapped him in, Jim said to Matt, 'Is Willy OK? He's acting sort of strange.'

'Don't worry, he's just had some painkiller.' Matt replied as he fastened his seat belt.

Willy was now slumped in the back seat, muttering and humming.

At Bullaroo Station, Peggy was waiting with the ute, and looked concerned as they helped Willy in to the vehicle, still muttering and humming.

'What the hell's wrong with him?' she asked anxiously.

'Don't worry, he's fine. Just had some strong painkiller,' Matt said, trying to reassure her. 'Very nasty tooth – worst I've seen for a while,' he added.

Back at Roebourne, Matt watched Jim fly off, and climbed wearily in to Mary's car.

'Had a good day?' she asked as they sped back to town.

'Not bad. Not bad at all,' he replied.

Chapter 17

Two weeks had passed, and life was running smoothly. His visits to Onslow were uneventful, and he had successfully taught the Matron how to measure blood pressure, much to her delight.

Also he had arranged for a new Traeger two-way radio to be installed in her hospital.

He called at the post office for his mail, and learned that Bess had made a complete recovery. Physically that was, for she bore an indelible scar of hatred, and growled whenever Matt appeared.

There was a letter for him from Bill Corbett, hoping that he had settled in well, and inviting him to the station for the coming weekend if he was free. Perhaps he could give them a call on the morning radio schedule. He included a 'mud map' so that he would not get lost. Matt felt a twinge of guilt at not having contacted Bill as he had promised.

The next morning Matt called up Spinifex Plains. A woman's voice responded, and identified herself as Elizabeth. Matt told her about Bill's letter, that he would be delighted to come out to the station for the weekend. He asked that the message be passed on to Mr Corbett.

Elizabeth said that she was pleased that he could come, and she would pass the message on to her parents.

Her parents? Bill had not mentioned that he had a daughter. Through the day he kept remembering her voice, and somehow it seemed to trouble him.

On Friday afternoon Matt filled the ute with petrol.

The Health Department provided a 44-gallon drum of fuel, which the local garage man dumped in the middle of a dusty patch behind Matt's garage. There was a hand pump with it. When the drum cooled down in the middle of the night, the top indented with a loud 'Bang!' like a gunshot. For a few nights he woke with a start, but after a while he barely heard it.

Before bed he packed a bag, including slacks and a blue jacket and tie, not knowing what level of formality to expect, then slept soundly until daybreak.

Dressed in khaki slacks and shirt, he ate toast and jam for breakfast, washed down with a cup of tea, then walked over to the hospital.

Mary was busy sterilising bundles of dressings in the old autoclave when he arrived, and looked hot and bothered. 'One of these days that bloody thing will blow up,' she muttered, glaring at the steriliser leaking steam. She turned as he entered.

'Well! Off for the weekend?' she said brightly, brushing a strand of hair from her face.

'Any problems for me?' he asked, fingers crossed.

'No, go and have a good time,' she replied. 'Drive carefully, and look out for kangaroos. They run across in front of you sometimes.'

'OK. You know where to find me if needed.'

Matt had driven only a few hundred yards past the last house in town when the bitumen surface of the road changed to dusty corrugated gravel. Driving at slower speeds was a bone-shaking event, but at the recommended forty-five to fifty miles per hour, the bumps diminished as the vehicle floated over the top of the corrugations. More comfortable, but hazardous, as Matt found when he negotiated a bend, only to find the vehicle drifting off the road, unresponsive to the steering wheel! With difficulty he regained control, and thereafter drove with great concentration.

In the morning sunshine the countryside looked brilliant. The bright red earth was dotted with grey-green spinifex bushes, and the distant hills were deep blue against the azure sky. Here and there were stunted trees, and red rocky outcrops. A flock of pink and grey galahs swooped by, their harsh cries reverberating in the morning stillness.

He slowed down as he approached a line of green gum trees, recognising this to be a creek.

The track descended sharply to the dry creek bed crossing, but off to his right there was a long stretch of reed-lined water, with white wading birds. As he drove up the incline on the other side, he saw high above a great wedge tailed eagle hanging motionless in the clear morning air, watching.

He drove for nearly two hours, passing through several creek beds, some with a few sleepy kangaroos that moved away as he approached. They mostly slept through the day.

At last he came upon some sheds off to the right, with wooden pens beside them. Shearing sheds he guessed. He was getting close.

He drove around a grove of trees, and in front of him stood the old stone homestead, with wide bungalow-style verandas and a green corrugated-iron roof.

Surrounded by green lawns with flowering poinciana trees and date palms, it looked like a beautiful oasis.

He drove slowly up to the house, and pulled up in the shade of a big tree.

As he climbed out, a familiar voice greeted him. 'Hello Matt! Welcome to Spinifex Plains.'

Bill Corbett approached with his hand extended and a wide grin. They shook hands warmly.

Bill picked up his bag and led the way to the veranda.

Inside the house the air was cool, and it took him a moment to adjust his eyes to the reduced light as they stood in the wide passageway. A woman approached.

'Joan, this is Matt Harrison.' Bill said.

She held out her hand. 'Hello Matt, welcome to our home,' she said in a soft pleasant voice. She was slim and tall, with fine features and pale skin. She had luminous dark eyes and dark hair. In the dim light she looked younger than Bill. She wore a blue blouse and dark brown slacks.

She must have been very beautiful when she was young, he thought.

'Bill, show Matt his room, and the bathroom, I'm sure he wants to freshen up. Then we'll have a cup of tea on the veranda.'

Matt came out to the veranda having unpacked his bag and tidied himself up.

Bill and Joan were sitting by a wicker table in matching cane chairs with cushions. There was a tea tray with cups and saucers, and a plate with a cake under a glass cover.

'Good! Come and sit down,' said Bill. He joined them at the table.

'Ah, here's the tea,' he said looking up.

A young woman approached carrying a teapot and a hot water jug. As she bent to place them on the table, a strand of golden hair fell across her face. Matt looked at her in awe. She was beautiful!

As she sat down with them Joan introduced her. 'Matt, this is our daughter Elizabeth.' She looked at Matt with a radiant smile that showed her even white teeth.

'We spoke on the radio. Nice to meet you, Matt.'

He rose from his seat. 'How do you do, Elizabeth?'

'Such formality,' she said with a little laugh. 'Everyone calls me Lizzie.'

As Joan poured tea and handed round the cups, Matt's eyes were drawn to Lizzie.

Like her mother she was tall and slim, but her skin was golden brown, and her eyes were large and the colour of caramel toffee. Her golden hair was loosely tied back with a black ribbon, and though she wore no lipstick, her full lips were a perfect pink.

She wore men's moleskin trousers and elastic-sided boots, and a pink open-neck shirt with rolled up sleeves. Her young breasts jutted proudly beneath her shirt. As Matt looked at her their eyes met and he felt his colour rising.

'Well Matt, tell us about your experiences so far. All running smoothly for you?' Bill asked.

They sipped tea as he told them about his adventures. They laughed heartily at the tale of the postmaster's dog, and sympathised with Willy in his traumatic dental experience.

'Well, if I get tooth ache, I'm flying South,' said Lizzie firmly.

'Good idea,' Matt replied. They all laughed.

'Now then, while you girls get on with women's business, I'm going to show Matt around the homestead.' Bill stood up.

He led Matt around the corner of the veranda. 'The house was built about fifty years ago, using local stone for the walls. They were made thick and strong to resist the cyclones, and the house always stays nice and cool.' Off the veranda was another building. 'That's the kitchen,' he said. 'Having it away from the main house reduces the fire risk, and also it doesn't heat the house up.' He opened the door. 'Come and have a look.'

The kitchen was enormous. Likewise made of stone, there was a great iron wood-fired stove in an alcove, and another more modern stove beside it. 'We don't use the old stove much these days, but it is useful if we have a big party. That's an Aga stove.' He pointed at the other. 'Comes from England, and mostly are used in the country there. They are wood-fired too, but well insulated, and don't heat the place up so much.'

While they looked around two native girls in clean dresses and white aprons and bare feet were working quietly at the kitchen table preparing food.

There was a cold-room off the kitchen, with frozen meat hanging from hooks, and a well-laden storeroom as well.

In response to Matt's surprise at the quantity of the stores, Bill pointed out that when the rain came, the roads became impassable, and they needed always to have a good reserve of food. 'You'd be surprised how many mouths we feed here,' he added with a chuckle.

Bill then showed Matt the old shearers' bunkhouse that was behind the kitchen. In recent times the shearers were housed nearer the sheds with their own cookhouse, and the old bunkhouse had been done up as comfortable, though spartan, accommodation for men when they had weekend parties, and was known as 'the Bullpen'.

They sat down to a lunch of cold mutton and salad, with icy lemon squash. The temperature had gone up considerably.

'Yer can't get much work done in the heat,' said Bill, 'so we start at first light, then knock off for a few hours in the middle of the day – like they do in the Mediterranean countries. We have dinner late, when it cools down.'

After lunch they retired to the 'cool house'.

The cool house was a large wooden frame covered in wire mesh. This in turn was covered with thatch-like brush, thicker on the roof than on the walls. The brush was held in place by another layer of wire mesh. As they walked in the temperature was noticeably cooler.

'There's a sprinkler on the roof that keeps the thatch damp, and it works like a big Coolgardie Safe,' Bill explained.

Matt looked blank. 'A what?'

Bill laughed. 'I guess a Pom wouldn't know what that was,' he said.

'Yer see, in the gold-rush days, the town of Coolgardie was the centre of activity, and the heat was as bad as it is here, out in the desert country near Kalgoorlie.' Matt vaguely recalled hearing the name Kalgoorlie before he came to Australia.

'The diggers worked out a system for keeping their food cool, with a wire mesh box covered in hessian bags, and a big dish of water on the top, with holes in it so the water kept the bags moist. Nature did the rest with the cooling evaporation. They called it a Coolgardie safe.'

There were cane lounges and chairs, and a cane table laden with magazines and newspapers.

'This is our retreat from the heat,' Joan said. 'Just make yourself comfy.'

She and Bill stretched out on lounges, and Matt and Lizzie sat on chairs by the table. In a matter of minutes both Bill and Joan were sound asleep, and snoring quietly.

'Bless them,' said Lizzie with a smile. 'They are both getting too old for the work they do – Dad especially,' she said quietly.

'Tell me about yourself,' Matt asked, fascinated by the golden girl. 'Have you lived here all your life?' He offered a packet of cigarettes.

Lizzie shook her head, raising her hand. She said quietly, 'Dad doesn't like people smoking in here.'

'Quite right,' Matt responded, pocketing the cigarettes.

'Why don't we go for a drive? I can show you around a bit of the property. Or is it too hot for you?'

'Great idea,' Matt said rising from the chair. 'I'm pretty well acclimatised now, you know.'

Lizzie got up with a glance at her dozing parents. 'I'll meet you out the front. You'll need a hat, there's no roof on the jeep.'

Matt collected his safari hat from the ute and a moment later Lizzie rounded the corner in a dusty old khaki ex-army jeep, with a beaten up bush hat on her head.

'You look like a big game hunter,' said Lizzie laughing.

Matt took his hat off and looked at it then put it on again. 'First time I've worn it,' he said with a sheepish grin.

'Get in. It looks great.'

'We'll go a few miles along the river,' she said as Matt settled himself on the dusty hard seat.

As they drove Lizzie answered Matt's question.

'Going back twenty years or so, things were fairly primitive up here in the north, so Mum went down to Perth for the last part of her pregnancy, and that's where I was born. Just as well too, as it was complicated, and as a result she couldn't have any more children.

'I spent my early childhood here on the station, and later went down to boarding school in Perth.

'When I left school I came home for a year, but Mum wanted me to see some of the world, so she and I went to England by ship, and spent six months touring England and Europe.

'When we got home, I felt unsettled in the isolation here, so I enrolled in university and spent the next three years doing degrees in Commerce and Economics. Since then I've been back here helping run the station, and I help with the books too.'

They reached a gate, and stopped in a cloud of dust.

'You open it, then close it after I drive through,' she said.

Back in the jeep, she said, 'You must always leave a gate as you found it up here – open or closed.'

As they drove towards a line of trees, Matt saw a large group of kangaroos hopping along away from the approaching vehicle.

'There are more kangaroos on the property than anything else,' she replied to Matt's comment.

'They eat all the feed, and breed like flies.'

'Where are all the sheep I've heard about?'

'All out on different paddocks where there is more to eat. We can only run one or two sheep to about four acres at the moment, because of the drought.'

They drove into the trees and came to a beautiful stretch of water lined with reeds and shaded by gum trees.

'This is our swimming pool,' she said. 'I spent my life here when I was a kid.'

She stopped the engine and the silence seemed profound.

'The pool never dries up, no matter what happens, and when the big rains come, the whole river runs. But that hasn't happened for a few years now.'

As they sat watching a flight of ducks skimmed in and landed in the water.

'Back home I read about billabongs. Is this a billabong?' Matt asked.

'Well, I suppose so, but we don't call them that. I think that comes from the eastern states – we just call them pools.'

They drove on, and came to the shearing sheds. She pulled up again. 'Come in and have a look.' She led the way.

They walked past the wooden pens and up a ramp. Inside, there were rows of shearing bays and machinery. The air had a strong, musty animal smell.

'We shear some of the best merino wool in the country,' she said, stooping to pick up a piece of wool from the otherwise clean floor. 'Here, feel the texture.' She handed it to him. It was creamy white and tightly wavy. It felt greasy.

'That's where lanoline comes from. The whole place seems greasy when the shearers are working. You must come out and watch when shearing starts, it's quite a performance.'

'Who does the shearing?' Matt asked. 'You people?'

'Hell no,' she said. 'A team of professional shearers comes around the stations; about twenty men in the team, all skilled in their job. Shearing contractors make big money, and work their teams hard. The men get well paid, mind you.

'All we have to do is provide food for them. And believe me, that's no mean task! Mum used to do the cooking in the old days, but now they bring their own cook. The shearers have enormous appetites, and are very fussy about the cooking!

'The wool is baled up and trucked to the port, then taken south by the state ships. After that, things get back to normal until next time.'

'So when is this big event? Matt asked.

'About September usually,' she replied.

It was late afternoon when they headed for the homestead. On the way, Lizzie drove past a row of neat cottages, standing in the shade of a grove of trees. Each had a fenced garden with lawn and a vegetable plot. Aboriginal children were playing on a swing beneath a tree.

'This is where the Aboriginal stockmen live with their families,' Lizzie said, as the smiling children waved to her. 'We have about ten at any one time, but they come and go as they please.

'They live in family groups and their extended family could be six to eight people. The men are marvellous stockmen and natural mechanics, and the women and girls learn how to cook and sew and do house work.'

'I see what Bill meant when he mentioned the number of mouths to feed,' Matt said as they drove on slowly.

'We provide flour, tea and sugar, and tobacco, plus odds and ends they want, and they eat only kangaroo meat, which is plentiful, as you saw. Usually the men shoot a few 'roos and bring them home at the end of the day.

'The workers get paid, but not much, and they can buy things from our store, such as clothing and odds and ends, but basically we give them everything.'

'I asked one Aboriginal patient if he lived at the Reserve,' Matt said, 'and he seemed quite insulted. He told me proudly that he lived on a station, and that he was a stockman. I can see why now.'

'Yes, they take pride in their work and seem very happy to live here. Every now and again they wander off on "walkabout", though. It's an ancient thing, part of their culture. God knows what they do, but they turn up again weeks later and carry on as though nothing had happened.'

Back at the homestead Bill greeted them as they stopped the jeep.

'You look hot and dusty, Matt. Come and I'll show you the shower, then we can sit and have a cold drink.'

The shower was located under the huge water tank that stood beside the house on a wooden tower, with enclosed sides. When Matt turned on the tap, a deluge of cold water fell like Niagara Falls from the huge showerhead. It was the best shower he ever had!

There was a cool breeze wafting through the trees as they sat on the veranda having drinks before dinner.

Matt had changed into slacks, and collar and tie, plus a jacket, but when he came out to the veranda, Bill was in an open neck white shirt and white slacks and sent Matt back to dress more casually.

Now they were all relaxed, with long icy drinks in hand. Lizzie looked gorgeous, in a simple white dress, and a gold bracelet on her suntanned wrist. Her hair was tied back with a black ribbon.

'Well, did you have a good drive around?' Bill asked.

'Yes indeed,' Matt replied. 'Lizzie showed me right round the station.'

'The station is more than a million acres, Matt, you saw one little corner,' Lizzie said smiling. 'It takes days to drive right around, and when the stockmen are mustering for shearing, they are gone for weeks.'

'To put it simply,' said Bill, 'the sun comes up on one side of the station and goes down on the other. This is an enormous country. You can fly around an area the size of England and it will fit in just one corner here, and contain only a few hundred people, if that.'

'The concept is a bit hard to grasp,' Matt said weakly.

'Wait till you've flown round a bit more, and you'll soon see what I mean.'

They sat down to dinner at eight, when the evening had cooled down. Joan and Lizzie had done the cooking, but two Aboriginal girls quietly and efficiently waited table. Bill carved a leg of mutton at the table and Joan served vegetables from silver dishes. A silver gravy boat on its dish was passed around.

After dinner they went out for coffee on the lawn. The grass was wet from the sprinklers, and the air was cool and sweet scented from the flowering trees.

'You know, this really is God's own country up here.' Bill said stretching out in a comfortable cane chair. 'Just look at that sky.' Above them the stars blazed in the inky blackness.

They sat talking for an hour, then Bill got up and stretched. 'Well, I'm off to bed.'

'Yes, me too,' said Joan rising from her chair. Matt got up. 'By all means stay and talk,' she said with a smile. 'The old folk have had enough for one day. Goodnight.'

The date palms rustled in the breeze as they sat under the stars talking quietly.

'Dad told me about your awful tragedy,' Lizzie said unexpectedly.

After a long pause Matt answered. 'It's in the past now, and I don't think about it any more. I came here to start again in a new country with new people. At first it didn't seem possible, but time heals, and my little family are now just a beautiful memory. I will always love them in my heart.'

'I'm sorry Matt, I shouldn't have said anything, but I wanted to tell you how sad I felt.'

In the dim light Matt could see tears glistening in her eyes.

'Thanks Lizzie.' He leant over and patted her hand. 'I think it's bed time.'

Matt awoke to a clatter and loud voices outside his window. He opened the curtains and looked out. Bill was standing talking to two stockmen in a jeep. He looked at his watch – six o'clock.

He wandered off to the shower and returned refreshed. At seven the gong sounded for breakfast, and he headed for the dining room.

Lizzie and Joan were already there, helping themselves to scrambled eggs and bacon from the hot box.

'Good morning,' Joan greeted him. 'Hope you slept well.'

'Like a log thanks,' he replied.

'Just help yourself to breakfast.' She waved at the buffet.

'Bill had his breakfast early, and has gone off to repair a broken mill,' Joan said as he joined them at the table.

'We'll drive out and see how they are getting along later,' Lizzie said to Matt.

After a leisurely breakfast, Lizzie drove her jeep round to the front of the house where Matt stood in the shade waiting.

'Where's your famous hat?' she asked. 'You'll need it.'

'Ah,' said Matt and sped inside, returning with it.

'It's about a five mile drive,' Lizzie said as they drove off, leaving a dust trail behind them. They chatted as they drove, and Matt did 'gate duty' as he had been instructed.

Along the way Matt commented on the parched earth. 'What do the sheep live on?' he asked. 'All there is seems to be sticks, stones and spinifex.'

'Yair, it looks that way, but they manage to forage out food enough, providing the kangaroo population doesn't get too big.'

'And how do you contain it?'

'She leant forward and patted the leather scabbard on the side of the vehicle that held a rifle. 'With these.'

Finally they reached the windmill where there was a hive of activity. Bill was down on his knees working on a greasy metal pipe. He had grease up to the elbows. He looked up and gave a cheery wave.

'Come to help?' he called out.

'No, just to watch,' Lizzie replied.

Two stockmen were leaning over the edge of the well, and the top of the third man's hat could be seen inside the well. One was passing down tools.

'She's just about fixed, anyhow,' Bill said.

They sat watching for a while then Lizzie went to the front of the jeep and brought back the canvas water bag that hung on a rail at the front. They took turns swigging the surprisingly cool water. 'You get dehydrated very quickly out here,' she said, passing the bag to Matt again.

'Why don't you take Matt off and see what sort of shot he is?' Bill called out.

'Great idea,' she replied. 'This is getting a bit boring.'

She started the motor, and they drove off in a swirl of dust. They stopped at a dry creek bed, and she climbed out, with the rifle.

'Ever fired one?' she asked.

'Never,' Matt said as he climbed out and brushed off the dust.

'During the war all the ammunition we had was used on the Germans, and even then it was in short supply.'

'OK.' She produced a tin can from amongst the junk in the back of the jeep, and walked over to the bank of the creek bed, placing it on the ground, about twenty yards away. She came back to the jeep and picked up the rifle.

'This is a Remington .22 calibre rimfire pump-action repeating rifle, and it is as dangerous as hell, so always remember that.'

For the next five minutes Lizzie gave Matt a lesson in firearms safety, and showed him how the ammunition was loaded in a tube magazine under the barrel, and how the handgrip under the barrel worked like a pump, reloading the rifle after each shot.

She demonstrated by firing a few rounds into the embankment. At the crack of the rifle, birds flew startled from the trees around them.

She placed the rifle on the bonnet of the jeep.

'Now rest your elbows on the bonnet, and sight along the barrel, putting the front post in the V notch of the back sight. Then line up the tin, and squeeze the trigger slowly, concentrating on the sight picture.'

Matt did as instructed, but jerked the trigger, and the shot went wide.

'Good try, but you must hold the rifle steady and squeeze.'

She came close and leaned over him, adjusting his position. Her nearness and warmth suddenly aroused him. The earthy sweet smell of her body awoke old memories and sensations that he thought were lost forever. He struggled to concentrate on the tin can, which now seemed of minor importance. He squeezed the trigger and the tin can leapt in to the air.

'Well done!' Lizzie cried, giving him a thump on the back.

After about ten minutes, Matt was shooting well, and had a natural ability, Lizzie told him.

'You should have a rifle of your own up here you know,' she said as they drove off.

'What ever for?' he asked.

'If you are stranded in the outback you need food and water. Your ute is well supplied with a big water tank and the water bag, and you can shoot a 'roo or even a bush turkey if you're lucky, and have tucker until someone finds you.'

'Sounds like a lot of fun,' he said without enthusiasm.

'Believe me, people have died in the outback, mainly because they were unprepared.'

They drove on in silence, while Matt was preoccupied and struggling with his new emotions.

As casually as he could manage, Matt asked. 'Well Lizzie, you know all about me, what about yourself? Is there a man in your life?'

She paused, and then said. 'No, not really. Well, sort of.' She paused, and Matt waited.

'There's Jack Morgan. He is the overseer on his uncle's station, Mount Cooke. He seems to think that I fancy him – which I don't – but he tells people that I'm his girlfriend.

'He can be very charming, but there is something about him that frightens me. I don't know what it is; he just seems to have a dark side.' She stopped, and laughed. 'Anyhow, that is my love life, as far as it goes.'

They arrived back at the homestead hot and dusty, and were met by Joan on the veranda.

'Go and freshen up then come and have a cold drink in the cool house,' she said.

As they sipped their icy lemonade, Lizzie told her mother of their morning's activities, and of Matt's prowess with the rifle.

'Well good for you,' she said. 'You need to be able to shoot, living up here.'

'So Lizzie told me,' Matt replied with a straight face. 'She said that the big kangaroos often attack and are extremely dangerous.'

Joan raised an eyebrow and looked at Lizzie, who blushed and retorted. 'What nonsense, I said no such thing.' They all laughed.

When Bill got back and freshened up, they had a leisurely cold lunch, and then returned to the cool house, as the temperature had soared.

For the next couple of hours they chatted, read magazines or dozed until the heat of the day had passed.

They had afternoon tea, after which Matt said he must get back to town and prepare for the week's work. He packed his belongings and said thanks and goodbye to Bill and Joan in the cool house, then carried his bag out to the ute, parked in the shade.

Lizzie walked out with him. A light breeze had sprung up and the air was much cooler.

'Lizzie, thank you so much for a wonderful weekend, I can't remember when I last enjoyed myself so much,' Matt said, shaking Lizzie's hand.

'Thank you for coming,' she replied. 'I hope you will come often, and feel that this is your home in Australia.' She leaned forward and kissed him lightly on the cheek.

He looked in to her eyes and said softly. 'That would be wonderful. Goodbye.'

As Matt drove back to town his mind ran over the events of the weekend. It had taken him completely by surprise. He asked himself: 'Could I fall in love again?'

Chapter 18

About seventy miles from Spinifex Plains, Jack Morgan sat on the veranda of Mount Cooke Station with a cold bottle of beer in a corrugated cardboard tube on the table beside him. They were packed like that in wooden boxes for shipping north, and it kept them cool for longer.

On the other side of the table his uncle Bruce was slumped in a cane chair snoring. A rifle with a telescope sight rested against the chair, and on the table was a half empty bottle of scotch whisky.

Jack ran the station now, and Bruce spent a lot of time sitting on the veranda with his whisky bottle and rifle. His favourite occupation was shooting crows, and to attract them, he had shot a kangaroo a couple of hundred yards from the house early that morning. The crows were now feasting on the carcass, but no longer in danger from Bruce in his present state. He had shot a couple earlier in the afternoon.

Jack sat brooding. He had been on the station for nearly three years now, hoping that Harry would finally retire and go south, but the old man just hung on, clinging to his bottle and his beloved high powered .250/3000 Mauser rifle. He had told Jack that the station would be his when he died, and that couldn't happen soon enough in Jack's opinion.

Jack was a big man. He was over six feet tall and deeply suntanned, with a broad chest and bulging muscles. He had blond hair and a square jaw, and would have been handsome had it not been for his blue eyes, which seemed too close together, and had a shiftiness about them.

Jack had spent his school days as a boarder in an exclusive private school, sent there when his parents separated. His mother died soon after. She had committed suicide.

He left school without matriculating, and went on to an agricultural college for the next two years. He then became a jackaroo on a station in western Queensland.

Jack's father and Bruce had shared the station for many years, though Bruce had never married, and lived in bachelor's quarters while old Jack, his brother, had lived in the homestead with his wife. Like Bruce, old Jack had a weakness for the bottle, which had ultimately caused his wife to leave him, suffer severe depression, and ultimately taken her own life.

Later, when old Jack died of lung cancer, Bruce found the station too much for him, and wrote to Jack in Queensland, asking him to come home. By that time Jack was restless, and was ready to move on from Queensland. Besides, he had got an Aboriginal girl pregnant, and the station owner had threatened to write and tell his father. His death had been timely.

He finished off the beer, drinking it from the bottle. He belched then stood up and stretched, looking out at the gathering dusk.

At least there was some life in Queensland he thought. There had been a decent sized town to drive into for a good time. Here there was nothing. He was bored.

He looked at the sleeping man.

'Hey Bruce!' he bellowed. The old man jerked upright.

'What … What's wrong, Jack?' he muttered, still half asleep, his mind fuddled with liquor.

'Do yer want to stay there all night?'

The old man rose unsteadily to his feet, picked up his rifle, and followed Jack inside.

'Make sure you've unloaded that bloody thing,' Jack growled as he put plates on the table, and lit the kerosene lantern. The power plant had broken down, and they were waiting on a part to come up from the south.

They sat down to their evening meal of cold mutton, boiled potatoes and tinned peas.

'I hate tinned peas,' whined the old man, glaring at the plate Jack had put in front of him.

'Well don't bloody eat 'em.'

They sat and ate in silence.

'What would you say if I told yer I'm going to get married?' Jack said.

'I'd say you're a bloody fool.' The old man growled. 'We're not making much money these days, and a wife'll cost yer plenty. Anyhow, who is she?'

'Bill Corbett's daughter – but I haven't told her yet.'

'Yer don't tell 'em son, yer ask 'em.'

Jack grunted and went on eating. In his mind he went over his plans.

Chapter 19

The main road north was bituminised as far as Carnarvon, about six hundred miles north of Perth, but for the next thousand miles, it was gravel. When the road grader had been over it the surface was good, but it quickly became corrugated, and broke down into potholes. Once the rain came, it turned into a quagmire of mud, scarred deeply by wheel tracks. The big trucks tore the road to pieces and it became impassable. When it rained, the police in each town closed the roads to all traffic to prevent this happening, but still the trucks drove through, risking a heavy fine in order to deliver their cargo.

Sid Baker had driven heavy transport all his adult life, and in the last five years had worked for the North West Transport Company carting cargo as far north as Derby in the Kimberlys. It was easy driving in good weather, but hazardous in the wet, with the risk of being stranded for days on end by swollen rivers and closed roads. He had made up his mind to quit the company after this trip and spend more time with his family. The long lonely stretches of the north no longer interested him. He planned to get a job driving trucks around the city.

He had left Perth in early March and reached Carnarvon in a couple of days without any mishaps. The weather report said rain developing. There was a tropical cyclone off Cocos Islands and it was heading towards North West Cape, a few hundred miles north of Carnarvon.

He had checked that his cargo was secure before starting out on the gravel. He would have to move fast to beat the rain. Sid drove steadily and as fast as he dared on the dusty corrugated road, as the clouds gathered, and the wind became gusty. A hundred miles on, the rain started.

The next town north was Onslow, and he had a couple of hundred miles to go. Already the road was getting slippery, and he had to drive more slowly to keep control.

By six o'clock the rain was coming down steadily and the visibility was poor in the gathering dusk. Under normal circumstances he would drive a few more hours, then pull off the road and sleep until first light. But now he knew that if he stopped, he would probably be stranded for days.

He pressed on, leaning forward and straining his eyes to see the road in front through the driving rain. He reached a creek and found that it was running with a few inches of water. In a few hours it could be impassable. In low gear he hauled across, and slithered up the embankment on the other side, with the engine roaring.

On he drove across the desolate sodden countryside. Usually there were kangaroos to avoid on the road, but even they had taken shelter from the weather.

Sid had been at the wheel for nine hours non-stop and he was desperately tired. He reached over to the glove box and located a bottle of pills. A couple of these would smarten him up, he thought as he swallowed the Dexedrine tablets. He rarely took them, but they were good for situations like this.

Another hour, and he was feeling quite alert. The road had become dangerous and it was hard to see the edges, as water covered the ground. He was glad to have the high powered lights that the company had installed on their trucks. He crouched over the steering wheel, and peered through the rain into the pathway of light.

Suddenly, all hell broke loose! Hidden from sight by water, his front wheel went down a deep pothole, tearing the steering wheel from his hands as it spun. The truck lurched to the left and rolled over into the shallow ditch on the side of the road, spilling cargo into the mud.

Sid was thrown across the cabin, and finished up bleeding and unconscious in the mud that oozed in through the broken window. In the blackness the only sound was the falling rain, and a slowly spinning truck wheel.

When he regained consciousness he was completely disorientated. The truck lay on its side, and above him the rain beat down on the drivers side window. It was pitch black. He tried to sit up but the pain in his leg made him scream. Slowly he felt along his leg, and when his hands felt bone protruding from the warm sticky blood, he passed out again.

Matt was doing his morning clinic when Mary knocked on the door and came in.

'RFDS base on the radio want to speak to you. There's been an accident.'

Matt dropped everything and hurried to the radio.

'Port Hedland Base, this is Matt Harrison, over.'

'Hello Matt, this is Joe Bailey. There's been a road accident south of Onslow. The driver was found this morning by a stockman at Bonnagilla Station, with concussion and a compound fractured leg; God knows what else. Over.'

'OK Joe, what's the plan? Over.'

'The plane is on the way, and we think you had better go out with it to collect him. He sounds as if he's in a bad way. Over.'

'Roger that, what's the ETA? Over.'

'Plane should reach you in twenty minutes. We've got serum on board, but you need to take your own gear.'

'OK Joe, I'll be waiting on the strip. Over and out.'

The hospital had a comprehensive medical kit for such emergencies, and Matt and Mary heaved equipment into the back of the ute, together with the stretcher, and a Thomas splint for the broken leg. Together they drove out to the airstrip, and pulled up at the shed to wait.

Urgently they made their plans. Mary was to prepare the theatre for surgery and get the instruments sterilised while Matt was away. Also she would send a message round town alerting the blood donor panel to be on standby.

Fortunately there had not been much rain in their area, and the clouds were already clearing as the cyclonic depression turned away from the coast.

The Cessna skimmed to a perfect landing, and taxied over to the shed. Matt drove out under the wing, and greeted Jim Dickson as he opened the door. He had left the engine idling. The three of them loaded gear onto the aircraft, which already had the back seat removed and the stretcher in place.

'OK Mary, we'll see you later,' Jim said looking at his watch. It was nine thirty.

'We should be back by about two thirty or three this afternoon, all being well. I'll get Hedland to call you up when we're on the way back and give you an ETA.'

She waved as Jim gunned up the engine and they taxied off.

Once they gained cruising altitude, Jim set a course for Bonnagilla Station. Hedland had advised him that the station airstrip was 'all weather', which was fortunate, as a lot of rain had fallen in that area. They flew over the featureless earth for an hour and a half, then finally Jim leaned over and nudged Matt who was dozing. He pointed down.

Far below, Matt saw a station homestead. Bonnagilla! Jim's navigation was spot on. They descended quickly and flew over the strip at low altitude, checking the condition. There were a few puddles, but otherwise it looked safe. A truck was parked beside the airstrip, with a group of people standing next to it. They waved. They made a bumpy landing on the strip, and taxied to the truck.

A suntanned man with a worried expression greeted them.

'G'day,' he said, holding out his hand to Matt. 'I'm Rob Ward. One of my boys found this fella about three miles down the road. His truck had rolled over. He's in a pretty bad way. We did what we could, but he's lost a bit of blood.'

Matt climbed onto the back of the truck with his bag, and knelt beside the man on the mattress. He was conscious, and in a lot of pain. His face was ashen.

'I'm going to give you an injection to help pain. What's your name?'

'Sid Baker,' he whispered.

'OK Sid, just relax, you're going to be alright.'

Quickly Matt ran his hands over his body. He had a compound fracture of his left lower leg, and possibly some broken ribs, but no other obvious major problems.

'Hey Jim! Pass up the Thomas splint, and get the stretcher up on the truck please.'

With Jim's help, he slid the splint over the broken leg, fitting the padded ring of the splint in his groin. He padded the ankle, and wrapped the cord around, then knotted it securely. Gently, but firmly, he stretched the leg out straight. As he did, the broken ends of the bone disappeared back into the wound with a dull 'clunk' that made Sid groan with pain. He then tied the foot to the end of the splint frame, immobilising the leg. 'Thank God for morphine,' he thought.

He poured disinfectant over where the bone had protruded, and applied a firm dressing to the wound, and small dressings to the cuts on his face. With some cloth and water from a water bag, he wiped off the dried blood on his face.

'There. You look better already,' Matt said with a reassuring smile.

He poured some water into a mug, and raised Sid's head so he could drink.

'Thanks, Doc,' he muttered.

They carefully transferred him to the stretcher, and with the aid of the station men they carried him to the plane. Once on board, Matt inserted an intravenous needle and put up a bottle of plasma. Sid's blood pressure was low, and his pulse was weak and rapid.

Matt took the rubber pump bulb off the blood pressure apparatus, and connected it to the air inflow tube on the plasma bottle. With the reduced atmospheric pressure in flight, he would need to pump some pressure into the serum bottle to keep it flowing.

Jim started the engine.

'G'bye, Rob,' Matt shouted to the station owner. 'Thanks for the good work. I'll let you know how he's getting on.'

Rob nodded and smiled, as he waved farewell.

The flight home seemed to take a long time. Matt sat beside Sid and watched the intravenous drip, pumping air into the bottle when the flow slowed down. His pulse was stronger, and he seemed comfy.

Jim radioed Base and told them to advise Mary of their ETA.

It was half past three when they touched down at Roebourne, and found Mary waiting with the ute. She had Mibbin with her. Matt sat in the back of the ute with Sid on the stretcher as Mary drove to the hospital. The morphine had worn off, and Sid groaned as the ute hit bumps in the road. Matt patted him on the shoulder. 'Nearly there.'

They settled him in a bed, gave him some more morphine, then Mary and the nursing aide cleaned him up and took off his muddy bloodstained clothes. Matt took a sample of blood and spent the next fifteen minutes determining his blood group; O Positive. He then got into the ute and drove round town with his list of donors.

By five o'clock, Matt had cross-matched two donors, and taken two pints of blood, one of which was dripping in to Sid's arm.

X-rays were next on the program. The machine was portable, and Mibbin wheeled it into the ward. Matt took one of Sid's chest, and a couple of the leg. He then went to the dark room, and developed the films – his first ever!

The quality was fair, and the chest seemed OK. He could not see any fractured ribs, but that was often the case with simple X-rays. Anyhow, the lungs looked normal.

The leg was another matter. Both bones were fractured, the Tibia and the fibula, and the alignment was poor. He would need an anaesthetic to straighten the bones and repair the wound before encasing the leg in plaster.

Two hours later Sid had colour in his cheeks and was relatively pain-free. He was out of shock. Matt sat down beside him. 'Sid, we need to give you an anaesthetic to straighten the leg, and clean up the wound. Then I'll put it in a plaster cast. As soon as we can, we'll send you south. We'll send a telegram to your family and your boss to tell them what's happening, but we can't do that till the morning now.' He took the details, and a message for his wife.

By eight o'clock Mary had the operating theatre ready, and they wheeled Sid in. Susan, the nursing aide, was dressed in theatre gown and mask, and stood beside Harry holding his hand.

Matt injected some pentothal into the intravenous drip tube, and after a moment, Sid was sound asleep. Next he injected some scoline and turned the mixture of nitrogen and oxygen on at the anaesthetic machine. As the scoline paralysed Harry's respiration, he 'breathed' him with the rubber mask over his nose and mouth, squeezing the rubber anaesthetic bag until he was completely relaxed, then he took a laryngoscope and slipped a rubber tube down in to Sid's trachea, and connected it to the anaesthetic circuit.

He stood 'breathing' Sid gently with the bag until his own respiration returned. The scoline wore off quickly. He then turned on the tap connecting the ether bottle, so that ether vapour entered the anaesthetic tubing. Gradually the ether deepened the anaesthetic, and Sid's breathing became deep and regular. By listening to the breathing, Matt could now judge the depth of anaesthesia, and increase or reduce the amount of ether with the tap. Ether was a safe anaesthetic.

As Matt and Susan scrubbed up, Mary sat by Sid's head, listening to his breathing and monitoring his pulse. She watched his pupil size too, as another check on anaesthetic depth.

With Mary directing her, Susan undid the sterile packs, and laid out the instruments. Matt cleaned up the leg, and painted it with iodine disinfectant while Mibbin held the end of the splint off the table. At last the leg was draped and sterile. With a probe, Matt felt in the wound, striking the overlapping ends of bone. At the foot end, Mibbin had a firm grip on the cord that was tied around the ankle.

'Right Mibbin, pull hard,' Matt said as he felt inside the wound with metal levers. With a sudden 'clunk' the bone ends came in to apposition. 'Right Mibbin, tie it firmly to the end of the splint.'

The ring of the Thomas splint was snugly settled into the groin, so that traction could be applied, stretching the leg and thus overcoming the bone overlap. The broken bone ends were now lined up end to end. Matt had applied a tourniquet loosely above the knee, in case of haemorrhage, and the wound was now bleeding profusely.

'Now Susan, start twisting the tourniquet.' As she did the blood flow diminished.

Matt cleared the blood from the wound with the 'sucker', and located the torn artery. He tied it off. He then debrided the wound, cleaning out blood clot and cutting away dead tissue.

'Right Susan, slowly release the tourniquet.' He watched closely as the wound started to ooze a small amount of blood. Good! No arterial 'bleeders' now. He tied off a couple of veins that were starting to bleed, then after pouring in penicillin powder, he sutured the wound, leaving a small rubber tube in the lower end to drain any accumulation of blood.

He put a dressing over the wound, and then with Mibbin's assistance, he X-rayed the leg.

'You OK Mary?' he asked.

She nodded. 'He's doing well.'

'Back in a minute,' he said as he ducked through the door to his consulting room, and into the darkroom where he ran the plates through the developing tank.

The bone position was acceptable. The tibia was nicely lined up, but the ends of the fibula were still a little out of line. That didn't matter at this stage, and if necessary, could be attended to at a later date, down south.

With Mibbin and Susan helping, they carefully removed the splint, having first immobilised the whole leg in a plaster of Paris 'back slab'. They then applied a padded dressing over the wound and completely encased the leg in plaster, leaving only his toes protruding, and a window over the wound.

Matt washed his hands again and stitched up the minor lacerations on Sid's face, while he slept on peacefully. The anaesthetic was long since turned off, and the tube removed from his throat, but he would not wake for fifteen minutes or so.

Back in the otherwise empty ward, Sid started to come around.

'Nurse! I'm going to be sick!' he called. Ether had that effect.

Susan brought a bowl, and Sid dry retched. 'Jeesus, I feel terrible,' he muttered.

They settled him in the bed with his plastered leg up on pillows. His toes were a good colour.

Matt helped the girls clean the theatre, and then they sat down and had a cup of tea. It was after midnight.

'I'm going to sleep here in the ward,' Matt said. 'You girls get off to bed. Just leave the morphine cupboard open.'

Matt gave Sid a shot of morphine, then threw himself on the next bed. He was asleep in minutes. He woke once in the night, and found Sid sleeping peacefully. When he next awoke, he found Mary standing beside his bed with a steaming cup of tea.

'Good morning. Did you sleep well?' she asked.

Matt sat up and rubbed his eyes. 'Like a log. Thanks for the cuppa.'

Sid was propped up on some pillows drinking water, and looked a good colour.

'Well, how do you feel?' Matt asked as he sipped his tea.

'A bit knocked out,' Sid replied. 'I'm pretty vague about what happened, and don't remember much – just bits here and there.'

Matt told Sid the story as he knew it, but couldn't tell him about his truck.

'We'll radio Bonnagilla station and tell them how you are, and I'll ask about your truck. You're lucky they found you and got the rescue organised so quickly.'

'Yair, please thank them for me,' he said.

'Now doctor,' Mary said, 'I'm sorry to tell you that there is work to do today, and I suggest you go home and clean up, then come back and we'll give you a good breakfast to start the day.'

Chapter 20

The week passed quickly. Bonnagilla Station was glad to get the good news about Sid, and in turn replied that they had salvaged his truck, and loaded the cargo again. There was water damage and a lot of broken glass that turned out to be mostly from smashed cases of beer. The North West Trading Company was flying a replacement driver to take the truck to Onslow for repairs.

Sid had made good progress, and his leg was comfortable. The minor cuts and bruises were on the mend, and his chest didn't hurt if he breathed quietly. He was still bed-ridden.

'Right, Sid. Time you got yourself moving!' Matt announced as he finished examining him on his morning round.

Slowly and carefully he was helped out of bed, and given a pair of crutches. With Mary on one side and Matt on the other, Sid slowly moved across the ward. and back.

'Good start.' Matt said. 'You're off to Perth on Monday's plane, so you had better get some practice on those sticks.'

'Well, let's hope that's it for the week,' said Mary as they sat over a cup of morning tea. 'Got any plans for the weekend?'

'Not really. I've got to write a report for Sid to take south, but apart from that I thought I'd have a quiet one.'

'If you don't get a better offer, you're welcome to have dinner with me this evening. I've got some nice steak from the south, and I'd appreciate a hand with the barbecue.'

'Sounds great. I'll bring something to drink.'

Later in the afternoon, Matt ventured into the pub. He went in through the lounge and peered around the door of the bar. Maisie the barmaid was wiping down the bar, and there was only one customer, who was concentrating on his glass of beer.

'G'day, Doc,' said Maisie cheerfully. 'Yer wanna beer?'

'No, no thanks Maisie. I wondered if you had a bottle of red wine.'

'Lemme see,' she pondered. 'I think there's one in the 'fridge. Been there for a couple of years.'

She opened the big refrigerator and rummaged about in the bottom, ultimately producing a bottle.

'Yalumba Four Crown Claret,' she read slowly. 'This what yer want?'

'Well, what's it like?' Matt asked.

'I wouldn't know, Doc, yer see, I'm not a wino,' she drawled with a crooked grin.

Matt paid for the bottle and hastily retreated.

The barbecue went well, however Mary did not entrust the cooking to Matt, even though it was, she said, 'men's work'.

They sat out on the veranda of Mary's quarters and chatted as they ate their steak and fresh salad, by candlelight, and watched the shooting stars blaze through the moonless black sky. Later they sat back, smoked cigarettes and sipped the last of the wine – which had turned out to be quite pleasant, considering its dubious history.

'Where do you come from Mary?' Matt asked.

'A country town in Victoria,' she replied. 'Dad was a farmer, but sold up when Mum died, and moved into town. I was an only child, and went off to Melbourne to do my nursing training.'

'So what got you up in the north? Not much of a social life for a young woman here, I wouldnt've thought.'

'Well,' she paused. 'I guess I was running away really. You see, I was engaged to a bloke, but it fell through when he found someone else, and I didn't want to stay around, so, I answered an advertisement, and here I am. With no future plans and no prospects.'

They sat in silence for a while and looked at the sky.

'Are you running away too?' she asked.

Matt thought for a moment. 'Yes, I suppose I am, though I hadn't thought about it in those terms.' He paused. 'You see, we had a terrible car crash, and my wife and daughter were killed. I couldn't go on working at my hospital, so I came here – to learn how to live again I suppose.'

Somehow he felt at ease with Mary, and was happy to talk about his past. They sat talking quietly for another hour then Matt thanked Mary for the meal, and went home.

'Are yer there, doc?' A voice filtered in to Matt's dreams. He woke with a jolt and looked at his watch – six thirty.

'Coming!' He pulled on some shorts, and went to the back door. Bert Harris was standing with a grin on his face.

'Bert! What can I do for you?' he asked, suppressing a yawn.

'G'day, Doc, sorry if I woke you. A few of us is goin' fishing, and wondered if you'd like to come along.'

'Now?' Matt asked, looking at his watch again.

'Well, yes. Yer see the tide goes out in a couple of hours, and then we can't launch the boat. We stay out all day then come in with the evening tide.'

'Right,' said Matt. 'Give me ten minutes.'

'We got everything, food, beer, bait and lines,' Bert called after him.

They stopped at the hospital as Matt dashed in and left a message with Susan. He'd gone fishing, and wouldn't be back till dark.

The road to Point Samson was bituminised, and bore quite a lot of traffic, as the State ships berthed at the big jetty, and the blue asbestos from the mine at Wittenoom was exported there. Also, the China Navigation Company ships called in occasionally, with tourists and cargo.

They reached the port just before eight, and found Harry Dobbs the postman, and Mike Jackson waiting for them. Mike was the manager of Dalgety's store where Matt did most of his shopping. You could buy anything there from beer to bulldozers.

'About time youse guys!' Harry called out. 'The tide's turning.'

They set to, and launched the little cabin cruiser from its trailer, down the ramp into the water, and all climbed aboard. Harry and Bert were serious fishermen, sharing the boat. Harry pushed off, and Bert started the big Johnson fifty horsepower outboard motor.

There was a small cuddy cabin, and a canvas awning to protect them from the sun. There were two large iceboxes each containing a block of ice, and one part-filled with food and beer. The other contained fresh bait. Also, there was a large water tank provided drinking water – in case the beer ran out. It was a glorious morning, with only a light offshore breeze as they motored out to sea.

'Thought we'd 'ave a go for some mackerel,' Harry shouted to Matt as they roared along.

'We'll get out near the islands, then put out a couple of lines.'

They headed towards the Dampier Archipelago – a collection of little islands and reefs – then slowed down in the lee of a small barren island. They baited the ganged hooks with long thin fish from an icebox then set out again, trailing the lines from the stern.

They idled along at about five knots for the next hour, with not a sign of a fish, Harry steering and Bert at his side. Matt and Mike held the two short fishing rods. As they ran close to a reef, a great manta ray raised its flap from the water. 'Beautiful aren't they,' Mike said. 'And harmless,' he added, then glanced up.

'The sun is high over the yard arm,' he said. 'Let's splice the main brace.'

Matt looked at him with a puzzled expression. 'Time for a drink,' he explained. 'Hey Bert!' he shouted. 'What about a beer?'

'Bloody good idea,' he replied and pulled a cold bottle from the icebox. He filled four aluminium mugs and handed them round. Matt took a long swig and put the cup down on the seat. As he did, the rod in his hand jerked, and the reel screamed as the line sped out!

'Christ! What do I do now?' he yelled.

'Just hang on,' Harry called, slowing the engine.

Bert sat down beside him. 'Now as the line slackens, reel it in,' he calmly instructed. Matt reeled in, but off went the fish again, tearing line off the reel.

Bert leaned over and adjusted the reel brake. 'That makes it harder for 'im to run, and 'e tires sooner,' he explained. 'Good! Keep playin' 'im!' he called excitedly.

For the next ten minutes Matt sweated and strained, slowly bringing the fish to the boat. Once it leapt high out of the water, flashing silver in the sunshine. Finally exhausted, it was dragged alongside the boat where Bert leaned over with a gaff, and expertly caught it in the gills then heaved it aboard.

Matt stood and looked at the beautiful mackerel that lay flapping in the bilge. It was the first fish he had ever caught, and he felt a pang of remorse as he looked at the glittering creature that he had destroyed. 'That's a beauty, Doc,' said Harry, giving Matt a thump on the back. 'About thirty pounds I'd reckon.'

At lunchtime they dropped the anchor in shallow water near an island, and Mike set about gutting the mackerel. He threw the guts over the side and wrapped the fish in a wet hessian bag then stowed it in the little cabin.

'How about a swim?' Matt suggested.

'Wouldn't recommend it,' drawled Harry. 'Ave a look at that.' He pointed over the side. Cruising under the boat were half a dozen sizeable sharks, feeding on the offal.

By the end of the day they had caught one more mackerel, and two trevally, which Bert said were good eating. They arrived back at Point Samson at full tide, and winched the boat up the slipway.

They had agreed to store the fish in the big refrigerator room at Dalgety's over night, and divide it up in the morning. 'I'll bring plenty of fish 'round to the hospital tomorrow,' Bert told Matt as he dropped him off at his house, tired, sunburned, and smelling of fish.

On Monday morning, Matt and Mary had Sid out of bed and practising on his crutches.

Matt had spent Sunday writing a report, and sorting out X-rays to go south while Polly cooked up a great lunch of fish and chips for everyone. They congratulated Matt on his catch, and wished Sid a speedy recovery, drinking a farewell toast with homemade lemonade.

With a stiff plastered leg, Sid wouldn't fit inside the ute, so they put him on the stretcher, and slid him in the back, under the canvas-covered frame. Mibbin got up with him, and Mary and Matt climbed in the front. The plane was due in at ten.

As they drove to the tin shed, the DC3 made a graceful landing, right on time. They waited until it had taxied up and the engines had stopped. Johnny wheeled out the steps and opened the door, as Matt drove as close as he could to the plane. Sid was manhandled up the steps and into the plane where they had a special seat for him with room for his plastered leg.

'Well, goodbye Sid,' Matt said giving him a pat on the shoulder. 'If you come up this way again, drive more carefully.'

Sid gave a grin. 'Doc, don't worry. I'm not comin' north again, and I wanna thank you for everything. You and Matron both.'

They watched as the plane took off and disappeared into the clear sky, then drove back to the hospital. A small group of people waited outside the surgery door. 'Business as usual,' Matt said to himself as he walked to his office.

Chapter 21

Three months had slipped by and the weather had changed. The temperature was still in the eighties and nineties, but the nights were pleasantly cool.

The town boasted an out-door picture theatre, where the audience sat on wooden benches under the stars, and watched the movies – or the stars, depending on the film. Matt regularly attended the Saturday night entertainment, mainly as there was nothing else to do, apart from go to the pub. Sometimes he took Mary, and they would go back to her quarters for supper. They had become good friends – nothing more.

Matt had visited Spinifex Plains on several occasions, and had spent sunny afternoons with Lizzie. She had taught him to ride a horse, and they rode to the swimming pool and swam in the deep cool dark-green water, with the sun filtering through the trees above them.

On each occasion, he had driven home unable to think of anything but Liz, and the disturbing thought that he seemed to be falling in love with her. She in turn seemed warm and friendly, and Matt wondered what she thought of him.

The following Saturday he was visiting again for a weekend, on the occasion of the annual cricket match.

Bill had told him that the match had been played at Spinifex for as long as he could remember, and it was always held in June, with the cooler weather. The match was the 'Townsfolk versus the Stations'. This was a rather loose arrangement, and town folk were often recruited into the Stations team and vice versa. Bill had in fact asked Matt to play in his team, when he found out that he had played in the First Eleven at school.

By rotation, this year Bill was Captain of the Stations, and had enlisted as well as Matt, some good men from surrounding stations.

From previous experience it was accepted that there should be fourteen to fifteen men in each team, as the trials of the day often saw two or three drop by the wayside, with heat exhaustion, injury, or too much booze.

Wives and families came along, and a great party with a barbecue was to follow. Accommodation was provided, though the townsfolk usually all drove home that night – unless incapable!

The ladies were catered for inside the homestead, though often two or three to a room. The men were to be accommodated in the 'Bullpen' or on stretchers under the trees in the garden, placed there mainly for those who succumbed through the evening.

Food was largely provided by the station folk, but to cover the costs of drink and sundries, a levy of two pounds per man was set.

To cater for the barbecue, Bill had taken a couple of men out to hunt wild cattle, and had shot a 'scrub heifer', which had been butchered, and hung in the cool room for a few days, whilst the town butcher had made a mountain of sausages for the occasion.

Early on the Saturday morning Matt set out for the station. He had asked Mary if he could drive her, but she declined, saying that she had gone to the match last year, and had decided that she would 'give it a miss' this time.

As he drove he came across more and more cars, all heading for Spinifex, and sending up a pall of dust as they drove in convoy in the still fresh morning air. A number of vehicles were already parked when Matt drove in, and the station was a hive of activity.

The 'paddock' behind the homestead made a perfect cricket ground, being quite flat, and devoid of any vegetation. When it rained, it was a quagmire, but now it was baked hard.

The oval was marked out with white painted rocks, indicating the boundary, and the pitch had been carefully laid out in concrete years before, and maintained in excellent condition. Beside the grounds Bill had erected a large marquee with the sides rolled up, providing a shady place for lunch, drinks and spectators to sit.

The annual match was a very serious affair, and custom dictated that the teams turn out in whites, and that the rules of cricket be strictly observed. Last year, the 'Town' had won, and now the Station team sought revenge!

The Town team was captained by Dalgety's Mike Jackson, who had played A grade cricket in his youth, and included Bert Drummond, the publican, usually called 'Bull' – short for 'Bulldog' – Constable Pete Harris from Roebourne, and also Jack Morgan from Mount Cooke, who had a reputation for his formidable fast bowling.

Bull had driven out in his truck, with a couple of cold kegs of beer, which were immediately unloaded into the cold store, and boxes of plates, cups and glasses to cater for the mob.

At ten sharp, the coin was tossed, and the Town team went in to bat. Bill introduced Matt to the other members of his team, and then placed the field, with Matt in slips, and Vic Armitage, Overseer of Nullagong Station, opening the bowling. Vic, still in his early thirties, was a good fast bowler. Mike Jackson and Bull Drummond were opening batsmen, but by the third over, Bull was clean bowled by Vic for only three runs.

By midday, the Town team were six wickets down with only eighty-two runs on the board. Mike had made more than half of them before Matt caught him in slips.

Jack Morgan was the next batsman. He sent his first ball off for a four, then quickly ran up fifteen runs. At the next over, Bill handed the ball to Matt. 'See if you can move him,' he said with a wink.

Matt was a spinner, but very much out of practice, and Jack sent his first ball to the boundary. His second ball went for two runs, but the third was pitched higher with more spin. Jack stepped forward planning to send it over the boundary, but the ball angled sharply off the pitch and took out the middle stump. Jack looked at the stumps, amazed, then turned, red-faced and scowling, and strode back to the marquee.

'Bad luck,' said Mike, giving Jack a pat on the shoulder as he sat down. Jack scowled again and poured himself a beer. 'Bloody Pom,' he muttered under his breath.

At one o'clock they stopped for lunch, and by then the last batsman was in, with the score a respectable one hundred and twelve. Matt walked back to the marquee and saw Lizzie standing with her mother serving sandwiches and tea.

'You look hot and bothered,' she said as Matt approached.

'You've got no idea what it's like out on that field,' he gasped, gulping down a glass of water before accepting tea and sandwiches.

'You're doing a good job out there Matt,' she said, smiling at him.

'It's a long time since I've played cricket,' he said, as he munched a sandwich.

'Well don't worry, a fair bit of beer will have been consumed by the time play starts again, and the 'Town' batsmen all had a few when they came off the field.' Matt looked over at some of the town team with beer glasses in their hands.

Play resumed at two o'clock, and after the last Town batsman was dismissed, the opening Station batsmen quickly put up thirty runs.

Jack Morgan was put in to bowl, and in a matter of minutes the first wicket fell with his furious attack. Matt was the next man in, and faced the bowler. The first ball was wide but flashed past at high speed. The second ball was just as fast, but accurate, and he managed to block it. He tensed himself as Jack walked back for his next delivery. It came like a bullet. Matt stepped forward and connected perfectly with a square cut, sending the ball high over the boundary for six, to the roar of appreciation from the spectators.

Jack Morgan was puce with rage as he thundered down to the wicket to deliver his next ball. At high speed it bounced short, then rose sharply in a pink blur to shoulder height, striking Matt a glancing blow on the side of the forehead.

There was a gasp from the crowd, as Matt dropped his bat and fell to his knees stunned by the blow. The players gathered around, except for Jack Morgan who stood with hands on his hips and a leer on his face. 'Cop that, yer Pommie bastard,' he said to himself.

They helped Matt back to the marquee, by this time with a large bruise coming up on his forehead. He was laid down on a cane lounge, and given a drink of water. Bill leaned over him with a worried expression. 'Matt. Are you alright?' he asked.

Matt looked up at him trying to focus on his face. 'That was some bouncer!' he said weakly.

'Yes, and I bet it was done on purpose.' Bill turned to see Lizzie standing with an angry face and an ice pack for the injury.

'Aaw no,' said Bill, 'it was an accident.'

Lizzie gently placed the pack on his forehead, and looked into his face with concern. 'Are you comfy Matt?' she asked.

He smiled up at her 'Yes Liz, thanks, I'm just fine. I'll be out on the field again an a few minutes.'

'You will not,' she replied firmly. 'You've done your cricketing for the day.'

Matt tried to sit up but was overcome with dizziness, and slumped back. 'Perhaps you're right,' he conceded.

By five o'clock the match was nearly over. With three wickets to spare, the Station team had almost equalled the Town score. Some of the town folk had already packed up and left, and by five thirty the batsmen had toppled the score and stumps were drawn, with victory to the Station team.

Liz had taken Matt up to the homestead in her jeep, and he was now lying in the cool house on a couch, sipping a cold drink. Some aspirin tablets had relieved the pain, and he was feeling more like himself.

By seven, the barbecues were ready for cooking, and folk had gathered on the homestead lawn. A good deal of beer had been drunk, and the party was happy and noisy. Matt had recovered enough to join the party, but was fussed over by Lizzie who wouldn't let him out of her sight.

Matt walked over to Jack who was standing alone holding a glass of beer. Matt held out his hand. 'We haven't been introduced,' he said with a slightly lop-sided smile. 'That is, not counting the cricket ball.'

Jack ignored the outstretched hand. 'Too bad about yer head,' he growled. 'Might be worse next time.' He turned and walked off, leaving Matt astonished.

'Don't take any notice of him,' Lizzie said, coming up to his side. 'He's a rude pig.'

For the rest of the evening she stayed by his side. They sat at long tables and ate their steak and sausages, after which Mike made a speech, congratulating the Station folk on their win, and thanking them for a great day. Bill responded for the Station team, and the party roistered on for a few more hours. Not so Matt, who by this time had a cracking headache.

Bill had organised a bed for Matt on the back veranda of the homestead instead of the bullpen, where he would be closer if he needed any help in the night. He was quite concerned for him. Matt said goodnight to Bill and Joan then changed into his pyjamas in the bathroom. He came out on the veranda to get into bed and was surprised to find Lizzie waiting for him.

'I just wanted to tuck you in and see if there was anything you need,' she said, coming close.

She looked so beautiful in the dim light, her golden hair loose around her face, and her eyes shining. Matt reached out and drew her to him. Their lips met in a sweet gentle kiss.

'Goodnight beautiful Lizzie, and thank you for caring for me.'
'I love you Matt Harrison,' she whispered. 'Goodnight.'

The next morning Matt was woken early by the mournful cry of crows in the trees. He gingerly felt his face. It hurt. He went to the bathroom and was shocked to see in the mirror that the bruise had spread down the side of his face, and that he now had a black eye. Refreshed with a shower and shave, he dressed and packed his bag, then took it out to his ute.

As he walked in to the house he met Lizzie in the passageway. 'My God!' she exclaimed, looking at his face.

'Pretty isn't it?' he replied with a grin.

'We have a buffet breakfast on the side veranda so come along before the mob eat it all.' She led him by the hand.

A long trestle table was set up on the veranda, on the shady side of the house with tables and chairs on the lawn. A row of entrée dishes standing in a tray of hot water contained bacon, scrambled eggs, sausages and potato cakes.

Matt helped himself to eggs and bacon, and a potato cake, then joined Liz at a table. There were only a few people sitting eating, as a lot had already left, with only a cup of tea for the road. In spite of his appearance, Matt felt fit and well, and brushed off the sympathetic comments of those he bumped in to. Bill and Joan appeared, and inspected Matt's wound with concern.

'My real problem will come when I get back to town. They'll ask about the fight,' Matt laughed.

'Don't worry, the whole town will know about it by now,' Joan said with a smile. 'You can't keep things quiet in a small town you know.' Matt thanked them for their hospitality, and said that he must be on his way. Lizzie walked out to the ute with him, and as he opened the door she put her hand on his.

'Matt, about last night,' she paused, and blushed becomingly. 'I shouldn't have said what I did. – I'm sorry.' She looked at her feet. Matt took both her hands in his and looked into her eyes. 'Lizzie, if you meant it, don't be sorry.'

'I did mean it Matt, I truly did,' she whispered.

'That's good Lizzie, because I love you too.'

She looked up at him with tears in her beautiful eyes, and he kissed her gently on the lips. A car door banged, startling them from their intimate moment. Matt looked up to see the furious face of Jack Morgan glaring at them, as he revved his engine and roared off in a cloud of dust.

'I must go,' Matt said, climbing in to the ute.

'Drive carefully,' she said, smiling through the tears.

Matt drove slowly back to town deep in thought.

Chapter 22

The next week was busy. By the end of it he had pulled out four teeth, treated a goat with milk fever, and delivered twins. His dental skills had improved no end, though he found Aboriginal teeth a problem. The high fluoride level in the water gave them strong white teeth, but the 'bulgai' rotted their gums and caused ulcers. Pulling out a decayed molar was difficult, and he snapped off the root occasionally, which necessitated digging in to the cavity to lever it out – a messy business!

Matt was pleased to hear that the travelling dentist was coming to town in a few weeks, and Mary was compiling a list of patients for him. He, of course could fill tooth cavities, whereas Matt's only option was to remove the offending tooth. As it turned out, the dentist was something of a mixed blessing.

On Friday afternoon, Bert Harris looked in the surgery door. Matt was at the desk, writing notes.

'G'day, Doc,' he said with a shy grin. 'I wondered if yer'd like a trip to Cossack to see the old Port. We could go there early tomorrow for a couple of hours. That's the best time to see it.'

'Sounds great Bert,' Matt replied.

'Good-o, I'll pick yer up at six thirty,' he said, and disappeared.

They turned off the bitumen road to Point Samson and bumped along the track to Cossack. The sky was clear, and the sun was just rising.

'Tell me about Cossack, Bert,' Matt asked.

'Well, Doc, a bit over a 'undred years ago, Cossack was the base for the pearling industry, and it was quite a town. It was named after a ship – HMS *Cossack* – that the first Governor came to Western Australia in. But that wasn't its original name. It was first called 'Tien Tsin' after the boat that brought the early explorer Walter Padbury.

'It had four pubs and a big population, and was the first port in the northwest coast. But the port was in the shallow estuary of the Harding river, and the sailing ships anchored out in deep water, sending cargo and passengers over the sand banks by lighter.' He paused to light a cigarette.

'What about Roebourne?' Matt asked. 'Was the town there at that time?'

'My oath it was,' said Bert, the cigarette in the side of his mouth. 'Roebourne was the "Queen City of the North", and the stepping off place for the Pilbara gold rush back in about 1865. 'Ad a population of about four thousand, they reckon. 'Undreds of prospectors came up by ship and landed at Cossack, then went on to Roebourne. From there they travelled 'undreds of miles, often on foot, pushin' their gear in a wheelbarrow. A lot died in the heat, and a few got rich.'

Through a clearing in the scrub they caught a glimpse of water. 'Ere we are,' said Bert, slowing down as they rounded a bend. In front of them lay Cossack – or what remained of it.

Bert went on. 'When they moved the pearling fleet to Broome, the town started to die, and when they built the deep water jetty at Point Samson in about 1902, that was the end of Cossack. By the time the first war started, there were mostly old folk remaining, but the last of them died years ago. Now it's a ghost town.'

Matt was astonished at Bert's knowledge of the early history, and said as much. Bert grinned widely. 'It's me 'obby,' he said.

They drove up to the water's edge where an old wooden wharf lined the shore, with worn timbers cracked and broken by time. Bert stopped the car and the silence enveloped them. Seagulls stood on the timbers and watched.

They opened the doors and stepped out. The water was like glass and there was not a breath of wind. The birds watched without moving. They wandered around the old buildings with walls of stone, still standing strong. Their wooden and corrugated iron roofs were long gone, blown away by fifty years of cyclones and neglect.

'That's the old Court House,' Bert pointed, speaking almost in a whisper, as though not to disturb the tranquillity. They wandered on. One old stone house held the remains of the last solitary inhabitant – an ancient Japanese woman, who stayed on long after the pearling industry moved to Broome and the town slowly emptied out. Broken furniture and paper bearing Japanese characters were strewn about, all that remained of her existence.

They walked up the hill to the cemetery, which was in two parts, the Japanese, and the European.

'Mostly pearl divers,' said Bert, in a whisper, for the place seemed full of ghosts of the dead. He pointed to the ocean. 'Look out there. That's Foam Passage. The bright blue ocean looked peaceful and still in the morning sunshine. 'When the wind gets up and the tide is running it's a bloody death trap,' he said.

The European part of the cemetery told tales of tragedy. Matt walked slowly along reading the headstones. Five children and their parents drowned in Foam Passage: 'In loving memory'. Matt stood in the stillness of the morning and tried to visualise the horror of a lighter capsizing in the turbulent passage infested with sharks. Another headstone: 'In memory of William Bonnington. Feloniously slain'; yet another, 'Died of fever'. Markers of harsh and brutal times gone by.

They walked back to the ute, still talking in whispers as if afraid to disturb the ghosts. As they turned and slowly drove away from the wharf, a swirl in the water and the glimpse of a black fin warned of the dangers that lurked below the surface.

They drove slowly back along the rough track, crossing a tidal creek on a rickety little bridge. The tide was well out, and the muddy creek bed was strewn with rocks. Bert stopped the ute. 'Ow about we catch some mud crabs?' he said with a wide grin.

They walked down through the mangrove bushes to the muddy creek bed. Bert had a hessian bag, and a pair of old workman's leather gloves. 'Ere, put this on.' He handed Matt the right hand glove, and put on the left hand himself. 'I'm left handed,' he said by way of explanation. He bent down and carefully turned over a rock. Nothing. Under the next rock lurked a large crab, greeting them with huge claws ready to attack. Deftly, Bert scooped it up from behind with his gloved hand and put it in the bag. He caught four more, watched in fascination by Matt, who valued his fingers too much to do battle with those giant claws.

As they walked back to the ute, Bert, holding the bag carefully, said. 'Once I put the bag over me shoulder, and one of those buggers grabbed me on the bum. I couldn't get it to let go and me mate had to break the claw with a pair of bolt cutters. I never did that again,' he said ruefully, holding the bag well away from him as he walked.

As they drove home, Bert said, 'Would yer like to have tea with us tonight? We'll be cooking the crabs, and there's just me missus and me, and the kids, but they eat early.'

That evening, Matt walked down to Bert's place, carrying a couple of bottles of beer – the standard visiting gift.

'G'day, Doc,' Bert beamed as he opened the door. His wife stood in the background. 'Doc, this is me missus, Thelma.' She smiled, and shook Matt's hand with a surprisingly firm grip. She was about mid thirties, Matt guessed, and lean and suntanned, like most of the northwest women.

'Glad yer could come, Doc, we're 'aving chilli crab.' She smiled, showing tobacco-stained teeth.

'Sounds great,' Matt said, and followed her through the house to the porch. Bert followed, carrying Matt's beer. They talked about Cossack as Thelma went back to the kitchen to prepare the meal.

'Where are the kids?' Matt asked.

'They've gone over to the neighbour's for the evening. More peaceful that way,' he said with a grin. He passed Matt a glass of beer. 'Cheers!' They raised their glasses.

The meal was outstanding. The great meaty crabs were cooked in spice and chilli, and the huge claws were cracked to let the sauce in. With slices of bread and butter, they mopped up the sauce, washing it down with cold beer. It was Matt's first experience both with crabs and with chilli, and he loved them both.

They sat picking the remains of the crab from the shell, and drinking beer, as Bert told more tales of the early northwest days. He'd been born and raised in these parts, and the stories were handed down from his parents.

As Matt walked back to his place after saying goodnight and thanking his hosts, he thought what wonderful folk Bert and Thelma were. How different from any people he had ever met at home; that went for everyone in these parts. The 'Nor'westers' truly were the salt of the earth.

The weeks went by quickly, with weekly visits to Onslow, and occasional weekends at Spinifex Plains. Bill and Joan now treated him as one of the family, and were well aware and silently approving of the growing affection between Matt and Lizzie.

One of Matt's tasks was to act as Quarantine officer, as occasionally

'China Navigation Company' ships from Hong Kong called in to Point Samson. With British officers and Asian crew, they carried passengers and cargo.

On the first occasion, Matt sat waiting on a bag of blue asbestos, fiddling with the silky strands of asbestos fibre that lay about. The ship was slowly coming alongside, hindered by the tide that was still running. After Matt had completed his routine inspection, he received a message from the Captain, asking Matt to join him on the bridge for coffee. The Captain was a lean, tall good-looking man of about fifty, suntanned, with silver grey hair and twinkling blue eyes. He was pleased to find that Matt was English, and they sat and chatted about the Old Country over their coffee.

Matt then took him for a drive around the town, and during the conversation, the Captain mentioned his love of hunting and shooting, and wondered if Matt could arrange something for him on his next call. Matt discussed the question with Mike Jackson, who he knew was interested in shooting, and together they arranged a hunt for the Captain's next visit.

A month later, his ship, the *Qantung* arrived at Point Samson at six thirty on a Saturday morning, where Matt stood waiting as the ship berthed. Captain Robinson greeted him cheerily, and was delighted to learn that a hunt had been arranged.

After the formalities of quarantine were completed, Matt was escorted to the Captain's day-cabin where they had a cup of coffee and discussed the plans for the hunt.

They walked from the jetty to Matt's utility. The Captain, now dressed in an immaculate khaki safari jacket, trousers and a bush hat to match, brought along a beautiful leather case containing his own rifle, and his cabin boy, Archie, to carry it. Archie, whose real name was Ah Chee, was a small wiry Chinese lad who looked no more than fifteen. Apart from the rifle case, he had a leather 'shooting bag' over one shoulder, containing a box of ammunition. He followed behind.

They drove into town, and met Mike, and also Peter Harris the policeman, who Matt felt would give some authority to the hunting party. Peter was also a keen shooter, and knew where they could find some game.

They drove in Mike's truck for about an hour, out towards the barren coast where feral donkeys and goats roamed, and usually a good number of red kangaroos. Mike and the Captain sat in the cabin in relative comfort, while Matt, Archie and Peter stood on the truck tray behind the cabin, holding on to the handrail.

They stopped in the shade of a small gum tree, and Mike produced cold bottles of ginger beer from an icebox. While they drank, the Captain lovingly opened his rifle case. It contained a beautiful double barrel rifle in 300 magnum calibre, hand-made by Holland and Holland of London. Mike's jaw dropped when he saw it. A gunsmith's masterpiece, with 'scroll' hand engraving on the burnished metal and an oil-finished stock of exquisite burl walnut, which gleamed softly in the sunshine.

The Captain picked up the barrels and fitted them to the stock, then raised the rifle to his shoulder and looked along the barrels. He put half a dozen large brass cartridges in the pocket of his jacket.

'Jeesus!' Mike said. 'I've never seen a rifle like that before!'

'I had it made for me,' the Captain said, beaming with pride. 'Hunted tiger with it in India.'

'Well, I hope you don't find this too much of a comedown,' Peter said, with a straight face. 'If we're lucky we might find some 'roos and a goat or two.'

Pete had a battered ex-army .303 rifle, and Mike, his trusty 303/25 that sported a telescope sight. Matt had a pair of binoculars, having offered to be a scout rather than shoot.

They set out on foot, with Peter in the lead, rifle over his shoulder. The Captain walked beside him, with Archie at his heel, carrying the double rifle, the bag of ammunition, and a water bag. Mike and Matt brought up at the rear, and after a short distance, Matt relieved the overburdened Archie of the water bag.

The terrain was rocky and bare apart from spinifex bushes, and undulated in a series of low hillocks. 'Watch where you put your feet,' Pete told the Captain. 'This place is lousy with snakes.' The Captain had a quick anxious look around him.

About three hundred yards ahead, Matt spotted some goats standing in the shade of a gum tree. They crept forward. At two hundred yards the goats saw them and started to wander away.

'Now's your chance Captain,' Pete whispered.

The Captain raised his rifle. BLAM! BLAM! The rifle bucked as he fired both barrels in quick succession, and a large billy-goat leapt into the air then fell motionless. The remainder of the group broke into a gallop and disappeared behind the hill.

'Good shot!' said Mike. 'Makes quite a bang, that thing,' he said nodding at the rifle, his ears still ringing from the explosions.

The Captain 'broke' the rifle, and extracted the spent cartridges then blew smoke from the barrels. The still air was heavy with the smell of burnt cordite.

'Do you think I could have one of those?' Mike asked, pointing at the shiny brass belted magnum cases in his hand.

'Surely,' said the Captain with a smile, passing one over. It was almost twice the size of his cartridges!

They walked up to the dead beast.

'Are they edible?' Matt asked.

'Yer'd 'ave ter be bloody hungry,' Pete said with a grin. 'Yer can smell 'im from 'ere.'

The goat truly did stink, and the flies were starting to swarm around the blood that oozed from the wounds. 'Unless you want the horns, we'll just move on.' Pete said. 'The crows and eagles will clean 'im up.'

They walked for a couple of hours in a great circle, and shot a couple more goats, the Captain demonstrating his marksmanship on each occasion. Peter had guided them back to the truck, where they had cold drinks and sandwiches in the shade, fighting off the hoards of bush flies.

They climbed back on the truck and drove back inland in search of kangaroos. As they approached a creek bed with its green trees, Pete spotted some. They slowed down, and came to a stop a couple of hundred yards from the trees, as the group of kangaroos stood on their hind legs watching them.

'You take the one on the left Captain,' Pete said quietly.

The silence was shattered by the crash of three high powered rifles. Archie dropped to the ground, and crouched in fright with his hands over his ears. Three large red kangaroos lay dead on the ground, as the others fled into the trees.

The Captain was delighted with the kill, and insisted that the carcasses be gutted and loaded on to the truck to take back to the ship. 'I shall freeze them and when we get back to Hong Kong, I will have them served as 'Scottish venison,' he announced. Mike looked at Matt, who rolled his eyes but said nothing.

Back at the wharf, a trolley was found, and the bloody carcasses were trundled out to the ship, where Archie was to arrange their storage. The Captain shook hands all round and thanked the three for the excellent day's shooting. He then strode up the gangway with his precious rifle case in his hand.

'Rule Britannia,' said Mike quietly as the Captain turned and waved a salute from the deck.

They walked back to the truck and all three climbed into the cabin. 'Right fellas, let's go back to my place and have a beer,' Mike said as he started the truck. 'It's been a long hard day!'

Chapter 23

The dentist came to town.

Matt set him up in the only separate room that had its own power plug. It happened to be the mortuary, though Matt didn't say so. Anyhow, it had not had much use over the past six months, and the dentist seemed quite happy with the accommodation.

Mary had booked a couple of dozen people to see him. His patients paid cash. Matt leant against the door and watched as the balding tubby dentist toiled away, sweating profusely in the unaccustomed heat. In quieter moments he tried to engage him in conversation, but found him uncommunicative to the point where Matt left him to his own devices.

He stayed at the pub, and completed his work in two days, then drove off to the next town north.

Three weeks later, the first of his patients returned with toothache. The filling had dropped out. Matt reluctantly pulled out a few teeth from the justifiably annoyed victims, but others who could afford it chose to travel south for repairs.

The next event on the social calendar of the little town was the annual meeting of the Roebourne Racing Club, which took place in mid-August. It was a gala weekend, with the traditional Dalgety's Cocktail Party on Cup Eve, and a dance on the Saturday night.

The race course, a relic from days gone by, had a small 'grandstand', which offered some protection from the sun, an ill defined race track, and a finishing post. These were the only permanent fixtures, all else was brought in for the occasion.

Matt received a letter from the chairman of the Racing Committee inviting him to be the Club's medical officer, which he accepted politely, pondering whether there really was any alternative.

The week before the meeting was a busy one for the town. The pub accommodation was fully occupied by tourists, bookmakers,

Station folk and visitors from Port Hedland, Onslow and Wittenoom.

The Main Roads Department grader had been brought in to level out the race-track that was in poor repair, and a number of caravans magically appeared, and set up near the grandstand, advertising food and soft drinks. The grandstand was undergoing a major overhaul and repair by a team of Public Works carpenters, who also refitted the 'bar' underneath. On the day, the pub would annex this and serve cold beer to the thirsty punters.

Matt had received an invitation to Dalgety's party. Attendance was 'by invitation only', but it seemed that most of the townsfolk, and all the surrounding station people were included, so nobody felt left out. He had offered to escort Mary, but fortunately she had arranged to go with some town friends. Lizzie and parents were coming to town, and planned to stay at the pub.

On Friday after lunch Matt drove to the other side of the river, where the racecourse was located, and found a row of ex-army tents had been erected. One of these bore a Red Cross on the canvas roof, and was his first aid station. The others were occupied by out of town people who could find no other accommodation. Behind the tent row was a temporary ablution block.

Inside the first aid tent, he found a stretcher, and a table and two chairs. He was to bring anything else he needed. He made a list of his requirements, and headed back to the hospital where he collected the equipment and stacked it in his surgery.

At about five he dressed for the evening, and drove round to the pub, where he found Bill and Joan with Lizzie, sitting in the shady beer garden sipping cool drinks.

'Ah!' said Bill rising from his chair. 'I hoped you would show up.' Matt shook his outstretched hand, and sat down next to Lizzie, who gave him a sweet smile. 'Can I get you a drink?' Bill asked.

'No thanks, I'm just fine,' he replied.

They chatted about the next day's racing program. Bill didn't have a horse in the events. He had in previous years, he said, but decided he was getting too old to be bothered now.

At six they walked around to Dalgety's where the whole back yard was lit with coloured lights, and chairs and small tables were spread around in groups. A bar was set up at one end, with a keg of beer, and a large container of fruit punch. A couple of young men stood behind the bar pouring drinks, while another with a frosty jug of foaming beer walked around topping up glasses. Already there were a few dozen people standing with drinks and chatting, and trays of sandwiches were being offered around.

Mike and his wife Anne greeted them at the door. 'Hello Lizzie,' he said, shaking her hand. 'Hi Matt. Don't think I've seen you since the great hunt.'

Lizzie looked quizzically at Matt. 'Great hunt?'

Matt rolled his eyes. 'You don't want to know about it.'

They circulated through the growing crowd, with Lizzie introducing Matt to station people he hadn't met. Horses were the main topic of conversation. In the corner of the yard, Matt saw Jack Morgan. He was standing on his own, with a glass in his hand. He caught Matt's glance and wandered over.

'Well Doctor, I hope your head has recovered,' he said affably.

'Yes, thank you Jack. No permanent damage,' Matt replied cautiously.

Jack turned to Lizzie. 'Will you be at the dance tomorrow night Liz?'

Matt looked at her.

'Yes Jack, I'm going with Matt,' she replied coolly.

'Good.' He leered at her. 'Better save a few dances for me. I want to have a talk with you,' he said enigmatically, then turned and walked away.

'A very strange man,' Liz said looking after him with a worried expression.

'Take no notice,' Matt said taking her arm. 'Come and have something to eat.'

At about nine, they walked back to the pub arm in arm. The party was still in full swing, and would remain so until the beer ran out. In the cool of the evening, they sat in the quiet beer garden. 'Penny for your thoughts,' said Matt. 'You seem to be far away.'

'I was thinking about Jack,' she replied. 'He frightens me Matt. I don't know what it is about him, but he scares me.'

Matt put his arm around her. 'Well, you have nothing to worry about. I will look after you.' He drew her to him and kissed her tenderly.

By midday Saturday the race course was buzzing with activity. A pall of dust hung in the air, stirred up by cars and horse floats arriving. The track marshals had driven round the course and checked its condition, and the hot dog stall was doing good business.

The local Aboriginals had arrived in numbers, all dressed in their best attire, queueing for pies, hot dogs and soft drinks. Groups of Aboriginal women sat on the ground on rugs, playing a game of cards that was fast, furious, and completely incomprehensible to the onlooker.

Matt had set up the first aid tent, and had Mibbin on stand-by. All was prepared. At ten to one Matt wandered over to the grandstand. There were three 'bookies' with umbrellas and blackboards, busily collecting bets for the first race, which was to start at one. Matt collected a hot dog and a bottle of Coca Cola, and took a seat in the shade to watch the race. There was no sign of Lizzie or her parents.

The first race went by in a cloud of dust. There were four horses running, and they crossed the line roughly in the same order that they were in after the start. Matt closed his eyes. It was going to be a long afternoon.

'What's this? Sleeping on the job?'

Lizzie stood in front of him, a smile on her face and hands on hips.

Matt opened one eye and growled. 'You want to come to my tent?' They laughed. He went and bought her a Coke and a hot dog, and they sat in the shade watching the passing parade of people and horses.

The main event for the afternoon was the Roebourne Cup. Bill and Joan had joined them in the grandstand, and on Bill's recommendation, Matt had put a fiver on a horse from a nearby station which he thought had a good chance, though it was not the favourite.

It was a six-horse race, over one-and-a-half miles, and as the horses came into the straight towards the finishing line, the jockeys on the leading two horses were standing in their stirrups, leaning back and pulling their mounts. An angry roar rose from the crowd as they crossed the line, with Matt's horse in third place.

The protest flag was raised, and ultimately the first two horses were disqualified, leaving Matt's horse the winner at ten-to-one!

Matt raced off with his ticket to the bookie, and came back with a fist full of notes, grinning from ear to ear.

At the end of the afternoon, tired, dusty and sunburned, they drove back to the pub, and sat in the cool beer garden sipping cold drinks. Bill and Joan had not planned to go to the dance, to be held in the Masonic Hall just up the road, and opted for an early night at the pub. Matt drove home to change, having arranged to pick up Liz at eight o'clock.

The dance was well under way when they arrived, with a small band from Port Hedland beating out the music. The band consisted of a middle-aged bespectacled lady on the piano, a grey haired man playing the clarinet alternating with a saxophone, and a portly bald man playing the drums. The music, however, was surprisingly good, though the dances themselves came from a different age. The Pride of Erin, Boston Two-step, Gay Gordons and the Barn Dance featured with Foxtrots and Quicksteps. Soft drinks were served, but no alcohol, though this was of little importance as there was plenty being consumed outside the Hall.

Lizzie and Matt had just finished a dance when Jack Morgan came up to them. His face was flushed with alcohol, and he looked dishevelled.

'Ah Lizzie, I think the next dance is mine,' he said, taking her by the arm and turning his back on Matt.

Jack whirled Lizzie off in a fast quickstep, and Matt leaned against the wall and lit a cigarette, watching as they circled the room amongst the dancers on the crowded floor.

'Hello Matt.' A voice beside him made him turn. It was Anne and Mike.

'Hello Anne,' Matt replied. 'Nice party last night, thanks,' he said as he shook Mike's hand.

'Thought you'd be with Liz Corbett tonight,' Mike said with a grin.

'Yes, well I am, or rather, was. She's dancing with ...' his voice trailed off as he looked to the other side of the room. Jack Morgan, firmly gripping Lizzie's arm was guiding her out the door. The expression on her face alarmed him.

'Excuse me,' he said and walked over towards the door that led out to and out to the veranda. As he reached the door, he was almost knocked over by Lizzie, as she rushed inside, red in the face.

'Lizzie! What's ...'

'Come on, we're leaving,' she said, taking him firmly by the arm.

They left through the front door, without speaking to anyone, and they were half way to the pub before she stopped and fell into his arms sobbing.

'Do you want to tell me what happened?' he asked quietly.

She was silent for a moment. 'He … he held me against the wall, and kissed me, and…' she paused. 'Then he tried to put his hand up my dress.' Another long pause. 'Then – I slapped his face as hard as I could and ran.'

In the dark, Matt tried to suppress a smile. 'Well, I guess he knows where he stands now,' Matt said.By the time they reached the pub she had regained her composure, and they walked out to the beer garden and sat in the cool.

'I'd best be off,' Matt said. 'You'll be driving home tomorrow I guess.'

'Please don't go yet,' she said reaching out to take his hand. 'I won't see you for a while I suppose. We start shearing in about four weeks, and we'll all be flat out with mustering till then.'

'Hey, you said you'd invite me out when you started shearing. Does the invitation still stand?'

She smiled, her white teeth catching the light.

'Of course it does. I'll radio you once we are under way. There's a lot of organising to do before then, and Dad needs all the help I can give him.'

'Why doesn't he have an overseer or manager?'

'He did have one last year, but he left. They are not easy to come by you know.'

They sat talking quietly for half an hour, still holding hands.

'Must go,' he said finally, and leaned forwards to kiss her cheek, but she turned to him and put her arms around him, looking into his eyes. 'I love you Matt,' she whispered, and kissed him passionately.

Matt lay in bed wrestling with his emotions. Lizzie was a wonderful person, and he did indeed love her, but it was too soon. He had only just come to terms with Penny's death, and he felt guilty. Although he knew he would never find another like Lizzie Corbett, he wasn't ready to commit himself. He drifted off to sleep, and dreamed he was making love with Penny. He woke disturbed, and troubled by the consequences of his erotic dream.

Chapter 24

Early the next Thursday morning, Matt sat at his desk writing his report on the previous day's Onslow trip. Mary put her head in the door.

'Matt, Hedland base want you on the radio'.

'What's up?'

'They didn't say'.

Matt followed Mary to the radio, and sat down. Mary stood behind to listen. He picked up the microphone and pressed the button.

'Hedland this is Matt Harrison. Over.'

'G'day Matt – Joe Bailey. We may be looking at a problem, so I thought I'd better warn you, out.'

'OK Joe, tell me.'

'For the past twenty-four hours we've been receiving radio messages from a yacht coming up the coast, a ketch called the *Marie,* out of Fremantle, and heading for Darwin. The messages are a bit scrambled, but it seems that there are four on board, and one is a woman. She and one of the men are extremely seasick. I've tried to contact them, but they don't acknowledge my calls'.

'OK Joe, I'll stick around, and leave the receiver on for your call.

Matt thought no more about it, and went back to his report, followed by a small clinic of minor ailments. At ten thirty, Mary called Matt to the radio.

'Matt, I've just picked up a distress call from the boat. They've hit a reef, and are stuck. They hit fairly hard and one of the men fell and injured his head. He's unconscious.

'I managed to get an answer from the guy on the radio; said his name was Fred somebody, I didn't catch it. He doesn't know where they are but they passed Onslow yesterday morning, and he thinks he can see land on the horizon. I'd reckon they are off the Dampier Archipelago. There's lots of reefs out there.'

'So what's your plan Joe?'

'I'm going to set up a land and sea search, asking the coastal stations to patrol their area, and the plane will do a grid search around Dampier area. I want you to get up a sea search if you can.'

'OK Joe, I'll see what I can do. Do you want me to call you?'

'No, just stay on the air, and we'll update you.'

'Cup of tea time!' Mary called from the veranda.

They sat over tea discussing the problem.

'All sounds a bit weird to me,' Mary said. 'If they've sailed from Fremantle, you think they would've sorted out the sea sickness problem by now, or called in at Onslow.'

Matt rang the PWD and spoke to Bert, and told him the story.

'Well,' Bert said after a pause, 'the tide is about to go out, and if we want to use the boat, we'll need to launch it right now.'

'Do you need a hand?'

'No thanks; I'll get some of the boys to help. You better stay with the radio.'

Half an hour later Joe called again.

'Matt, they've got off the reef, but the boat is badly damaged, and taking water. Fred said the pump was holding it, and they were under sail again. He tried the engine but it wouldn't start.'

'So what now?'

'Just wait and see. They may turn up at your place.'

'What about the head injury?'

'Still out cold he said.'

'Any idea where they are?'

'Two DC3s picked up their signal, but the bearing they got was somewhere inland, so that was no help.'

Matt returned to his daily tasks, but kept near the radio. At eleven forty-five he was called again.

'Matt, it's turned into an all time disaster!' Joe's voice faltered with emotion.

'The pump failed, and they started to sink, so they launched the dinghy. The two sick ones got in and Fred tried to lower in the unconscious guy, but they nearly capsized the dinghy, and the man fell into the water. The two in the dinghy couldn't hang onto him, and he started to drift away, and before they could unhitch the dinghy to go after him, th… the sharks took him!'

'Jeesus,' Matt whispered to himself, and shuddered at the thought.

There was a silence while they both struggled with the situation.

'Matt?'

'Yes Joe.'

'I want you to get out to the Archipelago, and search from there to Depuch Island. Can you do that?'

'We're on our way. But you'd better have Jim look out for us from the air.'

Matt rang Bert, and was told that he was already at the jetty, putting fuel in the boat.

With Mary's help he loaded the emergency kit in the ute, and a box of food that Polly had thoughtfully prepared, together with a large thermos of hot tea. He stopped briefly at his house and stuffed a jumper and some trousers in a bag then wrapped an old blanket around it, and drove to Point Sampson.

The boat was floating in deep water at the end of the jetty, and Bert waved as he drove up. He told Bert the story as they loaded the boat.

'Those poor bastards,' said Bert shaking his head.

'Have you got any warm clothes?' Matt asked.

'Yair, and a blanket and some emergency grub.'

'OK let's go!'

It was twelve thirty when they set out, and a stiff easterly was blowing as they motored out towards the Archipelago. The waves were steep and choppy, and in no time they were soaked with spray. With the wind behind them though, they didn't feel cold.

At one thirty they had reached the islands, and sheltered in the lee of one to take stock. Matt searched the horizon with the binoculars, whilst Bert organised a cup of tea, and some of Polly's hamper of corned beef sandwiches.

They cruised around the islands, keeping a sharp lookout, with no result. At one point they saw the RFDS plane in the distance.

'Doc.' Bert shouted. 'If we're goin' to Depuch Island we'd better start now. It's a good fifty miles, and we'd be lucky to get there by dark.' Matt nodded, and they turned east and butted into the wind and waves across open water.

After three hours they were soaked to the skin and shivering with cold. The boat had taken a lot of water, and Matt was busy working the bilge pump. At least the exercise helped to warm him.

Five o'clock, and still there was no sight of land. The sun was dipping to the horizon. Bert stood with his feet braced, gripping he wheel and watching the compass as the little boat bucked and tossed in the choppy sea. Another hour and the sun had gone, but in the darkening eastern horizon shape of a small mountain could be just made out. Bert pointed. 'Depuch Island!' he shouted.

At seven thirty they were anchored in the lee of the island, and sheltered from the wind. They were tired, cold and hungry. Bert lit the hurricane lamp.

They stripped and put on dry clothes, then wrapped themselves in their blankets, which had remained dry in the little cuddy-cabin. They finished off the luke-warm tea, and Polly's sandwiches, then had a slab of fruitcake.

'Well, I reckon I'm feeling better. 'Ow about you, Doc?' said Bert with a grin.

Using their wet clothes, they had mopped up the cabin floor, and cleaned up the mess.

'We better get ourselves organised, it's gunna be a long night,' he added.

They sat smoking cigarettes. The wind had dropped off and the water was flat, with only a little swell to rock the boat gently.

Matt pumped Bert's local knowledge. 'Tell me about Depuch Island,' he asked.

'Actually it's a little volcano,' Bert said taking a drag on his cigarette. 'Named after one of the frogs on Baudin the explorer's ship *Geographe*. They charted a lot of the West Australian coast, and you know what, Doc? We're bloody lucky! We could've become a French colony!'

They chatted and smoked for the next hour, watching the blazing stars in the velvet-black sky, punctuated by meteorites that flashed across the heavens and burned out. The night grew cold. They lay on the cockpit floor wrapped in their blankets, and with their bags for pillows, and tried to sleep. The boat rocked gently and water lapped soothingly against the hull.

Matt lay shivering with cold. His teeth were chattering. Suddenly he remembered! In the emergency bag was a bottle of brandy! – Strictly for medicinal purposes, of course. Matt crawled over and dug it out, then pulled the cork.

'Bert?'

'Wot.'

'Are you asleep?'

Pause. 'Yes.'

'I've got something for you.'

Bert sat up, clutching his blanket around him.

'Have some of this.' Matt handed him the bottle.

Bert squinted at it and took a sniff. 'Nah, thanks, Doc, I'm a beer drinker.'

'Bert, this is medicine. Drink it! Doctor's orders!'

Bert dutifully took a long swig and choked. 'Jeesus, Doc! That's real firewater!'

He handed the bottle back, and Matt took a mouthful. It burned all the way down, but he could feel it warming his body.

'Well, how does that feel? Matt asked.

'Not bad. Not bad at all.'

'Want some more?'

'Ta.'

As they sat passing the bottle, Bert became talkative.

'Yer know, Doc, when I was a lad, me an' me mate used to go fishing off the jetty. The best time was at night, 'specially when the salmon was running. We'd go down with a blanket each and an 'urricane lamp, and catch a bag full.

'One night I was at the end of the jetty, and me mate Jerry was about fifty yards away. They weren't biting too well that night, and I dozed off. When I woke it was just gettin' light, and I could see Jerry's lantern, so I went down to see 'ow 'e was goin', but 'e wasn't there. I thought 'e might 'ave gone to the beach for a crap or something, so I walked in and whistled and called, but 'e never answered.

'Yer know, Doc, we never saw 'im again.

'They reckon 'e must 'ave 'ooked a big'un and lost 'is footing, but I never 'eard the splash. Because I was sleepin' yer see'.

Bert paused, lit another fag and took a drag.

'Ever since that time I've felt guilty. They never blamed me mind, but just the same I wasn't there to 'elp 'im when 'e needed me.

'Since then I've always 'elped to look for lost souls. It's me duty yer see.'

They sat in silence for a while.

'Well Bert, we'd best try to get some sleep,' Matt said, and lay down with his rug around him.

At first light they were both awake, having slept fitfully. There was no wind, and the ocean was flat calm. They started the engine and pulled up the anchor, then set off around the island. As they came round the point, Matt was surprised to see that the shore was only about five or six hundred yards away, but they could approach no further as the tide was low, and a reef barred their progress.

A shrill whistle drew their attention. On the shore they saw a jeep approaching with two men on board from a nearby station. They waved. The jeep stopped at the high water line and the men unloaded cans of fuel and a couple of boxes. They realised that the boat could not cross the reef, and as it was too far to call, they waved and drove off.

'Well,' said Bert, 'we might as well make ourselves useful for the next few hours. Let's take a run up the coast.'

For the next hour they skimmed along at top speed across the calm water, scanning with the binoculars then turned out to sea for a few miles. They returned to the island, having seen nothing. When they arrived, the tide had come in enough for them to cross the reef and motor to the shore, where they beached the boat.

To their delight there was a box of food containing eggs, sausages and bacon, bread and jam, a primus stove, and a frying pan. There were also some enamel plates, knives and forks, enamel mugs, and a tin billy with small jars of tea and sugar inside. There was a note in the box wishing them well, and asking if they would leave the fuel cans and dishes on the beach when they left. While Bert lit the primus stove, Matt carried the fuel cans to the boat and put them on board. They sat in the sand and feasted on fried eggs, bacon and sausages, then ate slabs of bread and jam, waiting for the billy to boil.

Breakfast over, they cleaned up and packed up the utensils. Matt found a pencil on the boat, and wrote a note to the station folk thanking them for their kindness, while Bert poured fuel into the tank. Just as they were ready to push the boat off the sand they heard the drone of an engine. It was the RFDS Cessna!

They watched as the little plane came down low as though it was going to land, and flew along the beach towards them with its flaps down. As it passed overhead at about a hundred feet, a tin was thrown out the window. Jim climbed steeply and waved as he banked the plane and headed back the way he came.

'They've found 'em!' Bert shouted with delight, and dashed off to retrieve the tin. He prised the lid off, took out the note and read it, then turned and walked back. Without a word, he passed it to Matt.

He read with disbelief.

'Sorry boys, it's all been a hoax. Get yourselves home, and thanks for your effort.' It was signed by Joe Bailey.

Dumbfounded, he looked up at Bert, who had tears in his eyes.

They pushed the boat out into deeper water in silence and climbed in.

Before he started the engine, Bert looked at Matt and said. 'Yer know what, Doc? If they ever catch the bastard who done that 'oax, I 'ope they cut 'is balls off.'

He started the engine before Matt could speak, and they skimmed out past the island and headed for home at top speed. They reached Point Sampson by mid afternoon, and with help from a couple of Bert's men, they pulled the boat up then headed for home.

After cleaning up, Matt wearily drove over to the hospital and returned the emergency kit, recording that the brandy had been put to good use. Mary told Matt that Joe wanted him to call, and that there were some very angry people round town. 'I reckon they would lynch that rotter if they caught him,' she said.

'Not if Bert got him first,' he replied with a wry grin.

On the radio Joe told him the story.

More than a hundred people had been out searching along the coast and of course there were no sightings. The radio messages kept coming, even though they were supposedly in the dinghy, with a portable radio they assumed.

On two more occasions, the DC3 planes recorded bearings that pinpointed a station inland. Finally, the Wittenoom police drove there to investigate, and found the place in a mess. Apparently the new cook had been left alone on the property while the manager had driven to Port Hedland to collect some equipment, and he had got on the booze. They found some notes and scribbling by the radio, and a pile of empty beer bottles but no sign of the cook. He had taken off.

Mary cooked some supper for Matt, who was exhausted and sunburnt, then packed him off to have an early night. Some months later Matt heard that the police had arrested a man in a Perth hotel, who had drunkenly boasted about his clever hoax in the north. He was now residing in Fremantle Prison.

Chapter 25

For the next two weeks, Matt was fully occupied with his work. The ketch *Marie* hoax was behind them, but not forgotten. A car pulled in to the Hospital. A man came to Matt's surgery door. 'Are yer there, doc?' he called. Matt was writing reports, and put down his pen. He went to the door.

'Can I help you?' he asked.

'Doc, it's my kid; I think she's got appendicitis. She's in the car, can I bring her in?'

Matt walked to the car, and on the way, the man introduced himself as Frank Edwards, the overseer at Yerilla Station about 100 miles out.

'Why didn't you call RFDS?' Matt asked.

'Well, I thought it would be quicker to drive her in myself,' he replied.

Frank opened the car door, where an anxious woman was comforting a young girl.

'This is my wife Margaret,' he said. 'And this is little Lucy.' Margaret gave Matt a nervous smile. The girl looked flushed, and winced with pain when Frank picked her up.

'Come into my surgery,' he said to them, and led the way to open the door.

'Just lay her on the couch there,' he told Frank.

'There we are, Lucy, nothing to be frightened of,' Matt smiled at her as he gently felt her abdomen. She was very tender on the right side, and certainly had appendicitis. The parents looked on anxiously as Matt examined her carefully.

'How old are you Lucy?' he asked.

'I'm nearly seven,' she answered in a little voice.

'Well Lucy, you have a bad appendix, and we are going to make you all better, but you will have to stay with us here for a few days.'

Little Lucy just nodded, and held her mother's hand tightly.

Matt went over to his desk, and made some notes, then pressed the button that rang a buzzer in Mary's office. A few moments later she appeared.

'Hello Mary, this is Lucy, and her Mum and Dad. Would you like to take her down to the ward and pop her into bed? She's got appendicitis.'

Mary smiled at Lucy. 'Perhaps Dad would carry her for me, she's such a big girl.'

She led the way as Frank carried the child out the door.

'Come and sit here, Margaret,' Matt indicated the chair by his desk. 'Lucy will be just fine. When did she eat last?' he asked.

'She had some cereal early this morning, but vomited it up. She's only had sips of water all day.' Margaret was nervously twisting a handkerchief as she spoke.

'Well,' said Matt, 'we will operate in a couple of hours' time, and by tomorrow morning, Lucy will be feeling much better.' He gave her hand a reassuring pat.

'Will you be staying at the pub?' he asked. She nodded.

'Then I'll ring you as soon as we are through, and you can come and sit with her as she wakes up.'

Margaret nodded again, seemingly overwhelmed with the events of the day.

Two hours later, the operating theatre was ready, and Susan was preparing the instruments under Mary's supervision. Lucy was lying on the table, already drowsy with the premedication drugs.

Matt sat down by her head, and with Mary gently holding her hands, he held a cloth mask over her nose and mouth and sprayed a little ethyl chloride onto the outside.

'Lucy, I want you to take a few big breaths for me,' Matt said quietly.

'I don't like it,' she said, holding up her hands to her face. 'It smells funny.'

'Well see if you can blow it away,' Matt said. Lucy took a deep breath and blew, then another. Her hands fell limp, and she was asleep.

Matt changed bottles and started dripping ether onto the mask, with a small rubber tube under the edge of the mask providing oxygen. For the next five minutes, he listened to her breathing, and checked her pupil size, as she went into the deeper stages of anaesthesia.

Mary stood beside him watching throughout, and when told to do so, she took over the mask and ether bottle, while Matt scrubbed his hands and put on his gown and gloves.

Still listening to the deep regular breathing, Matt painted the abdomen with iodine solution, and placed sterile drapes over the whole body, leaving only a small area on the right side exposed. Carefully he marked out the position for his incision then with a scalpel, he made a two-inch cut through the skin.

He worked quickly, and in a few minutes was through the peritoneum and inside the abdominal cavity. With two fingers in the wound he felt around, exploring the anatomy that he knew so well. He located the appendix, and presented it to the surface. It was plum coloured and distended with infection. Skilfully, he removed the appendix and closed the abdominal wound.

'Mary you can stop the ether now, she will coast OK for the last bit.' Mary took off the mask, but left the oxygen tube in the rubber airway in her mouth. With careful stitching, he closed the skin with a row of fine silk sutures. The whole procedure had taken only thirty minutes.

'Well, that one wouldn't have kept much longer,' Matt said as he took off his mask. 'It was ready to pop.'

Lucy was now breathing quietly, with an Elastoplast dressing over the abdominal wound. Susan had placed the appendix in a little jar with some preserving solution. 'Lucy wants to see it,' she said with a grin.

'Stay with her Mary, while I ring the pub,' Matt said over his shoulder as he went out the door.

Thirty minutes later Lucy was awake but drowsy, with her parents by her side.

'Don't stay too long,' Matt said, 'She'll be very sleepy, but better tomorrow.'

He looked into the operating theatre where Mary was tidying up.

'Thanks Mary, you did a great job,' he said with a smile.

She looked up. 'You weren't too bad yourself,' she replied. 'See you in the morning.'

Matt went home and poured a whisky, then heated up some baked beans and made some toast.

Next morning Matt was in the ward by eight. Lucy was propped up in bed, drinking some apple juice through a straw.

'Well, how's the patient today?' he asked, sitting carefully on the side of the bed.

'My tummy's sore,' she said, 'but I feel better.'

Just then her parents appeared. They looked anxiously at Lucy.

'Good morning,' Matt greeted them. 'Lucy's doing well.'

'Mummy, look at my appendix!' Lucy held up the jar. 'Isn't it horrible?'

Margaret leaned down and gave Lucy a hug. There were tears in her eyes when she stood up.

'I … I don't know how to thank you doctor,' she faltered.

Matt put his arm around her. 'Don't try, seeing Lucy getting well again is reward enough.'

Three days later, Lucy was up and about, eating normally, and ready to leave hospital.

'I need to see her in a week to take the stitches out,' Matt said as the parents gathered up Lucy's belongings. 'It's OK to go home if you want in the meantime.'

Matt saw them to the car.

'Doc, we both want to thank you for what you did,' Frank said as he shook Matt's hand.

'Frank, that's my job. That's what I do,' he replied, and gave Frank a pat on the shoulder as he held the car door.

'Give me a call on the radio in a couple of days and let me know how Lucy is getting on,' Matt said through the window. He watched as they drove off with Lucy waving out the window.

Chapter 26

Two weeks later, Matt was scheduled to do his usual visit to Onslow, but on this occasion, he was to call in on some outlying stations on the way home. This meant staying the night in Onslow, and making an early start for the three stations. The trip down was uneventful, with Jim Dickson circling Matt's house at seven thirty. Mary provided the taxi service to the airstrip as usual.

At Onslow, Tom the orderly met them, and cautioned them that all was not well at the hospital. The night before last he said, Maggie the cook and her husband Horrie had a flaming row, and in his intoxicated state, he had chased her around the hospital, firing his shotgun in the air. The police were summoned, and he was now languishing in gaol. As a result of all this Maggie had gone into a total decline and refused to do any cooking.

Matron Harper was standing on the veranda when they pulled up. She was not smiling.

'Look out,' Tom muttered as they opened the doors.

'Good morning Matron,' Matt greeted her with a smile.

'That it is not,' she replied with a grim expression.

'Ah, anything I can do to help?' he asked affably as they climbed the steps on to the veranda.

'Come on in and have a cup of tea, and I'll tell you the problems,' she said, melting a little.

Over a cup of tea, Matron poured out the story. With no cook, she had to do the cooking herself, and do all the hospital chores and, she announced with some finality, she was getting too old for all this.

After tea, with cake noticeably absent, she took Matt for a tour of the damage. There were sizable holes in the corrugated iron roof all round the enclosed veranda, where patient's beds stood. All were empty except one, which contained Alf Gill, a grossly overweight cook from an outlying station who was having breathing problems.

'I'll just have a listen to Alf's chest while I'm here,' said Matt, pausing at the bedside. Matron gave a grunt, and walked off. Matt used the moment to get more information on the shooting.

'I tell yer, Doc, it was pretty bad. That 'Orrie came rampaging round after Maggie, blasting off with 'is gun. Honest, I was shit scared, and got under the bed. Then Jack Wilson the cop turned up and there was a brawl, with 'Orrie finishing up in 'and-cuffs, an' bein' marched off to the slammer.'

'What about Maggie?' Matt asked.

'Well, she just bawled 'er eyes out, and said she quit. Then Matron did 'er block an' thumped 'er one.'

Matt's jaw dropped. 'What happened then?'

'She stopped bawling and went to 'er room. She won't come out.'

'Then,' Alf said, 'then, she wanted me to get up and do the cooking! Me! A bloody patient!

'I told 'er that I had rights, and that don't include doin' the cookin.' An' then she said to me. "Well you old bugger, you can bloody well live on yer 'ump. I'm not gunna feed yer." The old bag.'

Matt stifled a laugh. 'Well OK, I'll see what I can do for you Alf.'

The morning went smoothly in the clinic and was followed by lunch, consisting of sandwiches and tea.

'What news of Maggie?' Matt asked mildly.

'She won't talk and she won't come out,' Matron replied. 'But she'll get hungry sooner or later, and that'll bring her out,' she said with conviction.

'Well now, we can stay at the pub tonight if you like,' Matt said.

'No, I've got beds made up for you here, but you better 'ave dinner at the pub, because I'm not cooking any.'

'Would you like to join us at the pub for dinner then?' Matt asked.

'No, I've got to be here, there's a native girl 'aving a baby any minute now.'

At the end of the afternoon clinic, Jim looked in the door. 'How about we go down to the pub a bit early and have a couple of beers?'

'Damn good idea,' Matt replied, as he packed up his equipment. Tom drove them down to the Beadon Hotel. It was five thirty.

The hotel was an old two storey stone building that had weathered the cyclones over the years, without so much as losing its roof. It was in fact the gathering point when the town was threatened with a cyclone. They walked into the front bar, and Tom ordered three beers. As they stood sipping, Tom said to Dulcie the barmaid. 'Too bad about Horrie. Not much fun in the can.'

'Well I don't know,' Dulcie drawled. 'They've been out fishing all day.'

'Who has?'

'Jack Wilson and 'Orrie,' she said, filling a glass. 'Jack needed a bit of 'elp with the boat, and 'e reckoned that 'Orrie wouldn't be any trouble, 'im still 'aving a bloody 'angover.'

'Well I'll be damned!' Matt said, listening to the conversation.

'Horrie's not a bad bloke when he's sober,' said Tom. 'Jack will probably turn him loose tomorrow.'

'Well I hope so for Matron's sake,' he replied.

As they stood drinking, Matt commented on the large mural, which was a beer advertisement. It showed a painting of an atomic explosion over an island in the ocean, and a caption 'Swan Lager! It Beats the Bomb!'

Tom explained. 'After the war, the Poms – oops, sorry – the British tested an atom bomb off the coast of Onslow on the Monte Bello Islands, and the locals all heard the explosion, and saw the mushroom cloud. It ruined one of the best fishing areas, and no one can go near the island now. The Swan Brewery cashed in on the act.' Matt sipped his beer, and looked at the garish lethal scene.

They went in to the dining room and sat down. There was no menu, and after a pause, a young coloured girl brought in vegetable soup. Plates of meat and vegetables followed, then bowls of tinned fruit and tinned cream. They ate in silence.

Back at the hospital, Matron announced that Maggie was feeling better, and had come out of her room. She had decided not to quit, and had cooked sausages and eggs for the patients – and a large plateful for herself.

Next morning they were up at six, and had a quick cup of tea and some toast before driving out to the airport. Matt waved to Tom as they bumped their way out for take-off. It was a glorious still morning.

Levelled out at four thousand feet, Jim set a course for the first of their destinations; Boolawon Station, located about one hundred and fifty miles inland from Onslow. Matt watched out the window as the featureless earth slowly drifted by. It was as barren as the face of the moon. There were no landmarks to identify, and navigation had to be dead accurate, or the tiny station would be passed by unseen.

He settled back in his seat and closed his eyes, thinking about Lizzie Corbett, and how she had come in to his life when he least expected it. The hypnotic drone of the engine lulled him into a sleepy state as he thought about the beautiful girl, and the curious chain of coincidences that had brought them together. Could he marry again? He needed a woman in his life to fill the yearning emptiness that Penny's death had left. In his sleepy state he fantasised about their future together. They could marry at Spinifex Plains, then fly south for the honeymoon, then back to England to his parents and his old hospital

He jolted to reality! How would Lizzie cope in that cold alien environment away from her family and friends? How could she live in a pokey little apartment, alone night after night while he was on duty? Wide-awake he pondered on this. If he were ever to marry her, he knew that he would have to live in Australia.

He thought about this new scenario that had never occurred to him before. Could he leave England forever? Suddenly Jim nudged him and pointed down. Boolawon station lay below.

'What a navigator,' Matt thought as he smiled and gave a 'thumbs up.' It was nine thirty.

They pulled up beside an old Ford car on the side of the airstrip. A suntanned, middle-aged man in khaki greeted them. 'G'day! I'm Ken Whittaker. Welcome to Boolawon. The missus has got morning tea all ready.'

They shook hands all round and climbed in to the dusty car.

The homestead was stark compared with Spinifex Plains, made of mud brick and timber, with a corrugated iron roof. There was no lawn, only a few peppercorn trees in the red earth around the house, offering little in the way of shade. On the veranda two women stood smiling as they climbed the steps.

'This is my wife Betty, and her sister Maude.' They shook hands as they made their introductions.

'Just in time for morning tea,' Betty said brightly. 'Come along.'

Inside the house the air was stifling and hot. She led the way to the back veranda, where there was a table set up for morning tea, with hot buttered scones and jam, and a large sponge cake under a glass dome.

Betty was about forty, Matt guessed, and like so many North West women he'd met, she was lean, wiry and suntanned. She was dressed in khaki slacks and a faded green cotton shirt. She chattered brightly as she poured tea, and passed around a plate of scones.

Maude was older, and said little. She looked ill, Matt thought. Her pale skin seemed to be tightly stretched over her face, and her greying brown hair was pulled back in a bun. She wore a simple cotton dress.

Betty had been a nurse in England, and had met Ken in London during the war, when he had flown in bombers over Germany. After the war they married, and Ken brought her back to his home, the North West. Apart from an occasional trip south, she had lived on Boolawon station ever since, working beside Ken as he built up the station and wrestled a living out of the harsh land. It had been a struggle, but they were happy, and their only real sadness was that they had no children.

After the substantial morning tea, Betty led Matt aside. 'Doctor, I'm sorry to bring you all the way out here, as we only have a couple of patients for you. I really wanted you to see Maude. I'm so worried about her; she is losing weight, and seems to have no energy. I've asked her what's the trouble, but she just puts on a brave face, and says she's alright. Sometimes, she seems to be in pain.'

She told Matt that a few years after the war, Maude had come out to Australia to live with them when their widowed mother had died. Her fiancé had been shot down in the last days over Germany, and she had never recovered from the loss. She had no wish to face the real world any more.

She walked Matt around to the shady side of the house where a little group of Aboriginal women sat on the ground. A tall well-built Aboriginal man leaned against the veranda post smoking a cigarette.

'This is Billy Banjo, our head stockman,' Betty said. Billy stood up straight and grinned. 'He has had tooth ache for a few days, and I'd like you to have a look at him. Also, we have two pregnant girls who need checking.'

'Right,' said Matt. 'Billy first. Give him a glass of water, to rinse out his mouth while I get my bag.'

Billy had a decayed molar, so he was given an injection, and told to wait. There was a cyclone bed on the veranda, and Betty had placed an old screen by it. With Betty in attendance, he carefully examined the two girls, noting the size of the womb and the lie of the baby. Both were due in about six weeks he thought.

Next, Matt expertly removed Billy's molar, without so much as a groan. His dentistry had come a long way!

Back in the house, Maude was sitting in the parlour reading a book.

'May I join you, Miss Maude?' Matt asked.

'Certainly, Doctor. Do sit down.' He sat beside her.

Matt chatted about England, and quickly put Maude at ease. In the conversation he talked about the contrast to his previous medical responsibilities, and the isolation here in the north. Medical check-ups were important, he said, and then carefully enquired whether she had any health problems. Maude hesitated, then seemed to crumble. She told Matt about the pain she suffered, that seemed to be getting worse over the last month, and now kept her awake at night.

'Perhaps I could have a look at you in your room,' he suggested quietly.

Twenty minutes later, Maude was dressed again, and joined Matt who waited in the parlour.

'It's cancer, isn't it Doctor?' she said as she sat down.

Matt hesitated.

'It's alright, you can be frank about it,' she added.

'Well, it certainly looks like it,' Matt said, 'but we need some special investigations to be sure, and unfortunately they can't be done up here.'

'What do you suggest, Doctor?' she asked in a quiet voice.

'Miss Maude, I think we should send you to Perth, where all the tests can be done. Only then can we assess the problem.'

After a long pause she said, 'And if I don't go?'

'Well, you can see yourself that things are getting worse, and you may suffer a lot more if nothing is done. Also, you must ask yourself whether it is fair on Ken and Betty, as they feel responsible for you.'

She bowed her head. 'I know you are right Doctor. Can I talk to Betty before I make any decisions?'

Thirty minutes later Jim and Matt were in the air, their next destination being Karrumbi station, some hundred miles on.

Betty and Maude had discussed the problem, and it was agreed that Maude should go south. Matt would make the medical arrangements, and radio Ken, so that he could arrange for her to go to Onslow to catch the plane. As they flew on, Matt thought about that lonely proud woman, who had effectively finished her life when the Germans killed her fiancé so many years before.

They arrived at Karrumbi at twelve thirty, and were met by George Baker in a dusty truck.

'Well,' he said after they had shaken hands all round. 'Just in time for lunch. The missus thought you'd be hungry after an early start, so we thought we'd eat first, then get you to look at the patients after.'

George's wife Barbara greeted them on the veranda. Karrumbi was an old station, built in the 1880s, and lovingly repaired over the years. It had a lush green garden with surrounding shady trees, and an aura of tranquillity.

George's father had come out from England as a child, back in the gold rush days with his father and mother. The old man had set up the holding, fighting off hostile natives, and struggling with the harsh environment. He had been a farmer in England, and decided that they should run cattle.

The old pioneer died, leaving George's father to carry on, and indeed, he made a great success of the property. By the time George grew up, Karrumbi was the biggest and best cattle station in the district.

'Welcome,' said Barbara, smiling as they stepped on to the veranda.

After introductions, Barbara led them into the house, and sat them in the sitting room, where a large wooden ceiling fan gently stirred the cool air. She served homemade lemonade ice-cold from a large jug.

'We have a few people for you Doctor,' she said putting the jug on the table, 'but no problems, so I thought you might like to eat first.' They finished their drinks, and followed her into the dining room. 'We're having a cold lunch, as I wasn't sure just when you would arrive.'

From the sideboard, she served cold chicken and sliced tinned ham, with lettuce, tomato, and cold boiled potato with mayonnaise.

After lunch, Barbara took Matt to an enclosed veranda at the back of the house, where a group of women and children sat waiting. First there were the children's inoculations, followed by two pregnant Aboriginal women for review, and another with tonsillitis. In no time, Matt had sorted them out, and was packing his bag. They made their farewells, and thanked Barbara for the excellent lunch, then drove out to the strip.

'One more stop,' said Jim as he ran through his pre-flight check. 'We should reach Mandarilla by two fifteen.'

Mandarilla was a big station, and owned by Thomas Hargrave, a Yorkshire farmer, who had inherited a good deal of money when his father died. He sold the family property near York, and with his wife Hetty and baby son, migrated to Australia, taking up Mandarilla a few years after the war, when the price was rock bottom. With sheer hard work, they had made a great success of the property, and his wool clip was top quality.

They touched down exactly at two fifteen, and were greeted by Tom. 'Well, I'm very glad to see you,' he beamed, first pumping Jim's hand then Matt's. He held the doors of the car open for them.

'It's been a long time since we've 'ad the doctor out here,' he said as they bumped along towards the homestead. 'Hetty will be right pleased to see you.'

Tom was a massive man, with a broad beefy face, and twinkling blue eyes. He spoke with a broad Yorkshire accent.

They drove into the sweeping drive, lined with poinciana trees up to the homestead, which was a sprawling bungalow with wide surrounding verandas, set in a lovely green garden. Big sprinklers were slowly turning on the lawn, and the air smelt of fresh mown grass as they climbed out of the car.

Hetty greeted them on the veranda, speaking with an accent as broad as her husband's. Her love of cooking was reflected in her ample proportions.

'Hetty love, this is Matt Harrison the doctor, and this is Jim, the pilot,' he introduced.

'I'm right glad to meet you both. We have been holding lunch for you, and I'm sure you'll be hungry by now.'

Matt opened his mouth to speak, but caught Jim's eye as he imperceptibly shook his head.

'Ah, that is very kind of you,' he managed, in a weak voice.

'We've got a few patients for you Doctor, but we'd best eat first.' Tom ushered them in to the house. 'You'll be wanting to freshen up first I'd imagine,' he said, and led the way to the bathroom.

'My God, I couldn't eat another thing,' Matt complained as he washed his hands.

'Well you'll just have to try hard, they won't take "no" for an answer,' Jim replied.

Back in the parlour, Hetty poured glasses of iced tea from a jug. 'Lunch will be ready in a moment,' she said, and left the men with their drinks. A smell of roasting meat filtered in to the room.

They sat down to the table, set for a main meal with the best silver. Hetty came in to the room with a tray, and set it down on the sideboard, then placed a large platter in front of Tom.

'Ah!' he said, his great face breaking into a smile. 'This be proper Yorkshire puddin,' he announced as he divided it into big wedges and put them on plates, passing them around. 'There's gravy in joog, 'elp yerselves.' His accent got broader.

Matt was relieved at the modest size of the plate of food, and made short work of it. He had never tasted real Yorkshire pudding before, and said so.

'Aye lad, yer don't taste it outside Yorkshire as a rule,' Tom replied. 'Will you have some more then?' Matt declined.

Hetty cleared the plates, and went to the kitchen, returning to Matt's astonishment, with a great leg of roast mutton, which she set down in front of Tom.

'Ah, that's more like it,' he said, his face lighting up again. 'Mind you, it should be a sirloin of beef – but the mutton's good.' He set to and vigorously honed the carving knife on a sharpening steel.

Tom sliced meat on to plates, to which Hetty subsequently added baked potato, cauliflower with white sauce and green peas. Another jug of gravy was passed around. Matt bravely tackled the pile of food on his plate, and almost ate it all, but finally his overloaded stomach rebelled, and he could not swallow another mouthful.

'Sup up lad,' Tom commented, noting that Matt had put down his knife and fork.

'You're not poorly then are ye?' he asked with a look of concern.

'No, well not really,' Matt struggled for words. 'I've been a bit off my food for a few days, a bit of a virus or something, I suppose.' He carefully avoided Jim's eye.

'It really is a marvellous lunch Hetty,' he said smiling at her.

'Ee we're not done yet,' she said, rising from her chair. 'There be apple pie and good cheddar cheese to come.'

Matt's heart sank and he glanced helplessly at Jim, who rose to the occasion as always.

'Hetty,' he said, looking at his watch, 'I don't think we have time for it, as we have a tight schedule, and the doctor still has to see your patients.'

Hetty looked crestfallen. 'Ah well, I'll do up a little parcel of it and you can eat on the way home. You'll be 'ungry by then I'm sure.'

An hour later, they were on the plane taxiing to the end of the strip with the parcel of apple pie sitting on the back seat.

Matt had attended to the patients' problems, which were all fairly straightforward and routine, and they had made their farewells to Tom and Hetty. They promised that they would come again, and next time would stay longer to enjoy their hospitality. Matt had his fingers crossed behind his back.

Levelled out at four thousand feet, Matt sat back and stretched, then closed his eyes and dozed for the rest of the flight.

Chapter 27

The next morning Matt was up bright and early, refreshed by a good night's sleep. He still felt overloaded with food from his travels, and settled for just a cup of coffee for breakfast.

Mary had met him at the airstrip as usual, and said that things had been quiet whilst he was away. He had politely declined her invitation to dine with her, saying without any detail that he had eaten a late lunch. As he walked through the door of the hospital she greeted him with a cheery smile.

'Good morning Matt, There's a message for you from Spinifex Plains. Lizzie wants you to call them up at midday.'

'Did she say what she wanted?' he asked.

'No details. Sorry.'

The morning clinic dragged on, and finally at ten to twelve the last patient left. It was time to call the station.

Matt turned on the transceiver and called up Spinifex Plains.

Immediately he was answered by Lizzie and felt a thrill of excitement at hearing her voice.

'Matt, we have started shearing, and dad wondered if you would like to come out for the weekend.'

'Sounds great Lizzie,' he answered. 'I'll be there by lunchtime. Thank your parents for the invitation.'

He signed off. Radio time was precious and open for all to hear; one didn't waste words.

Seventy miles away, Jack Morgan switched off his radio with a grim smile, and sat back in his chair, glass in hand. 'I'll get that bastard,' he muttered to himself.

Matt spent the rest of the day writing to arrange Maude's trip south. She would need an appointment with a physician, and no doubt hospital admission. With little knowledge of the system in Perth, he wrote to Peter at the Health Department, and explained the problem. No doubt he would advise him on how to proceed.

On his way to post the letter, he called by Mary's office. She had no problem with Matt's plan to go to Spinifex in the morning, as the hospital had been quiet for the last couple of weeks. 'Wouldn't mind getting out of town myself,' she said with a wry smile.

He posted his letter and collected a bundle of mail for Spinifex.

When Matt arrived at Spinifex, the station was a hive of activity. On the way to the homestead he saw thousands of sheep all herded in a paddock beside the shearing sheds, and on the other side of the shed, another paddock had large numbers of freshly shorn sheep. A couple of trucks and utilities were parked outside the living quarters, and smoke drifted out of the cookhouse chimney.

He pulled in to the homestead drive and parked the ute. As he climbed out, Lizzie appeared on the veranda. 'Hello Matt. Bring your bag inside.' As he stepped up on to the veranda she gave him a quick kiss on the cheek. 'I'm so glad you could come,' she said, leading him by the hand in to the house. She opened the door of the guest room and entered first. Matt followed with the bag, and put it on the floor.

'The place is very quiet, where is everyone?' he asked.

'Mum and Dad are up at the shearing shed. We are on our own.' She moved close to him and put her arms around his neck. The warmth and freshness of her body excited Matt and he held her close, feeling himself harden. She crushed herself to him and their lips met in a kiss that flared with passion. He drew her down on to the bed and their embrace became more urgent. His hands gently cupped her firm breasts as she whispered 'Yes, yes!' and slowly moved her body against his.

Outside, a car door banged! Lizzie quickly got to her feet. The moment was over!

Matt followed Lizzie out to the veranda, and was greeted by Bill. 'Ah there you are Matt. I saw you drive past the shearing shed, and thought I'd come in to make you welcome … But I see that Lizzie has already done that!' he said with a chuckle. Lizzie blushed.

'We were just about to drive up to the sheds to see how you're all getting on,' she said.

'Good,' Bill replied. 'Your mother needs a bit of help I think. The shearer's cook is playing up a treat, and is threatening to walk out. Joan is trying to pacify him.'

'Him?' said Matt.

'Yes, the cooks are mostly men. It's really hard work, and the shearers are a rough lot. Not many women would put up with the conditions, even though the pay is good. Not really our problem though. The shearing company employ their own cook, and he goes with the team from one station to the next. We just pay 'em.'

They climbed in to the front of Bill's ute with Lizzie between the two men. Matt was conscious of her warmth against his leg, and tried hard to concentrate on the shearer's problems.

The day was warm and still, and the shearing shed was bursting with activity. The pens were packed with sheep waiting to be shorn, and one by one they were herded up the ramp into the shed.

'Have a look at this,' Bill said to Matt as he leaned over the pen and parted the wool on the back of a sheep. Under the dirty surface covered with red dust he demonstrated four inches of rich creamy wool. 'That is best quality merino,' said Bill proudly. 'We'll have a good clip this year.'

Lizzie went off to find her mother, and Bill led Matt into the shed. The noise was terrific! The air was heavy and musty with the smell of sheep and human sweat.

Along one wall, six shearers were working. Each held a sheep between their legs, expertly manipulating them as they ran the power clippers over their bodies. The power supply came from a tractor parked outside, with a leather belt driving the shearing machinery. Overhead, wheels and shafts spun, with connecting rods down to the shears in each stand. The men were covered with sweat, and worked at a tremendous rate. Once finished, the sheep was pushed out a gateway leading to the back paddock, and the next sheep was shoved in. The fleece was rolled up and taken away by a rouseabout, then tossed in the air so it spread out and landed on a wooden bench. There the boss examined it and tossed it into the appropriate bin, where it was gathered and dumped in a wool bale under the mechanical press. When it contained enough wool, the presser, an enormous muscular young man, heaved on the lever, compacting the wool, and the bale was then sealed with metal bands. The bale was turned out of the press and with a black paintbrush and stencil, it was labelled, then carted away on a trolley to the storage area.

Matt watched in awe. Never in his life had he seen such an event, or a group of people working with such speed and team efficiency. Back outside he commented to Bill, who chuckled and said, 'They're a race apart, these blokes. They go from one station to another and work like blazes for weeks, then go back south with a fist full of money and relax for the summer. Not a bad life, eh?'

'If you can stand the pace.' Matt replied.

'Well, they've been going for two days now, and I reckon they'll be finished by next weekend. Then we'll all have a rest!' he laughed.

'Come on we'll see how Joan is getting on with the cook. They're a temperamental lot you know.'

They walked over to the cookhouse and opened the fly wire door. A rather dishevelled and wild-eyed man wearing a grubby white apron over his shorts and singlet stood clutching a meat cleaver, with Joan and Lizzie safely on the other side of the big table.

'What's the trouble cookie?' asked Bill in a voice as bland as he could muster.

'I've 'ad a gutful of those bastards!' he shouted, waving his weapon in the air. 'They're always pickin' on me and slingin' off at me cookin'.

Bill glanced at Joan and nodded at the door. She took Lizzie by the arm and led her outside. 'Alright then, tell us what happened to get you stirred up?' Bill asked.

The cook calmed down a bit and put the cleaver on the table. 'I'd rather talk to you on yer own Mister Corbett,' he said glancing at Matt. Matt took the hint and went out to join the women.

'What's happened?' Lizzie asked as Matt walked up to them.

'Nothing ... I hope,' he replied with a grin. 'They're having a nice chat now, without the meat axe.'

They walked over to the shade of the wool shed and waited for Bill. After a few minutes, Bill emerged and gave a 'thumbs up' as he walked over to them.

'Well?' Joan said. 'Did you find out what was wrong? He wouldn't talk to me.'

'Secret men's business.' Bill replied with a grin. 'I've just got to have a word with the team boss,' he disappeared in to the shed.

'Well, we might as well go and have some lunch,' said Joan and walked over to the ute. 'Bill can come back in the jeep.'

Over the lunch table Bill told them what had happened. 'Bit like the old story, "Who called the cook a bastard? – Who called the bastard a cook?" Don't worry, it'll all be blown over by now. As I said, they're a temperamental lot.'

They finished lunch, and Bill pushed back his chair and stood up.

'And now I have some news for you all,' he said with a serious expression. They all looked at him expectantly. 'I've got a new manager coming. He arrives next week from the south.'

'Dad, that's great news! But why the secrecy?'

'Well I didn't know for certain if he was goin' to take the job, and I got a letter from him this morning in the post. His name is Graham Martin and he's been working on a station out of Meekatharra for the past two years. He knows the job well. He's married with no kids and his wife Jill is coming on after he has got himself settled.'

'That's great news Bill,' Matt said. 'I think it's about time you slowed down a bit!'

Joan put her arm around him. 'Well then, we'll be able to go south for Christmas after all, won't we?' She gave him a kiss on the cheek.

'Let's go and have a look at the cottage,' Lizzie said. 'That's where the manager will live,' she explained for Matt's benefit.

'I think I'll just put me feet up for a while,' said Bill. 'You go with the kids,' Bill said to Joan as he headed for the bedroom. She looked after him with a worried expression.

As they walked towards the stand of gum trees that surrounded the little cottage Joan said, 'Matt I'm a bit worried about Bill, he's been overdoing it lately and he seems to be unusually tired.'

'Has he said anything about how he feels?' Matt asked.

'No, he's a stubborn old beast, and never complains, but I can tell he's not himself.'

'Well, a break down south is just what he needs I'd say,' he replied.

'Don't you get a holiday Matt?' Lizzie asked.

'Well, I don't really know, I suppose so,' he said with a puzzled expression. 'No one mentioned holidays,' he added. 'Anyhow, I wouldn't get one till I've been here for a year, and that's a while off.' He made a mental note to enquire about holidays next time he wrote to the Health Department.

The cottage was made of stone, with a corrugated iron roof and a wide veranda. Joan opened the front door and they followed her in. The air was cool and musty. 'Needs some fresh air in here,' Joan said going over to the window and opening it. The cottage was otherwise clean and would suit a couple well Matt thought.

'We will start in here on Monday,' Joan said to Lizzie. 'Should have it ship-shape in a couple of hours.'

Back at the homestead they found Bill on the veranda sprawled on a lounge, snoring. 'Let's go for a drive,' Lizzie said quietly, and led Matt out to the jeep.

September was almost over, and whilst the day was comfortably warm with a light breeze, summer was just round the corner, and soon the days would be blisteringly hot. They drove for half an hour towards the eastern border of the station where there was a creek that ran when it rained, and at other times was a series of pools where the birds congregated. Right now the countryside was bone dry, and a long plume of red dust followed them as the jeep bumped along the rough track.

About a mile away on the top of a stony rise, a man sat in his jeep and watched through binoculars as they drove past. He took a swig from the bottle of whisky beside him, and replaced the stopper, watching all the time.

They reached the trees that signified the creek, and pulled up in the shade beside a long pool with wading birds at its edge. It was like a scene from paradise, with still blue-green water surrounded by leafy gum trees, and behind, the low red stony hills stood clear against the azure cloudless sky.

'I love this country,' Lizzie said, leaning her head on Matt's shoulder, and gazing at the tranquil scene before them. Matt put his arms around her and tenderly kissed her. 'Lizzie, I didn't think I would ever love again after Penny was killed, but I was wrong. I love you deeply and I want to marry you.'

She looked into his eyes and whispered, 'Matt I love you too and I want to spend the rest of my life with you.' Her eyes drifted down to his lips and they joined in a long and passionate kiss.

BLAM!

The silence was shattered by a rifle shot! The couple jerked around to see Jack Morgan leering at them with a high-powered rifle in his hands, and smoke trailing from the barrel.

'What a charming little scene,' he sneered and moved closer, carefully watching them.

'Liz, get out and stand over there!' he pointed to a tree.

'You!' he said to Matt. 'Take out the keys and bring them here. I'm taking the girl with me and you are staying right here,' he said. 'They will find you in a day or so I guess, and by then we will be well away.'

'Jack don't be stupid! You will never get away with this!' Matt said walking slowly towards him. 'They will hunt you down and you will go to jail!'

'So what,' Jack sneered. 'At least I will have had the girl before you, yer pommie bastard.'

While he was speaking, Lizzie had edged towards the jeep, and made a sudden rush to the rifle in the leather scabbard!

CRASH! The blast of the high power rifle was deafening! Dirt kicked up beside Lizzie as she froze, her hand almost on the rifle!

'Move back you stupid bitch, or you'll get the next one!' She wilted in fear and moved back to the tree.

'Right! Throw the keys over to me,' Jack said, keeping the rifle trained on Matt. He threw them, and they bounced off a flat rock, and slid down into the shadow beside it. 'Now move back to the jeep and take out the rifle. Slowly!' Matt did as told.

'Now throw it in the water!'

Matt hesitated.

CRASH! The shot galvanised him in to action as the bullet kicked up sand near his feet. He threw the rifle into the pool.

'Now you start walking and don't look back!' Jack said, glancing towards Lizzie who was crouching beside the tree. Matt started to walk along the water's edge, and without taking his eyes off him, Jack stooped to pick up the keys.

AARRGH! With a cry of pain he sprang back, clasping his hand as blood oozed from it! A large brown snake had struck him from under the rock, and then slithered away to safety!

Matt turned at the cry and Lizzie leapt to her feet!

'Serves you right you rotten swine!' she screamed. Matt hurried back towards him.

'No you don't!' Jack shouted wild-eyed. 'Stay where you are!' He picked up the rifle that had fallen to the ground and shakily trained it in their direction.

Already Jack's hand looked bluish and had started to swell, and his eyes were mad with fear and hate. He tried to suck the poison from the back of his hand, and in he process, dropped the rifle again.

Matt slowly approached. 'Jack, you've been bitten by a very poisonous snake and unless you have help, you may well die, slowly and painfully. I am a doctor … I'll help you. It's my duty to help you.'

Jack looked at him, his bloody swollen hand still at his mouth, his face pale under his suntan and his eyes now wide with fear. His bravado left him and he sank to his knees.

'Help me! Please, Doc! I don't want to die,' he croaked.

'You deserve to, you lousy rat!' Lizzie said glaring down at him, having picked up his rifle.

'Quick Lizzie, we don't have a lot of time. Get the first aid box from the jeep, and the water bag.'

First he washed the blood and venom from Jack's hand, and then tightly bandaged the hand and forearm. 'Right. On your feet Jack.' They helped him in to the passenger seat of the jeep, with Lizzie driving and Matt squatting uncomfortably in the back.

They drove as fast as they could to the homestead, and while Matt transferred Jack to his ute, Lizzie quickly told her mother that Jack had snakebite, without explaining why he was there in the first place, and said she would go into town to help Matt. They drove off in a cloud of dust before her mother could properly grasp the situation.

Matt drove at high speed back to town, slowing only to cross over creek beds. Jack was sitting between them, slumped forwards. 'Christ my head aches,' he groaned. Matt threw him a quick glance.

'Give him a drink of water,' he said, and Lizzie leant forward and picked up the water bag from the floor.

As they pulled into the hospital Matt hooted the horn vigorously. Mary appeared at the office door, and Mibbin came running around the corner a second later. In no time they had Jack on a barouche, and wheeled him in to the empty ward.

'I'm goin' ter puke,' he groaned, and promptly vomited copiously on the floor. He lay back, ashen and sweaty. 'Doc, am I gunna be alright?' he asked in a quavering voice.

Matt was concentrating on putting an intravenous drip in to his other arm. 'Just lie quietly,' he replied. 'We're going to give you some antivenin, so just lie still.'

'Doc, I can't see properly, everything's double.' Matt glanced at Jack's face. His eyelids had started to droop.

Mary came in with an ampoule of snake antivenin from the fridge, and Matt drew it up in a syringe.

'Better have some adrenaline handy,' he said quietly to Mary. 'He may have a reaction.'

Matt turned the intravenous drip up so that it ran fluid into his vein, and then slowly injected the antivenin into the rubber tubing.

Mary rolled in the oxygen cylinder, and put a mask over his face as they watched for reactions to the anti-serum.

An hour later, Jack seemed to be breathing comfortably, and his condition had not deteriorated.

'I think we are winning,' Matt said quietly, checking his pulse and blood pressure. 'Time for a cuppa,' he looked up at Mary with a grin. They left Jack resting with Susan sitting beside him, and went in to the tearoom.

Lizzie, who had carefully stayed out of the way whilst the action was taking place, sat down heavily at the table. 'What happens now?' she asked Matt, her question having a deeper meaning. Matt glanced at Mary who was pouring cups of tea.

'I think he will make a good recovery now, and I don't think we will have any more trouble,' he said meaningfully to Lizzie. They drank their tea in silence.

Mary broke the silence. 'How did it happen?' she asked over her teacup.

'Oh Jack was over seeing Bill Corbett about shearing,' Matt lied, 'and he dropped his car keys in the wrong spot. A big brown snake took a dislike to him.'

'Not hard to imagine,' muttered Lizzie. Mary gave her a quizzical look.

As they were drinking their tea a vehicle pulled up and a door banged. A moment later Bill's face appeared at the door. 'Got a spare cup for me?' he said with a grin.

He sat down at the table, and was about to speak when he caught Lizzie's eye. She gave a slight shake of her head.

'So, how's the patient?' he asked.

'He should be OK, but will need careful watching for a few days,' Matt replied.

'Well young lady, I'd best be taking you home,' he said to Lizzie as he put down his empty cup. 'You can tell me all about it on the way,' he said meaningfully. 'Thanks for the tea Matron. G'bye Matt, sorry you had the weekend mucked up.'

'Thanks Bill, all part of the job,' Matt replied with a grin. 'Goodbye Lizzie, see you soon. It was a great day really.'

She smiled at him. 'Yes Matt, it was a great day.' She turned and walked out as her father looked from one to the other.

Mary stood next to Matt as they watched them drive off. 'Anything else I should know?' she asked him with a raised eyebrow.

'No, not really,' he replied with an innocent smile. 'Let's have a look at the patient.'

Four days later, Jack was out of bed, and though weak and shaky, he was ready to go home. His uncle had retrieved his jeep and was driving in to collect him.

Matt led him into his office, and shut the door. He walked over to his desk. 'Sit down, Jack,' he said, indicating the chair beside him. He pushed a typewritten paper across to Jack. 'Read this and sign it,' he said.

'What is it?' Jack asked, all traces of animosity now long gone.

'It is a statement of everything that happened, out there at the creek.'

'What are you goin' ter do with it?' he asked hesitantly.

'Nothing, providing you promise never to go near Lizzie again, or threaten her or me. I've thought it over Jack, and decided not to go to the police, who most certainly would have arrested you, and no doubt you'd go to jail. I thought I'd give you a chance to make good. But just remember. If you ever cause trouble again, I'll hand this to the police.'

Jack read the document, and signed it with Matt's pen.

'Doc, I don't know what to say. You saved my life, and I will always be grateful. I promise I'll never trouble you or Lizzie again.'

Matt took the paper, and put it in a drawer, then turned the key. He stood up and put the key in his pocket.

'Your uncle should be here soon, you can wait for him here on the veranda.' Matt pointed to the bench. 'You should rest up for a few more days, and come in to see me if you have any problems.'

Without another word, Matt turned and walked into the hospital.

Chapter 28

Things went quietly for the next couple of weeks. Lizzie had given her parents a watered down version of their encounter with Jack, and had managed to drive out to the pool and retrieve the rifle after a search. A quick clean and oiling had restored it to its functional state.

Of Jack himself, they heard nothing until several weeks later when he called in on the radio to say that he had found his uncle dead in bed, having presumably had a heart attack.

Constable Peter Harris had in his official capacity driven out to the station and brought the body in to the mortuary. As there was no background of medical problems, he told Matt that there must be a coroner's inquest into the death.

Accordingly Matt did a swift and efficient autopsy in the presence of the law, and demonstrated to Peter the blocked coronary artery, confirming that he did indeed die of natural causes. With the paperwork summarily dealt with, Jack's Uncle Bruce was quietly buried in the Roebourne cemetery.

A few weeks later, Matt was told by Mike that Jack had asked Dalgety's to sell the station and that he was leaving for Queensland as soon as a caretaker could be obtained.

'Good riddance,' he thought.

By late October, the days were becoming hot and the flies were noticeably more active. The perfect weather of winter was over.

Matt had received a message from Joan, asking if he would come out to Spinifex for the weekend, and look at a patient while he was there. He radioed back and accepted, speaking to Joan on the air. 'Yes Lizzie's well,' she said in reply to his question, and with no further information as to her request.

He set out early on the Saturday morning, to beat the heat, having included his doctor's bag with his overnight gear. The morning was clear and cool, and his mind wandered as he drove along the dusty gravel road.

Lizzie had agreed not to say anything to her about their plan to marry, as Matt had no answer for the obvious questions that would follow, such as, 'Where would they live?', 'What were his future plans?' He had lain awake at night pondering on this, and had reached some conclusions that needed exploring. And that needed time.

He realised that whilst Lizzie would go to England with him if he asked her to, she would never be happy so far away from the red earth of the North West. This was her country, and this is where they must live.

After some deliberating, he had written to the Secretary of Royal Australasian College of Surgeons in Melbourne to enquire if he was eligible to sit for their final examination in Surgery. He had given them details of his training and a copy of the letter that confirmed he had passed the primary examination of the English Royal College. Also, he sent a copy of his old Chief's letter. He had typed copies certified by Mike, who was a Justice of the Peace. He had told the secretary that he came to Australia to increase his experience by working in the remote areas before returning to England, but was now hoping to make Australia his home. (He thought that added the right tone to his enquiry.) At least with an Australian Fellowship all his options would be open. Two weeks had passed since posting the letter, and he was becoming a little anxious. Without this first step, he could take his plans no further.

He pulled into Spinifex, and parked under a tree. As he walked towards the homestead, Lizzie appeared on the veranda, looking fresh and delicious.

'Just in time for coffee,' she said after giving him a welcome kiss. 'Mum and Dad are in the cool house.' She led him by the hand.

Bill was lying on a couch, and greeted Matt cheerily.

'Will you have a cup of coffee?' Joan asked, picking up a cup from the tray.

'Yes, thank you,' he took the cup and settled in a chair.

'Well. Business first. What 's the problem?' he said with a grin.

Joan shot him a quick look. 'Oh nothing much, I'll tell you later.'

Matt caught the expression and changed the subject. 'Lovely drive out this morning,' he said.

Bill seemed to have missed the exchange, and they chatted on, while he quietly dozed. Joan got up and picked up the tray. 'Let's leave Bill to rest,' she said meaningfully, and walked out. The others followed. When they were out of earshot, Joan put the tray down and turned to Matt.

'I'm so worried about Bill,' she said. 'Lately he has been very tired, and complains of chest pain which he says is indigestion, but I think it is more than that. Matt, would you have a chat with him? Now would be a good time, while he is lying down.'

'Right,' Matt replied. 'I'll get my bag.' He walked back into the cool house and sat down beside Bill, who opened one eye.

'Sick of the female company already?' he asked with a grin.

'Time for man talk,' he replied. 'A little bird told me that you haven't been feeling too well lately.'

'Nonsense, I'm just fine,' he replied. 'Can't think what got into the little bird's mind.'

'Bill, are we going to do this the hard way? Joan is worried about you and asked me to check you over.'

'Aw well, all right,' he capitulated. 'I've been having a bit of chest pain. Nothing to speak of, mind you. I shouldn't have mentioned it.'

Matt quizzed him on his symptoms, and then suggested they go to the bedroom where he could give him the once over. When he had finished, Matt had a chat with Bill then left him dressing. He went outside where he found Joan in the garden with Lizzie, picking roses.

'Lovely aren't they? They grow well in the winter here, but this will be the last of them.' She spoke quickly, with tension in her voice as if dreading Matt's diagnosis.

'Joan, let's all sit down on the veranda. Bill will be out in a minute,' Matt said, gently taking her arm. 'The news isn't too bad.'

As they sat down, Bill joined them with a cheery smile. 'Well,' he said. 'Why all the long faces?'

He sat down, and they all looked at Matt.

'I've told Bill that he has a heart problem,' he said, going straight to the point. 'His blood pressure is raised, and his heart is enlarged. The pain he has been getting is called angina, and comes on when the heart muscle is not getting sufficient blood supply. It's nature's warning, and if ignored, could lead to serious problems.' He paused, noting the anxiety on Joan's face.

'I knew something was wrong,' she said. 'What should we do?'

'Joan, now that the new manager has settled in to the place, there's nothing to stop you going south, and that's what I want you to do. I want Bill to see a specialist as soon as possible.'

'I guess we can go at any time, but how do we get to a specialist?' Joan asked, her face drawn with concern.

'Don't worry about that, I'll have all the arrangements made by the time you are ready.' He smiled at Joan and patted her on the arm. 'Don't worry, I'm sure he will be alright.'

Graham Martin and his wife Jill were invited for lunch to meet Matt, and over the meal, Joan told them the news. Graham was about forty-five Matt guessed, and was tall, suntanned and strong, with a roughly handsome face and a pleasant manner.

'Well Bill,' Graham said. 'You can be sure everything will run smoothly here while you're down south. Jill and I feel quite at home here now. Will you take Lizzie with you, or would you like her to stay here with us?'

Since the Martin's arrival, Lizzie had got on well with Jill, and they were now good friends.

'Thanks Graham,' Lizzie answered for herself. 'I think I'd like to be there with Dad.'

'Right,' said Bill. 'That's decided. I'll book our flight to Perth for next week. Might as well get on with it.'

He stood up. 'Graham, we have a few things to talk over, let's go into the office.'

After breakfast next morning, Matt and Lizzie drove to the swimming pool. It was a lovely warm morning and perfect for a swim. On the way, Matt told Lizzie that he had written to the College of Surgeons in Melbourne to ask if he was eligible to sit for the Australian Fellowship, and how this would make future decisions easy.

'But won't you have to study for this exam?' she asked.

'Yes indeed!' he replied. 'Harder than I ever have before. Such a lot depends on passing it.'

They pulled up in the shade beside the pool. Both had their swim wear on and took their towels to the water's edge. Lizzie took off her shirt and sandals. She wore a fetching white one-piece bathing costume and looked terrific. They swam in the deep clear pool, then lay on their towels in the sun.

'What if the College won't let you do their exam?' she asked.

'I can't see why they wouldn't,' Matt replied, 'but they might need more information, or even an interview. Who knows? I guess they will get back to me.'

Matt drove back to town early the next day, as he had to organise things for Bill. He wrote to Peter McLean at the Health Department about Bill, asking him to arrange a consultation with a physician, and explained the problem. As Bill was going south that week, there would be no time for a letter to get back, so he asked for telegraph confirmation of his request. He walked to the post office and posted the letter so that it would catch the morning flight south.

Two days later he received a telegram from Peter saying that everything was arranged, and for Bill to ring him as soon as he arrived. He radioed the message to the station on the morning schedule, and spoke briefly to Joan. They would be coming into town early on Thursday to catch the flight south. Matt told her that he would meet them, and arrange for their ute to be garaged until they returned.

That afternoon he received a reply from the College of Surgeons. Yes, he could sit for the final examination in March! The letter enclosed a bill for the considerable examination fee!

The next morning, Matt picked up Mary, and they drove slowly to the airstrip while he told her of his intention to do the exam in March. 'Not heading back to Mother England then?' she asked with a knowing smile.

'Not for a while,' he answered.

Johnnie was waiting by the tin shed when they arrived, and a few minutes later Bill's ute pulled up in a cloud of red dust. Matt helped unload their cases, then took Lizzie aside and told her the good news.

'Oh Matt, that's wonderful!' She threw her arms around his neck and kissed him. Out of the corner of his eye he saw Bill watching them, and felt that some explanation was required. He turned to Bill and Joan, and told them that he had applied to sit for the Royal Australasian College of Surgeons final exam, and that he had just heard that he was eligible, and could sit next March.

Bill shook his hand vigorously. 'Well that's great news, I guess that means we will have you round for a while longer!'

'It will mean a lot of study between now and then I'm afraid,' Matt said with a grin. As he spoke, they heard the sound of the approaching plane, and all turned to watch.

Lizzie drew Matt aside. 'Do you think we should tell them about us?'

'No Lizzie, right now Bill has enough worries, and I think we should wait till he comes back. You could have a quiet word in confidence to your mother though, to sort of soften her up. It's really my job to ask your dad for your hand you know,' he said with a grin.

The silver DC3 had made a graceful landing, and was taxiing towards them. The thunder of its engines prevented any further discussion. She nodded and kissed him again.

Johnnie wheeled the steps up to the plane as soon as the engines died, and the door was opened.

'As soon as you get to the hotel, ring the Health Department,' Matt reminded Bill. 'Everything has been arranged for you.'

They shook hands, and Joan stepped forward and kissed Matt on the cheek. 'Thank you so much,' she said.

'Don't worry, he will be in safe hands,' Matt replied.

'I think they have already guessed about us,' Lizzie whispered in Matt's ear as she gave him a final hug.

'Goodbye darling, write and tell me the news,' he said, his arms around her. She kissed him quickly then turned and followed her parents to the plane.

With November came the heat, and all Matt's spare time was spent sitting under the ceiling fan in his house with a pile of textbooks and a jug of ice water. Two weeks had passed since the Corbetts had gone south, and he had received only a brief letter from Lizzie telling him that Bill was in a private hospital having tests, and was doing well. The specialist had said that his heart was not seriously damaged; however he would have to take life more quietly from now on. The next letter told him that Bill was out of hospital, and feeling well. They would be back at Spinifex in December.

Matt had written to Lizzie a couple of times, telling her what little news there was, and that he had his nose in his text books in his spare time. He had dutifully written short but regular letters to his parents since leaving England, and an occasional one to his old friend Tom, telling him about life in the remote outback, and how happy he was.

Now with Christmas approaching, it seemed a good time to tell them all of his future plans – as far as he could. He wrote to his old mentor Sir James Watson, and gave him a summary of his surgical adventures, and of his new plans to sit the Australian exam, pointing out that if he succeeded in passing, it would stand him in good stead when he returned to complete the English exam. (He was careful to keep his options open!)

He told Tom of his new love and his plans to practise in Australia, and looked forward to bringing Lizzie to England to meet his family and friends.

He told his parents about Lizzie, and said that he wanted to marry her and settle in Australia, but would certainly come home to visit, bringing his new bride.

That night he dreamt of little Chloe, but it was a happy dream, and when he woke before dawn, he lay thinking about his lost love ones. Perhaps they had visited him in his dreams. In his sleepy state he felt that Penny and Chloe would approve of Lizzie.

Chapter 29

It was a hot Thursday afternoon in early December, and the flies were particularly offensive as Matt stood in the shade of the tin shed waiting for the plane to arrive from the south.

The Corbett's ute had already been deposited at the strip by the local garage man, and with all windows wound up, would be like a furnace inside. Matt walked over and opened the door, letting out a blast of hot air, then wound the windows down. The flies droned around his head, and crawled on his face.

Johnny was waiting with him, and they exchanged a few words. He was not good on conversation, and soon they lapsed into silence, enduring the heat. The plane was late.

Lizzie had told Matt that Bill seemed well enough now, but in accordance with orders, was taking life quietly. They had agreed that they would announce their engagement at Christmas, and decide on a wedding date when he had completed his task in March. She said that she had quietly told her mother of their intentions, and although delighted, had promised not to say a word to her husband.

The drone of engines snapped Matt back, and they watched the DC3 circle and gracefully touch down, chased by a plume of red dust as it ran along the strip. It turned and taxied towards them in a crescendo of noise before the engines died. Johnnie bustled out with the steps.

Joan was first to emerge, and gave Matt a cheery wave. Bill followed, with Lizzie behind him. Matt's pulse quickened as he watched her descent the steps. She looked more beautiful than he remembered.

'Welcome back,' Matt said, shaking Bill's hand. He gave Joan a peck on he cheek, then embraced Lizzie.

'Warmed up a bit,' said Bill, spitting out a fly. 'Let's get the gear on the ute,' he said as Johnnie wheeled the bags over on his trolley. With the bags loaded on the ute, Bill suggested that they met at the pub for a cold drink before they set out to Spinifex, and led the way, setting up a cloud of red dust.

Lizzie climbed beside Matt, and they kissed passionately.

'Too damn hot for this,' Lizzie said, breaking away. 'Let's go!'

They sat in the shade of the beer garden, and sipped their drinks.

'Well!' said Matt over the top of his frosted glass of icy cold beer. 'Tell me all about it.'

'Ah!' said Bill, and reached into his coat pocket, producing a manila envelope. 'I nearly forgot. The specialist gave me this for you,' he passed it over.

'I'll read it later. Don't want to put a dampener on the occasion,' he replied with a grin.

'Now Matt,' said Joan. 'We would like you to come out to Spinifex for Christmas and stay with us for a couple of days, and have a bit of a break from work. Stay right through to New Year if you can.'

'Sounds great Joan, but I must be available at the hospital, so perhaps I could stay for Christmas, then come back again for New Year?'

'Yes,' said Lizzie warming up to the idea. 'We could have a New Year's Eve party!' They sat chatting for the next hour, then the Corbetts set out for the station while it was still light.

Matt drove back to his house opened a tin of baked beans for his supper. He sat at the kitchen table and opened letter. The report on Bill was favourable, and included his ECG and X-ray reports. His blood pressure had responded well to medication, and he now only needed periodic reviews.

As he sat eating his beans and buttered toast, it suddenly occurred to him that he needed to buy a ring for Lizzie! But where in this God forsaken place would he find one? The nearest jeweller would be down in Perth, more than a thousand miles away! He had an idea. He quickly finished his meal and drove round to Mike's house, next door to Dalgety's store. Mike and Anne were sitting on the veranda relaxing in the cool of the evening. Over the months, they had become good friends.

Mike greeted him, and offered a chair, while Anne went inside and returned with a jug of lemonade and glasses on a tray. Matt took them into his confidence about Lizzie, and explained his problem. How on earth could he get a ring in time for Christmas?

'You've come to the right man,' Mike said. 'Dalgety's has a finger in lots of pies, and we happen to have contacts in the jewellery world. I can get some sample rings sent up in good time, but we need to know what type of ring, and what finger size, and most importantly, what price range.'

Matt opened his mouth and shut it. 'Well, I have no idea what size for a start, any suggestions Anne?'

'I don't know really, but I would think her hands are about the same as mine in size. Anyhow it can be altered easily and quickly if it is the wrong size, so why don't we measure one of my rings?'

'Right. Next question. What type of ring? I think a single diamond would be right,' said Matt.

'That would be perfect! And in a white gold setting,' Anne added. 'Especially if its big!'

'Big diamond means big money,' said Mike. 'You had better decide what you could afford.'

'Well, I guess I could manage a thousand pounds, a bit more perhaps.'

'Right. I'll get a wire off to Perth first thing in the morning, and ask for a selection of rings to be sent up by registered mail as soon as possible, using Anne's finger measurement.'

'Mike, that's splendid. Thank you very much.'

They sat and talked for an hour, and Matt told them of his plan to settle in Australia, and his intention to sit the exam in March. Everything depended on his passing the exam.

A week later, Matt had a call from Mike. 'I've got something to show you,' he said. 'Can you come to the store?'

Half an hour later, Matt was sitting in Mike's office, looking at the most astonishing collection of diamond rings glittering on a piece of black velvet.

'Not a bad selection eh?' Mike said, picking up one and examining it closely. 'They are all in your price range, and about three quarters to one carat in size.'

Matt chose a brilliant solitaire white diamond set in white gold, and hesitantly asked the price.

'You get it at wholesale rate, and …' he consulted the accompanying paperwork, 'that will cost you eight-hundred-and--fifty pounds, my friend.'

Matt took out his chequebook to write a cheque. He looked up with a grin. 'No going back now, is there.'

'Not after I get the cheque!' Mike replied. He wrote a receipt, and put the ring in a little box. 'Do you want it gift wrapped?' he asked with a grin.

'No a paper bag will do fine.'

Mike looked at his watch. 'Five thirty, time to knock off. Come and have a beer, and show it to Anne.'

Mike locked the box of rings in the safe, and then they went in next-door and found Anne in the kitchen. 'Matt has something to show you, darling,' he said getting a bottle of beer out of the refrigerator.

They sat round the kitchen table each with a glass of beer, and Matt showed Anne his prize.

'Oh! It's lovely Matt,' said Anne admiring the glittering diamond. 'May I try it?'

Matt passed it over, and she slipped it onto her ring finger, holding her hand out to admire it.

'It really is just beautiful. She's a lucky girl.'

'We're not there yet,' said Matt. 'I have to ask Bill for her hand, and he might say no!' They all laughed.

The time up to Christmas seemed to fly by. Matt had spent every spare moment at his books, and whilst there had been no medical dramas, his workdays were busy with clinics.

On his last visit to Onslow, he had done some shopping at Jimmy Chung's Chinese store. Jimmy was also the local baker, and part of Matt's duty was as Health Officer, to follow up any complaints about food shops.

Over the past six months he had visited the bakery on two occasions following complaints of cockroaches in Jimmy's bread. On the second occasion, Matt had ordered the bakery to be closed, pending a thorough clean-up. On his next visit to Onslow the bakery was just as dirty as ever, but as there were even more complaints about the absence of bread in the town, Matt told Jimmy he could re-open, but to clean up the bakery. This was received with Jimmy's inscrutable smile; nods and promises, but nothing changed.

Jimmy greeted Matt warmly as he entered. 'Hello Doctor, you

come to close my bakery?' he asked with his usual smile.

'No Jimmy, I want to buy some Christmas presents.' Jimmy's face lit up.

After browsing through the masses of trinkets, he found a jade bracelet for Joan, and some pearl earrings for Lizzie, which Jimmy produced from under the counter. 'Velly special! Real north-west pearls,' he told Matt. A small lacquered doll in traditional Chinese clothes caught his eye, and he bought it for Mary. When he returned to the hospital Jim was waiting to fly him home, and on the way to the aerodrome he told him about his purchases.

'How were the prices?' he asked.

'Bit steep I thought,' Matt replied.

'Didn't you haggle?'

'No, should I have?'

'You ruined his day,' Jim replied with a grin.

Christmas fell on a Friday that year, and with three days to go, the heat had really set in.

The hospital had been quiet, and Mary had just left for the south on her annual leave. A replacement Matron named Margot was in charge. She was a middle-aged, pleasant, capable woman, who did relieving work in the outback hospitals, and had been in charge of one some years back. She had given up work when she married, but her husband had died of cancer, and she went back to part time work. Mary had given Matt a briefing before she left.

'How are you settling in?' Matt asked Margot as they sat having morning tea.

'Very well, thanks Matt, I can cope with the heat, but one never really get used to the bush flies,' she said, brushing one from her face.

They sat at a laminex topped table with chrome legs, and chairs to match, in a shady corner of the hospital veranda. Matt leaned his bare knee against the metal leg of the table. It felt hot. He glanced at the thermometer on the wall. It registered 110°F.

'Margot, I've been invited out to Spinifex Plains for Christmas. I'll check in on the radio schedule each day, and it's only an hour or so to drive back if I'm needed,' Matt told her.

'No problem Matt. You go and enjoy yourself. I'm happy to hold the fort.'

They chatted over their cup of tea, and Margot told Matt some of her experiences as a bush nurse.

On Christmas Eve as Matt drove out to Spinifex, he knew that Margot could cope in his absence. These women were a race apart he thought; the old matron in Onslow who had battled on for years; Mary, in her quiet capable way. These women had guts.

It was late afternoon when he arrived, hot and dusty. Lizzie greeted him as he pulled up, and kissed his sweaty cheek. He unpacked his bag and then headed for the shower room under the tank to freshen up. The deluge of cold water revived him immediately, and his thoughts wandered as he rubbed himself dry. Christmas Eve seemed a good time to take Bill aside and ask for Lizzie's hand. He wouldn't refuse, surely. Well maybe he would! He might want her to marry a wealthy pastoralist and take over the station in time. Now that was a real possibility!

He was deep in thought as he dressed in his long whites and a blue cotton shirt. Maybe it wasn't going to be as easy as he thought.

He walked out in to the veranda and found Bill and Joan sitting in deck chairs on the lawn under a poinciana tree that was in full bloom. Nearby a sprinkler made lazy circles and set up a mist of water that cooled the air.

'Ah! Welcome!' said Bill rising from his chair, hand extended. They shook hands.

'You look nice and cool Matt,' said Joan with a smile. 'Do sit down.' She indicated a chair.

'You're looking well, Bill,' said Matt with a clinical glance.

'I feel a hundred per cent thanks,' he replied. 'And thank you for your good organisation down south. Did you read the report?'

'I surely did. They said you would live to be a hundred,' Matt replied with a grin. Lizzie came out carrying a tray of drinks and canapés, and set them on the table.

'Well then, let's get the Christmas Spirit started!' said Bill, standing to pour drinks. 'It looks like champagne is the order of the day. French at that!' he said with surprise in his voice.

'Matt brought it with him,' Lizzie said. 'For the occasion,' she added meaningfully. They raised their glasses. 'Merry Christmas!' said Bill, and had a sip. Joan passed the canapés, and they nibbled in silence for a moment, expectantly.

'Well,' said Matt, clearing his throat. He paused.

'Well Matt?' Joan repeated.

'Nice champagne,' he said, taking a sip and grinning.

Matt turned to Bill. 'Bill, you remember I told you that I'm planning to sit the Australian exams in surgery next March?'

'Certainly do,' Bill replied.

'Well assuming I pass – and I think I've got a good chance – I plan to come back here for a while, then try to get a surgical job in the south, to build up my surgical experience.'

'And then?' Bill asked.

'Well that depends.'

'What does it depend on?' Bill asked.

'Well, here goes,' Matt thought, plucking up his courage. 'It depends on you really. You see, I am in love with Lizzie, and I ask for your permission to marry her.'

There was a long pause, with only sound of the insects in the gathering dusk. Bill raised his eyebrows and leaned forwards to Lizzie. 'Do you want to marry him?' He asked with a gentle voice.

'Oh yes, yes, Daddy! I love him.' She choked with tears, and put her hands to her face. Bill looked at Joan, who smiled and gave a little nod.

'Well then, you'd better get on with it,' he said rising from his chair with a broad grin.

They all stood up. Lizzie hugged and kissed Matt, who was shaking Bill's hand while Joan threw her arms around all of them in the huddle.

'Welcome to the family!' Bill said pumping Matt's hand. 'Everyone, raise your glasses!'

'To Matt and Lizzie! May they be as happy as we have been.' He slipped his arm around Joan's waist and kissed her tenderly. They all sat down again, looking at each other.

'Well, I think this is next,' said Matt, as he stood up and produced a little box from his pocket.

He knelt on one knee on the grass in front of Lizzie, and said quietly, 'Lizzie, will you marry me?'

Their faces were close, and her eyes sparkled with tears of joy.

'Yes darling, I will.'

Matt took the ring out of the box and slipped it on her finger. They kissed tenderly, as Joan and Bill clapped loudly. Lizzie held out her hand, admiring the sparkling diamond. 'It's lovely!' she said in an awed tone.

'Yes it is,' Joan agreed. 'It's very beautiful!'

'Well Matt, you must have felt confident I would say "yes" to have the ring already with you!' Bill said with a twinkle in his eyes.

'I was a Boy Scout when I was a lad, Bill,' Matt replied with a grin. 'Their motto was "Be Prepared!" – and I was.' He gave a scout salute and they all laughed.

Joan had prepared a full Christmas dinner, and they sat down to roast turkey and all the trimmings, whilst Bill poured champagne, and proposed toasts.

'Well I'm glad we organised a party for New Year's Eve. What a great occasion to announce the engagement!' Bill said, raising his glass to them.

Matt observed with mild concern that he was becoming flushed in the face with a combination of excitement, food and champagne, but said nothing, his role as medical adviser conflicting somewhat with his new status of prospective son-in-law.

After dinner they returned to the cool of the garden, now bathed in moonlight. 'Tell us about the exams Matt,' asked Joan.

'Well, that puts a dampener on the evening,' said Matt with a wry smile. 'The College of Surgeons are holding Examinations for the second part of their surgical qualification, and a lot of doctors will be sitting for it.

'I passed the first part in London some time back, and have been accepted as eligible to sit the Australian exam. If I pass it, I can use the letters "FRACS" after my name, indicating that I am a qualified Surgeon. At home it would be "FRCS", but now the qualifications are of equal status, and "FRACS" is as good in the UK as it is in Australia.

'All I have to do is pass it,' he added, with a twinge of anxiety in his voice.

'Then I guess we should be looking at a wedding in May, what do you think, Lizzie?' said Joan.

'And if I fail?' said Matt, now feeling depressed about it all.

'Well then, the wedding goes ahead as planned, and you knuckle down to more study my boy,' said Bill already assuming a parental role.

They talked well into the evening, and later, lying in bed in that twilight zone before sleep, Matt pondered on how for the second time in his short life, he had proposed marriage. He wondered if

Penny and little Chloe were watching from somewhere. He drifted off to sleep certain that they approved of his Lizzie.

Christmas day was hot. They had an early breakfast of tea and toast on the veranda, and exchanged presents. Matt had carefully wrapped his in bright paper he had bought from the Chinese shop, and ceremoniously handed them around.

Lizzie tore her parcel open like a child, and was thrilled with the pearl earrings, which she put on immediately.

Joan opened her parcel carefully and admired the beautiful deep green of the jade bracelet.

For Bill, Matt had found a very smart stockman's knife with a leather pouch in Dalgety's store, having noticed that his present one had the tip broken off the blade. Bill was delighted.

Prompted by Lizzie, Matt opened his presents. A plaited leather belt in a wooden box bearing the label 'Genuine cowhide stockman's belt'. The card read 'from Bill'.

'Thanks Bill – just what I needed.'

As he opened the next parcel, Joan said apprehensively, 'I hope they fit.' He opened the box and found a pair of rope-soled blue canvas espadrilles.

'That's exactly my size,' Matt exclaimed. 'Just the right thing for evenings on the lawn!' They all laughed.

The last was a small parcel, beautifully wrapped, with a card, 'Happy Christmas my darling. From Lizzie.' He opened it carefully, and found a black cloth purse inside the little box. Inside was a silver Ronson cigarette lighter. He leaned over and kissed Lizzie on the cheek.

'Now we are engaged, I'm not sure that it was a good idea. I think you should give up smoking Matt.'

'My God, it's started already,' Bill muttered, rolling his eyes.

'Yes, dear,' Matt said with a solemn expression. They laughed.

'Well,' said Bill getting up from the table, 'just because it's Christmas it doesn't mean there isn't work to do. I have to drive out and check a windmill. Would you like to come along Matt?'

Matt looked up, surprised. 'Of course Bill,' he replied.

Lizzie opened her mouth to speak, and caught her mother's eye, and changed her mind.

'Good idea,' Joan said. 'You two go off and talk men's business,' she said with a wide smile, laying her hand on Lizzie's.

They drove in silence across parched dusty paddocks, in the blazing heat. Not a living creature in sight, apart from an eagle hovering high above watching the ground for prey.

They came to a couple of stunted trees in the middle of a vast flat area, empty except for spinifex bushes, and 'willy-willys' of whirling red dust, sucked up in the heat. The emptiness stretched to the horizon. There they found the windmill; stationary in the still air, the trough beside it empty. Next to the trough lay a dead sheep.

Bill stopped the jeep in a swirl of dust. 'Let's get rid of that first,' he said, pointing to the fly-covered carcass. He turned the jeep and backed up to the dead animal, then climbed out and took a length of rope from the vehicle.

'Tie this on to the tow bar,' he said, handing one end of the rope to Matt. He walked over to the stinking carcass and tied the other end to its legs. The flies swarmed off the beast.

They towed the carcass a few hundred yards away from the trough, where Bill untied the rope. 'Crows'll clean it up.'

They drove back to the mill and stopped beside the tree that afforded meagre shade.

'Better have a drink,' said Bill, passing the water bag. 'You soon dry out in this heat.' Matt took a long draught of the water that was refreshingly cool and tasted of canvas.

Bill drank from the bag then they walked over to the trough, squinting in the heat and glare.

The mill pumped underground water from the well, which surprisingly was only about twenty feet deep. 'Plenty of water down there,' Bill said, peering down the well. 'Though you'd never guess it when you look around here.' He checked the pump, and the wind vanes, which seemed in order, then followed the pipe along to the trough. The float that controlled the valve had jammed in the off position, which had stopped the flow of water. In ten minutes Bill had it lubricated and working again. 'She'll fill up once the breeze blows,' he said wiping his greasy hands on a piece of rag.

They climbed in the jeep, and headed for home. In the intense heat and still air, Matt was dripping with sweat, but once the vehicle moved, the breeze cooled him down. 'Well Matt,' Bill threw him a sideways glance. 'What do you think of being part of the family?'

Matt was silent for a moment, not sure quite what Bill meant. 'Well, I'm not sure that you can rely on me to mend pumps,' he replied flippantly. Bill grinned widely.

'You remember when we first met in Perth,' he went on. 'You seemed so lost in the world. We talked about our different lives; how yours had come to a tragic crossroads, and mine, well, as an ageing pastoralist, with no son to take over my lifetime dream. It seems that destiny meant us to meet, and that your path was directed to our tiny town. D'you believe in destiny?' he shot a glance at Matt.

'If you had asked me that question then, the answer would have definitely been "no" but now, I guess I would have to agree with you.'

Since that time in the hotel in Perth, Matt and Bill had not really spoken a lot, and now they seemed to have re-connected.

'What are your plans Matt,' Bill asked, concentrating on the rough bush track. 'I mean, after you and Lizzie are married. Do you want to take her back to England?'

Suddenly Matt realised what this was all about. Bill was to lose his only child to an English doctor, and maybe never see her again. A breeze had sprung up, and they approached a line of trees, where a river had left a pool of water.

'Bill, why don't we stop a minute? Its hard to think straight bumping up and down in the heat.'

Bill slowed down and pulled up in the shade beside the long pool of dark green water, with wading birds feeding at the other end. A couple of sleepy kangaroos moved as they stopped, and settled down in the shade further away.

'Like Paradise isn't it?' Bill said in a soft voice. 'This is truly God's own country. All the heat and dust and hardship of life seem irrelevant when you come upon a scene like this.' He seemed to be talking to himself. He turned, and looked at Matt expectantly.

'Bill, when I first met Lizzie, I felt that we were meant for each other, and that feeling just kept growing. I never thought anyone would come in to my life again after …' He paused. 'I realised too that Lizzie belongs here, and that she could not possibly live in a strange country, no matter how much she tried. And so, it has all fallen in to place. Your "destiny" I suppose.

'Once I pass this exam in Melbourne, I can set up as a surgeon in Perth, and we will be only a step away from you all in the north. I could probably get a part-time job with the North West Medical service as 'Visiting Surgeon' too, if such a job exists.'

'What about your home in England?' Bill asked.

'I have a few friends, and my ageing parents – no one else. I hope that Lizzie and I might go and visit them; maybe on our honeymoon, then come back and make our new life here.'

Bill sat back and gazed at the peaceful scene. 'You know son, you have made me very happy.'

It was mid afternoon when they arrived back at the homestead, and as the jeep pulled up, Lizzie appeared on the veranda.

'I was worried about you. What have you been doing?'

'Secret men's business,' said Bill. 'Bring us some tea, woman.' Lizzie opened her mouth in surprise, and disappeared inside the house. They sat on the veranda with the breeze blowing across the lawns through the sprinklers. It felt wonderfully cool.

Joan came out with a tray of tea, followed by Lizzie with cake and a thermos jug of hot water. As they sat, Bill told them about the blocked valve on the trough. He made no mention of their conversation.

That evening, refreshed by a cold shower and a change of clothes, Matt joined them in the garden, wearing his new espadrilles. Bill poured beer for Matt and himself, and lemonade for the girls.

'Happy Christmas!' Bill toasted, raising his glass.

'It couldn't be happier,' Matt responded, and they all drank to that.

By mid January, Matt was well into his study program.

The New Year's Eve party had been a great success. About fifty people had come, mainly Bill and Joan's old friends from surrounding stations, and a few town people, including Mike and Anne Jackson.

Bill had shot and butchered a small 'scrub heifer', which was roasted slowly on a spit over the coals, then served with fresh home-baked bread and salads. Bull Drummond had arrived with a cold keg of beer, and Joan had made a bucketful of fruit punch.

Bill stood up after the meal, and announced the engagement of Lizzie and Matt, which was met with cheers and applause. There were toasts and speeches, and finally 'Auld Lang Syne' as the clock struck midnight, then everybody kissed. Most stayed the night, but a few town folk drove home.

Each weekend after that, Matt drove out to Spinifex and returned early on Monday mornings, to his clinic, the routine chores, and of course, the endless study program.

The weeks slid by.

Chapter 30

The cyclone season had come around again, and already a small cyclone had passed near Onslow, fortunately causing no damage, but bringing heavy rain to the area. Another had started to build up off Broome to the north, and characteristically it meandered slowly along the coastline, as if having a mind of its own.

Matt received a call from Hedland advising that his routine trip to Onslow was still on the next day, and he set about getting organised. He called up the Matron at Onslow, who had finally mastered the new Traeger radio set, though she still regarded it with suspicion, and often forgot to switch over to 'receive' after talking, thus blocking the channels. Matt had listened gleefully to the old lady roundly cursing 'the bloody newfangled radio' in fruity language before realising that she was still switched on to 'transmit'.

There were no special requirements for the trip, she told him, 'just a routine clinic.' Mary drove Matt out to the airstrip when the plane circled the hospital, and Jim greeted them with a rather worried expression.

'What's the problem?' Mary asked as they talked by the aircraft.

'Just that cyclone that's lurking off the coast,' he replied. 'Can't make it's mind up. Weather Bureau says we are OK, though.'

As they gained altitude, Matt could see the black clouds on the horizon over the ocean, and by the time they reached Onslow it had become overcast, with a gusty north-west wind blowing. Jim looked at the sky after securing the aircraft. 'I don't like the look of the weather Matt, let's get out of here as soon as possible.'

Tom Atkins drove up in the hospital car. 'I thought you guys might decide not to come today,' he said casting a glance at the sky.

'Yair, well we're here so let's get on with it,' Jim said climbing in. Matt got in beside the driver. The old Matron greeted them at the door.

'I think we'd better have a quick clinic,' she said. 'I don't like the look of the weather.' She led them in to the kitchen.

'Maggie!' she bellowed at the deaf cook. Maggie turned from the stove where she was stirring something, and raised her eyebrows questioningly.

'The doc can 'ave 'is tea in the clinic between patients.' Maggie nodded and grinned.

Matt worked quickly with the queue of patients waiting on the veranda. Every time he opened the door the wind seemed to be a little stronger, the sky darker.

At one fifteen, Jim looked around the door. 'Can we have a word?' Matt excused himself and joined him in the next room.

'Matt, we've got to get out of here quickly. I've been on to Hedland, and their Met report indicates that the cyclone has picked up speed and is heading for the coast between here and Roebourne.'

'Right,' said Matt, 'give me ten minutes.'

'I'll give you five or leave you here,' Jim replied. A quick glance at his face told Matt that he meant it.

Maggie had made some sandwiches for them, anticipating that they would not be stopping for a proper lunch, and together with a thermos of hot coffee, presented it all packed in a cardboard box. After making their hasty farewells and thanking Maggie for her trouble, they bundled into the car. As they sped to the airport, it started to sprinkle with rain.

In no time they were airborne and headed northeast towards Roebourne. To seaward the sky was black, with flickers of lightning in the clouds. Jim radioed the Base and gave his position. The radio was full of static.

Twenty minutes later conditions had deteriorated, and the plane was pitching and bumping. Jim leaned over. 'I'll have to fly lower, the clouds are closing off visibility,' he shouted.

They dropped to two thousand feet, but still the clouds rolled in. Jim was on the radio again, but now the base could not be contacted. The radio waves were jammed with static.

Jim leaned over again. 'We won't be able to get into Roebourne, so we can either go back to Onslow, or inland and around the weather.' It wasn't really a question, as Jim would make the decision. Matt nodded, feeling his stomach muscles tighten.

They went down another thousand feet and turned inland. Below Matt could clearly see details of the ground. He saw a herd of kangaroos hopping towards some trees, looking for shelter. The flight became more and more difficult, and the plane bucked and lurched in the gathering storm.

'Its no good,' Jim shouted. 'I'm just going to run with the wind and hope we can beat the worst of it. I can't hold this course.' Another twenty minutes went by and conditions seemed to improve. They were ahead of the storm, though it was still raining. Jim had a map on his lap and was peering out the window.

'We've been blown a fair way off course,' he shouted. 'I need to be higher to get a better idea of the land.' He took them up to three thousand feet.

Jim spent some time poring over the chart, and looking down at the ground. 'I'm not too sure just where we are,' he shouted, 'somewhere about here I'd guess.' He pointed at the chart, and passed it over to Matt. 'Keep a watch out for a homestead; Wallaroo Station should be somewhere in this area.'

Jim turned the plane north again, and kept calling on the radio. He received nothing but static. Below them the country was empty, like the face of the moon. No sign of roads or wheel tracks, or any other indications of habitation. The afternoon wore on.

'We should be heading towards Wittenoom on this course, so keep a sharp look out,' Jim shouted. Matt strained his eyes searching the horizon. Nothing.

Now Jim was looking really worried. He leaned over to Matt's ear. 'Matt, we are in trouble. We are OK on fuel, but this plane is not equipped for night flying, and if we can't find an airstrip, I'm going to have to put us down in the rough, and its better to make that decision whilst we still have enough light to do it safely.'

Matt just nodded. His mouth was dry; he had an awful premonition that this would end badly. He scoured the horizon with his eyes. In the distance he saw some hills and pointed. Jim nodded. Still no signs of life.

'Time to bite the bullet!' Jim shouted, and put the plane in a shallow dive. All the while he tried to contact the base with his 'mayday' call. He received no reply.

They flew at a couple of hundred feet, searching the ground for a suitable landing site. Jim pointed. Ahead was a flat clay-pan of red earth with no obvious vegetation, and beyond that, some trees, suggesting a creek bed. The rain had cleared.

'We're going in!' Jim shouted. 'Buckle up tight!'

Matt watched in horror as the ground came up towards them. He felt his pulse racing!

Jim throttled back and lowered the flaps, then edged the plane down. The ground rushed up to them and the stall klaxon sounded. They hit the ground with a heavy bump, then again as the plane bounced and slowed. All of a sudden the world seemed to explode! The earth was soft, and one wheel dug in to the ground. The plane pitched forward and swerved, then with a dreadful crashing grinding sound it came to a stop, nose in the earth.

Silence!

Jim shook Matt's shoulder. 'Are you OK?' he shouted, his voice thundering in the silence. Matt opened his eyes, and looked at Jim, then nodded. He was incapable of speech at that moment.

'OK let's get out of here,' he said, and pushed his door open. Matt did the same, and they shakily climbed out and slid down to the damp red earth. Both had bruised knees, and Jim had a nasty cut on his forehead, but otherwise they had escaped unhurt.

They limped around the plane surveying the damage. The propeller was bent, and the undercarriage almost destroyed, but the wings and fuselage seemed intact. There was no fuel leakage.

'Well,' said Jim. 'Could have been worse.'

Let's put a dressing on that cut,' Matt said. He climbed back into the plane and found the first aid box.

At the RFDS Base, Port Hedland, the alarm had been raised. Joe Bailey, the air controller, had received a report from 'Foxtrot Delta Zulu' on take off from Onslow at 1345hrs and since then he had only received messages scrambled by static, from which he gathered that they were not attempting to go to Roebourne, then later, that the plane was heading inland away from the storm. Even this was garbled and broken by the radio interference. Since then he had received no message, and had to assume that the plane had gone down somewhere south of Wittenoom.

It was too late in the day to start an aerial search, but by telegraph he contacted Meekatharra and sent a message to the RFDS Base there to stand by for a search in the morning. Hopefully radio communication would return by then. He had never known such a breakdown!

Joe then telegraphed Perth RFDS to advise them of what was happening. He had decided to spend the night at the base, as he had done before when there had been an emergency. He would continue calling the plane, and as soon as possible he would alert all the stations in the area when they came on the radio for the morning schedule.

Jim and Matt had taken stock of their situation and found that apart from Maggie's box of coffee and sandwiches, which were completely forgotten in the excitement, they had a tin of emergency rations – enough for a couple of days, Jim thought. There were two gallons of fresh water with the medical kit, and a hand basin and enamel jug that would serve to collect water if it rained again, or from the creek – if it was not dry. They would explore tomorrow, as it was now starting to get dark. They climbed back into the cockpit, and gratefully ate the sandwiches and coffee.

'We better make ourselves comfy for the night,' Jim said. 'There's the stretcher in the back if you want to take it out and sleep on the ground, or else you can stay in the cockpit. Either will be uncomfy.'

Matt opted for the stretcher, which gave Jim more room in the cockpit.

At dawn Matt woke, shivering with cold. Jim was already awake, and on the radio. He climbed out and greeted Matt. 'Get any sleep?'

'Not much.'

'Well I've contacted Hedland, but the trouble is, I don't know exactly where we are. They are organising a grid search, and are going to try to triangulate my radio signal, using the commercial DC3 plane's direction finding apparatus. There should be two planes in the area by nine thirty.

'They're spreading the word that we are alive and well.'

They walked over to the trees, and picked up some dry wood to make a fire. The creek bed was dry; the rain had made little impression this far inland. They collected some green branches too, so that they could make the fire smoky if they saw a plane.

By eight o'clock they had made a fire a short distance from the plane, and boiled some water in the enamel jug. They had coffee and condensed milk, and shared a tin of bully beef, with biscuits from the emergency ration.

By noon, the temperature had soared, and they sheltered from the sun under the wing. They were both thirsty.

Every quarter hour, Jim had radioed his call sign and a brief message, hoping that the planes with radio direction finding apparatus would pick up his signal.

'We've only got about six hours of radio time before the battery conks out,' said Jim, 'but we're sure to be picked up by then.'

All through the day two light aircraft flew over a planned area, where the controller guessed Jim might have put the plane down. There was no sign of them.

The two DC3 flights had picked up Jim's signal, but when the coordinates were charted, and the area flown over, there was no sign of the plane. They needed a third plane to get an accurate triangulation.

At the RFDS base Joe had broadcast to all stations news of the downed plane, and search parties were sent out from as many stations as possible in a wide area.

At Spinifex, Lizzie sat anxiously by the radio, listening for any news. She thanked God that Matt was alive.

By sundown, with no sign of an aircraft, Jim and Matt resigned themselves to the fact that there would be no more flights till the next day, and started to prepare for the night.

They had already used almost half of their water, and now rationed it. They ate some of their food supply then settled in for the night with fairly empty stomachs.

Matt woke shivering with cold. The luminous face of his watch showed one o'clock. He rolled himself tightly in the one thin blanket, and looked up at the night sky blazing with stars. He lay thinking about Lizzie, and all that had happened since he left England – a lifetime ago.

He woke with a start as dawn was breaking. A dark figure towered over him!

'Who are you?' he cried out in fright, struggling to sit up.

In the half-light the figure silently disappeared.

'Jim!' Matt shouted. 'Come out here!'

Jim appeared rubbing his eyes. 'What's up?'

Matt was on his feet, peering into the gloom. 'There was someone here,' he said. 'I think it was an Aboriginal.'

'Can't think who else it would be,' Jim answered with a trace of sarcasm. 'You must have frightened him off.'

In half an hour it was quite light, and they sat under the wing and summed up the situation. Water was getting short and the ration pack was half empty. By the end of the day the battery would be getting low if he continued the regular broadcasts. By noon the heat would be blistering again. Should they start walking? But in which direction? Their best bet was to stay with the plane. That was the 'golden rule' in the outback. Someone must spot it soon. – But then, it was a big country.

They sat and ate biscuits and had a sip of water. Both dirty, unshaven and becoming increasingly concerned about the situation.

Jim radioed the Base on the hour and told Joe of their situation. He didn't mention the early morning visitor.

At Hedland base Joe held a conference. The two town police officers, the head of the Public Works and the Main Roads supervisor were present. They pored over a large chart of the area.

Joe pointed. 'We've flown over these areas, and ground searched these areas.' He pencilled he chart. 'That means we should concentrate on these areas here,' he indicated. 'We will do some more work with the radio direction finders. With a third plane in the area they should be able to pinpoint them.'

The police were coordinating the ground searches, and had included the Wittenoom police, who would search to the south of the town. Public Works and Main Roads contacted their workmen in the area, and instructed them to alert the local Aborigines.

They all knew that people lost in the outback were in grave danger, and many had died of thirst. In this heat, they did not have a lot of time.

Matt and Jim walked over to the trees and picked up firewood. Their knees still hurt. 'This will be our lucky day,' Jim said gathering an armful of sticks. They walked back and re-kindled the fire.

As they crouched uncomfortably on the ground concentrating on their task, a shadow fell over them. They looked around, startled. Three Aboriginal men stood silently behind them.

'Hello!' said Jim as they struggled to their feet. 'Where are you from?'

The oldest of three with a grey beard answered. 'We bin local people. Some fellas with us from up north on walkabout. You better come with us. We take you to white fellas.'

'Is there a station near here?' Jim asked.

The old man shook his head. 'Maybe thirty mile,' he said.

'Where are the white fellas?' Matt asked.

'White fellas in copper mine,' he said. 'Bout five miles.' He pointed south.

'You betta come. No tucker here.' The other two Aborigines nodded their agreement.

'What do you think Jim?' Matt asked anxiously.

Jim scratched his chin. 'Well we're going to get bloody hungry and thirsty here if no-one finds us today, so maybe we better go with them.' Matt nodded agreement.

Jim turned to the men. 'OK, thanks, we will come with you, but we need to fix a few things here first.' The men nodded and squatted down in the shade under the wing, while Matt collected the remains of the water and food.

Jim tried the radio. The signal had almost faded out! 'Bloody battery has died on us!' he cursed.

'Which way are we going?' he asked the natives. They all pointed.

'OK Matt, let's build up the fire and put the green branches on. We will leave a sign on the ground too.'

With the empty bully beef tin he scratched a large arrow in the dirt pointing in the direction of their intended journey. Matt had a better idea. From the first aid pack he unrolled a white bandage and traced out Jim's arrow, pegging it down with small stones.

'They should be able to see that OK,' he said, standing up and regarding the large white arrow.

They set out on their long hike, with the Aborigines in the lead.

At ten o'clock that morning, flying at three thousand feet, the pilot of the RFDS plane from Meekatharra radioed in. 'Hedland Base, Hedland Base. This is Foxtrot Delta Tango. Do you read? Over.'

'Delta Tango, this is Hedland, go ahead. Over.'

'Hedland, I've just sighted the plane with a smoke fire. I'm going down to take a good look.' He pushed the 'stick' forward and descended to two hundred feet, and flew over the plane twice.

'Hedland, this is Foxtrot Delta Tango. I've buzzed the plane a couple of times but there's no-one about, and they've put an arrow on the ground pointing south.' He gave details of his position.

'Delta Tango. Roger that. Thanks for your help; we will take it from there. Over and out.'

Joe thumped the table angrily. 'The stupid buggers have left the plane! That's a certain way to finish up dead!' he muttered. He grabbed the phone and rang the police station.

It was about two o'clock in the afternoon when the little group reached the copper mine. Matt and Jim were limping badly, exhausted and dehydrated. They had finished all their water. Neither had a hat, and the scorching hot air seared their lungs as they struggled into the camp.

'Well what 'ave we got 'ere?' A tall suntanned man with a black beard approached them. He was dressed in dusty khaki shorts and shirt, and army boots.

'Im crash in plane,' the old Aboriginal said. 'We bring 'em to you.'

'Come and sit in the shade, you look done in.' He led them to a canvas tarpaulin with a table and chairs under it.

'Sit down, and I'll get you a drink.' He poured two mugs of water from the large water-bag that hung in the shade, and put them on the table. His accent was foreign.

Matt looked around for the Aborigines, but they had disappeared as silently as they had arrived.

'My name is Brakic, Miro Brakic, and this is my copper mine. Tell me what happened.'

Jim related the story to Miro, and told him about the search that had been set up. Had he not heard it on the radio?

'Unfortunately our radio is out of action,' said Miro with a shrug. 'We have ordered another one but haven't been into town to collect it yet.'

'Town? Where is "town"?' Matt asked.

'We drive to Wittenoom when we want something, but that's about sixty miles north from here,' Miro replied.

Jim asked, 'Is there a station closer?'

'Yair, there's Mount Hope. That's about twenty-five miles away.'

'Miro, could drive us there? A lot of people will be looking for us by now, and the sooner we make contact the better.'

'OK, I'll organise it for you. Help yourselves to water, and I'll get you some tucker – its not too flash, but.' He opened a can of meat and cut off some bread. 'We bake our own,' he explained, putting tin plates knifes and forks on the table. 'Eat up. I'll go find someone to drive you. They're all over at the mine.' He pointed over his shoulder with his thumb then walked away.

He returned about ten minutes later with another man, covered with grey-green dust. 'This is Drago. He'll drive you to the station,' he said. 'Have you had enough to eat?'

Ten minutes later after thanking Miro, they were bumping along in a jeep. Drago had washed his face, and turned out to be a handsome young Yugoslav, who had come to Australia after the war and teamed up with Miro to go copper mining. Apparently they were making it pay.

About an hour later they sighted Mount Hope; a run-down wooden homestead with a corrugated iron roof, and surrounded by red earth and dust. There were a couple of sheds nearby, and a few peppercorn trees for shade.

As they drew up, a dog rushed at them barking, and a woman came out on the veranda. Drago waved. 'Hello Mrs Johnson,' he said with a flashing smile.

They climbed out of the dusty jeep and climbed the steps on to the veranda. Jim introduced himself and Matt. Mrs Johnson's jaw dropped. 'You must be the two I heard about on the radio!' she exclaimed. 'Come inside I'll get some cold drinks.'

They followed her into the house, which was like a furnace, and sat around the kitchen table. She went to the kerosene refrigerator and took out a jug of lemonade. 'I made this only this morning,' she said, pouring a glass each for them. 'I'm afraid Brian is out on a mill-run with a couple of the boys, and won't be back be back till tomorrow afternoon at he earliest.' She was about fifty Matt guessed, and was wiry and deeply suntanned. Her leathery face was creased with lines, but her blue eyes retained their youthfulness, and sparkled when she smiled.

Drago stood up and said he must be getting back, thanking Mrs Johnson for the drink. She walked out with him, and they heard the jeep splutter in to life and depart.

'Mrs Johnson, may I use your radio?' Jim asked.

'Please call me Iris,' she interrupted. 'Of course, come with me.'

Five minutes later he returned to the kitchen beaming. He had spoken to Hedland, and one search plane was in the area. They would arrive in about twenty minutes and collect them.

An hour later they were aboard a Cessna 180 and heading for Roebourne to drop off Matt, then flying home to Port Hedland.

The ordeal was over!

Mary was waiting at the airstrip when they landed. Joe had broadcast the good news, and everyone was rejoicing. The Perth newspapers were running the story.

'God you look terrible!' Mary greeted Matt as he climbed wearily out of the plane. Without stopping the engine, the pilot gave a wave and taxied off, leaving them in a cloud of dust. He wanted to be home by sunset.

Matt sat in the ute and closed his eyes, his unshaven dusty face streaked with sweat, and his clothing filthy. After a pause, he grinned at her. 'You know Mary, that was quite an adventure.'

Two hours later, he was showered, refreshed and in clean clothes. The phone rang.

'Matt!' It was Lizzie. The family had driven into town on hearing the good news, and were staying at the Victoria Hotel. He hung up and drove to the pub, finding them in the beer garden.

As he walked in the few people sitting with drinks clapped loudly. He had become a celebrity! Lizzie threw herself into his arms and sobbed with joy. Bill pumped his hand, and Joan kissed him on the cheek.

'Well, there won't be any more flying for a while,' Matt said after telling them of his adventures.

'The plane will have to be dismantled and hauled out, with a lot of repairs to be done.'

'Don't worry, the RFDS will probably buy a new plane, and sell off the wreck. It was about due for replacement.' Bill knew a lot about the RFDS, as he had been on the Council for years.

They sat over dinner in the hotel then Matt drove home and crashed into bed to a dreamless sleep.

Life resumed its usual tempo, and February slipped by. As Matt turned over the calendar page in his office he realised that there were only three weeks until the exams! The break from his weekly trip to Onslow had given him extra study time, and any emergencies from there had been flown to Carnarvon, the next town south, by commercial transport.

He spent his last weekend at Spinifex before starting the marathon journey to Melbourne, but although they had a happy weekend together, he was pre-occupied with coming events. He drove back to town promising to send them a telegram if he passed the exam. Lizzie had corrected him to 'when, not if'.

He packed his bag with clothing appropriate for the big city, but had no idea what to expect in regard to the weather. Mary helped out by ironing shirts, and gave him an insight into what lay ahead. 'It's like a small version of London,' she told him, and added that the weather was totally unpredictable.

Mary waved him off as he boarded the early morning DC3 for Perth. A surgical registrar from Fremantle Hospital had been recruited as Locum for the next two weeks, and was due on the next plane north. Matt had elected to take the two weeks as 'study leave without pay'.

Chapter 31

At Perth airport, Peter McLean from the Health Department was waiting. 'Good to see you Matt!' They shook hands.

'Well you got quite a splash of publicity down here with your cyclone adventure,' he said with a grin as they collected the suitcase. 'My kids are still talking about it at school.'

They walked to the car. 'The Department have booked you in at the Esplanade Hotel again, and a car will take you the airport first thing in the morning for the Melbourne flight.' Peter opened the car boot for the suitcase, and they set off for the city.

'Jenny wondered if you would like to have dinner with us tonight, if you don't have any other plans.'

'That sounds great, thanks,' Matt replied.

They reached the Esplanade, and Peter lifted out Matt's case. They shook hands again.

'Thanks Peter. What time should I be at your place? And I'll need your address for the taxi.'

Peter grinned. 'If it's OK with you, I'll pick you up at six. The kids are looking forward to seeing you.'

The lady at the reception desk welcomed Matt warmly. 'Welcome back Dr Harrison, we read all about you in the papers. It must have been very exciting.' Matt thanked her and escaped with his key.

It was a lovely cool afternoon with a sea breeze blowing up the river. Matt lay on the comfortable bed with the French doors open, letting the breeze waft into the room.

'So much has happened since I was here last,' he thought. He dozed off.

He woke with a start when the telephone jangled.

'Hello?' It was Peter.

'Thought I'd ring before leaving home.' Matt looked at his watch; it was five minutes to six.

'Great. Thanks Peter, I'll be waiting for you at the door.'

Matt dressed in slacks and an open neck shirt, then walked down the gracious stairway to the lobby. He went into the bar and bought two cold bottles of beer, in a brown paper bag.

By the time he reached the front door, Peter's car arrived. Peter got out and opened the door for Matt. 'What's this then?' he looked at the paper bag.

Matt grinned and handed the beer to him. 'Old North West custom.'

The children were in the back seat and greeted Mat with excitement, both talking at the same time. 'Save it kids!' Peter yelled over the din. 'You'll hear all about it later I'm sure.' There was a reluctant silence in the back seat.

'Where are you going to stay in Melbourne?' Peter asked as they drove.

'Ah, well I haven't really thought about it,' Matt replied.

'I thought as much,' Peter said. 'And for that reason I contacted an old mate who is Super of St Vincent's Hospital, and arranged "digs" in the residents' quarters if you should want it. It's right across the road from the College of Surgeons.' Matt opened his mouth then shut it. He was overcome with this man's efficiency!

'What can I say?' he finally managed. 'You must be the most organised man I've ever met.'

Peter grinned. 'Working for the Government makes you that way.'

Jenny greeted them at the door, and gave Matt a hug and a kiss. 'Congratulations!' she said with a big smile.

'Oh yes, I forgot, congratulations on your engagement,' Peter followed.

'Thanks,' Matt replied, 'but how did you know about that?'

'There was quite a story about you in the *Daily News*,' Jenny said. 'You're a local hero!'

'Maybe I'll stay in Melbourne,' said Matt blushing with embarrassment. They went out on to the veranda and had a cold beer, then all sat down for dinner. Jenny had cooked a roast leg of lamb with all the trimmings. 'The children's favourite,' Jenny said.

Over dinner Matt gave an abridged account of his adventure, but particularly mentioned how the Aborigines had helped him, but disappeared before he could thank them. The children listened with wide eyes, and asked questions.

At the end of the evening Matt asked to ring a taxi, but Peter would not have it. He would drive Matt to the hotel. Matt waved

Jenny goodbye after thanking her for a marvellous meal, and settled back in to the car seat.

'Tell me your plans,' Peter asked, 'I mean, after you've passed this exam.'

Matt thought for a moment. 'I plan to live in Australia.'

Peter shot him a quick glance, but said nothing.

'A hospital appointment in Perth, and a private practice to back it up will keep us close to Lizzie's family – she would never be happy living in England.'

'But would you be happy in Australia?'

'I've grown to love the northwest, and I hope to be able to visit there as a surgeon, and provide a service they don't have now.'

Peter thought for a minute. 'How would you like to work at Fremantle Hospital? I think there is a vacancy coming up on their consulting staff, and you could get private rooms close by the hospital.'

'That sounds pretty good to me,' Matt said with enthusiasm.

'Well, you do your bit with the examiners and I'll have a quiet word with Dave Barlow at the hospital.'

At the hotel, they said goodbye and shook hands. 'Remember to ask for an early call,' Peter said. 'The car arrives at six thirty.'

It was just getting light as the car pulled up at the hotel. Matt was ready waiting. They arrived at the airport as the sun peeped over the Darling Ranges.

There was a small crowd of travellers, and they were called for boarding almost immediately.

Matt settled back in his comfortable plush seat on the Ansett ANA DC6B, as one by one the four great engines whined, coughed then thundered into life. This was the biggest plane he had ever been on, and capable, the brochure in the seat pocket said, of travelling at 320 miles per hour, over a distance of more than 4000 miles without refuelling. They would reach Melbourne at nine o'clock that evening!

Matt spent the day reading and dozing, thinking of the adventure ahead. He would be competing with well-trained postgraduate students with all the advantages of local knowledge, who had been in mainstream surgical training right up to the exams. 'Some handicap!' he thought.

Melbourne surprised him. It was indeed a little reminiscent of London, with its grey buildings and matching cold grey weather. A huge contrast to Perth!

He stayed the first night at a motel near the airport, as it was late when he arrived. The next day he phoned the Medical Superintendent of St Vincent's Hospital, who told him where to find his accommodation. He had allowed two days to acclimatise before the exams started.

Once he had settled in his digs, he went exploring, and started by crossing Victoria Parade to the College of Surgeons – an impressive building with a façade of stone columns, set in a small park. He entered, and located the Secretary, who welcomed him and took him for a tour of the College. By the time he left he felt more relaxed about the coming examination. He walked down Collins Street, and round to Bourke Street, admiring the shops along the way. Back in his little room he settled in for some last minute revision.

On the morning of the first exam he arrived at the College in good time. It was cold and drizzling with rain as he hurried in to the building.

For the next two days Matt battled through the written examination papers. Each night he ate at a small restaurant in the top of Bourke Street then returned to his digs and collapsed into bed.

On the last day the Clinical Exams were held at Royal Melbourne Hospital. One after another, Matt examined the 'short case' patients, and was questioned on his findings by an examiner, who made notes on a clipboard. Finally he was given his 'long' case. He spent an hour firstly taking a medical history from the patient, followed by a detailed physical examination. Once again came the inquisition, this time by two examiners.

Finally, at four o'clock it was over. The exam results, he was informed, would be announced in the College that evening at six o'clock.

Matt caught a tram to the city then walked up Collins Street. The air was fresh and clear, and he felt a sense of relief at having the exams behind him. He turned into Spring Street, and walked to the College. A few people stood talking in the foyer, and he walked over and joined them, introducing himself. It was five o'clock, and they had an hour to spend before the results.

'Come over to the pub,' one suggested, and the group walked

across Spring Street to the little pub opposite the College. The place was full of postgraduate students, drinking beer and discussing the exams. At ten to six, they drifted back to the College. The Secretary in academic gown directed them upstairs to the library, where they were to wait for the Board of Examiners to finish their meeting.

Finally the moment came, and the Secretary stood at the library door and called for silence. He then referred to the list in his hand and called the first name. The first examinee walked up to him. The system was time honoured. The Secretary either said 'Congratulations, Mister so-and-so,' directing the successful candidate along to the Boardroom; or 'I'm sorry, Doctor so-and-so,' in which case the unfortunate walked down the stairs to the exit. The names were called alphabetically, and by the time the Secretary reached Harrison, more had gone down the stairs than not.

As Matt walked unsteadily towards the Secretary he tried unsuccessfully to read his expression and barely heard his words. Convinced of his failure, he turned to go down the stairs.

'No! Stop Mister Harrison! You must go to the Boardroom!' called the Secretary.

Realisation dawned! He had passed!

The small group assembled outside the Boardroom were ushered in when the door was opened, and as they entered, the Secretary announced their names to the Examiners, who stood in a line resplendent in their black and gold academic robes. Once they were all assembled in a row, the President of the College made a short speech welcoming the successful candidates into the College, at the end of which, the line of Examiners then bowed to the somewhat bewildered and alcohol-affected graduates!

Then followed an informal gathering with sherry and trays of canapés. The President came over to Matt and greeted him. 'Well Mr Harrison, I read of your adventures in the north-west, and I am pleased that you also distinguished yourself in the examinations. Congratulations.' He shook Matt's hand warmly. 'Whilst we do not award honours as such in this Examination, I can tell you that your results were amongst those at the very top.'

Matt was speechless. 'Thank you sir,' he finally managed.

'Now come along over here, I'm sure you would like a College tie; they come in blue, green and maroon.' He led Matt to a table where ties were displayed. Matt selected a blue tie, and turned to thank the

President, who had moved away by then.

'That will be five pounds, thank you Mr Harrison.' The Secretary held out the tie. Academia had been displaced by Commerce!

It was too late to send telegrams, so Matt walked down to the top of Bourke Street and had a bowl of spaghetti at his little restaurant. Overcome with weariness, he returned to his digs and fell into bed.

Next morning he caught a tram to the GPO and sent off a series of telegrams; the first to Lizzie, and then one to the Health Department. He then sent overseas cables to his parents, to Tom, and finally one to Sir James Watson.

He was booked on the night flight back to the West, and returned to St Vincent's to pack his bag. He filled in the rest of the morning window-shopping around Melbourne, then caught a tram to the Botanical Gardens.

He bought a ham roll and a bottle of Coca-cola then wandered around admiring the autumn colours, and sat by a peaceful lake with drifting swans, thinking about the time he had sat with Tom beside the Serpentine. It all seemed so long ago. A different lifetime.

At six, he caught a taxi to Essendon airport. He checked in his bag then went to the café, where he had a hamburger and a cup of coffee, waiting for the boarding call.

The DC6B droned away through the night as Matt dozed. It seemed a longer journey going home.

At first light they were approaching Perth airport, and touched down at a little after seven, local time. Matt threw his suitcase into a taxi and headed for the Esplanade. Once there he showered and changed into fresh clothing, then went to the dining room for a good breakfast of bacon and eggs with coffee and toast.

Just after nine he rang the Health Department and spoke to Peter, who had already received the good news, and they arranged to meet at ten thirty at the Department.

'Congratulations Mister Harrison!' Steve Connor the Commissioner held out his hand, beaming at Matt. 'Come and have some coffee.' He led Matt and Peter into his office.

'Now what?' he asked when they were seated.

'Well Steve, it's back to the bush for now, and I hope I can stay on until May when we plan to get married. I guess I'll be due for some holiday pay, and that will take us home to England for a visit.'

'A visit?'

'Didn't Pete tell you we plan to live in Australia?'

'I thought you should tell Steve yourself,' Peter interrupted.

'Where do you plan to live?' the Commissioner asked, looking interested.

'Right here in the West!' Matt said with a grin. 'I'm going to apply for an Honorary Consultant position at a hospital, and start my own practice in General Surgery.'

'Well good for you,' said Steve, obviously impressed.

'Also,' said Matt, 'I hope you will consider setting up a part-time surgical appointment in the Department, to provide a visiting service to the north.'

'Well, let's take one step at a time,' said Steve. 'Why not go down to Fremantle and talk to Dave Barlow?'

Peter nodded in agreement.

Later that afternoon, seated in Dave's office, Matt outlined his plans. Dave listened in silence. When Matt had finished, he stood up and walked over to the window.

'Would you like a job here?' he asked over his shoulder.

'That would be just great,' Matt replied, his excitement rising.

'You've got to make a living too you know,' Dave went on. 'Hospital Consultant jobs are unpaid.' He turned around and looked at Matt. 'Also you'll have a wife to support. Thought about that?'

Matt well remembered Dave's confronting manner, and was careful not to over-react.

'Well maybe I could get a locum job or something until I've got settled,' Matt replied.

Dave's stern face cracked into a broad smile. 'Matt, I think you've fallen on your feet,' he said. 'It so happens that one of our senior surgeons is about to retire from the Hospital and also he is looking for an Assistant to ultimately take over his practice here in Fremantle.'

Matt's jaw dropped. 'What do I do next?' he asked, overwhelmed with the news.

'Nothing,' Dave replied. 'Go back to the North West and do your job. I'll do the ground work and write to you.' He looked at his watch. 'Time for a drink,' he announced.

Peter excused himself, with family commitments, so Dave took Matt in his car down to his Club in the city. They stood at the bar sipping beer. 'Do you remember what I said about drinking in the pub up there?' he asked Matt.

'I certainly do,' he replied. 'In such a small town if you have a drink with one, you'd offend the next person by saying "no thanks". It was good advice.'

Dave told him about the retiring surgeon, Mr James Price, who had been on the staff for twenty-five years, and had a thriving surgical practice in the area. It sounded ideal! Matt had met him whilst he was working at the hospital, and had a great respect for him.

Before they parted, Matt had told Dave that he and Lizzie would be travelling to England for their honeymoon, and would be away for a couple of months. This suited the Superintendent well, as the position in his Hospital wouldn't become vacant until the end of June.

The next morning Matt stepped on the DC3 and headed for home.

Chapter 32

The DC3 touched down at Roebourne late in the afternoon. Out the window Matt was delighted to see Lizzie waiting in her jeep, and when the plane doors opened she was standing at the bottom of the steps to greet him. They talked excitedly all the way into town, stopping first at Matt's place to drop off his bag, then on to the Victoria Hotel where there was quite a little gathering of locals to greet him, including Bill and Joan.

Later as they sat around the dinner table in the pub, Matt told them of his prospects in Fremantle. His whole life now seemed on a winning streak!

Next morning it was business as usual. The surgical registrar had left the same day as Matt arrived, and the veranda seat was full of customers waiting for him when he arrived.

Mary greeted him with a hug. 'Congratulations, Mister,' she said. 'Don't let it go to your head,' she added with a cheeky smile.

By the end of March preparations were well advanced for the wedding, planned for early May, and Joan and Lizzie seemed to have locked themselves in a world of female mystery. They talked about wedding dresses, bridesmaids, flowers, and a variety of topics that did not involve Matt. Bill reassured him that this was standard female behaviour at this time, and to just be patient!

The Reverend Philip Anderson was to marry them in the little old church on a hill overlooking the town, and after meeting the couple on his monthly visit from Port Hedland, he posted the Bans on the church door according to tradition.

Matt had received letters from England. His parents were delighted at the news of the wedding and also the exam results. They were looking forward to meeting Lizzie.

Sir James added his congratulations, going on to stress the importance of the English 'Fellowship' as the 'senior' degree, and that

Matt should take the opportunity of sitting for it whilst his knowledge was still fresh in his mind.

Tom, having passed his physician's exam, was now a Senior Registrar at his hospital, and was himself engaged to be married! He sent his heart-felt congratulations and looked forward to Matt and Lizzie's visit.

Dave Barlow wrote and told Matt that Mr Price, the elderly surgeon, was most willing to take Matt on as an 'associate', and would strongly recommend his appointment to the Honorary Staff of the Hospital. He hoped to meet Matt in the near future to discuss the issues.

Matt replied, thanking Dave, and told him that he and his bride would be coming to Perth prior to sailing to England, and that he would write to Mr Price himself.

It dawned on Matt that a return trip to England for two, plus expenses would not come cheaply, and he wondered how far his resources would stretch. Perhaps they could travel second class.

His dilemma was solved the following weekend at Spinifex. After dinner they were sitting in the garden under the stars, when Bill made his announcement.

'Kids,' he said. 'Joan and I have been wondering what we could give you for a wedding present, and we came up with an idea. It depends on what you think about it.' He paused, and they looked at him expectantly. 'We thought we would give you a first class return trip to England. What would you say to that?'

Lizzie hugged her father, and Matt kissed Joan then shook Bill's hand. 'That is a very generous gift,' Matt said, struggling with his emotions. 'I don't know what to say, except thank you both.'

Bill stood with his arm around Joan's waist, smiling broadly.

On Bill's advice, when Matt returned to work he wired the P&O office in Perth, and booked a first class return ticket for two, and asked for sailing schedules to be posted to him.

Matt asked Mike to be his Best Man, and Lizzie in turn asked Anne to be her Matron of Honour. The day was set for Tuesday, the twelfth of May, at eleven in the morning, and the reception would follow at Spinifex Plains – a late luncheon. Plans were laid down to the last detail.

A week before the wedding, Mike and Bert organised a 'town party' for Matt, who of course, would not be returning as town doctor. A replacement would be arriving a few days after the wedding.

The party took the form of a barbecue, held in the yard behind Dalgety's store, and it seemed that the whole town was present. Lizzie and her parents had driven in and were to stay the night in the pub.

Mike made a speech, saying how much the folk of the town had come to like and respect Matt, and Bert followed with a self conscious and touching short speech, ending with a presentation.

'We all chipped in for this, Doc, an' we 'ope that you and your intended find it useful. We all wish you both a long and 'appy life together.' He passed a large box to Matt. 'Careful! It's fragile,' he added. They all clapped and cheered.

Matt carefully put the box down beside Lizzie, and stood to reply. 'Ladies and gentlemen – friends, I don't know quite what to say except that my time here has been very happy, and I thank you all for making me feel one of you.

'We are going back to England, but only for a visit, then we return to Perth to live. I know that we will be coming back to Roebourne frequently, so this isn't really "goodbye". Thank you all for this party, and for your gift, which I know we will treasure.

'I'd like to conclude with my thanks to Bill and Joan Corbett for having such a wonderful daughter, and I ask you to drink a toast. To Joan and Bill!'

Amidst the applause, Lizzie gave Matt a hug. Later, Matt and Lizzie opened the parcel. It contained a beautiful Waterford crystal decanter and six glasses.

The twelfth of May dawned clear and cool. Matt woke early and lay thinking of the coming events. By now Lizzie and her mother would be getting organised to drive in to town. They had booked a room at the hotel for Lizzie to use for the day, and already her wedding dress was hanging up in the wardrobe waiting their arrival. Bill was coming a little later, as he and the Martins had some last minute details to organise at Spinifex.

At ten thirty Mike arrived at Matt's place spruced up in a suit. Matt had almost finished dressing, in a new lightweight suit he had purchased in Perth a year ago, but not as yet worn.

Sitting in a little box on the kitchen table was a white gold wedding ring.

'You'd better put that in your pocket,' Matt said, adjusting his tie.

At five minutes to eleven, Matt and Mike were sitting in the front row pew of the little church, which was rapidly filling up with guests and well-wishers. Matt could feel the sweat running down his back. He was unaccustomed to wearing a suit. The minutes ticked by, and Matt's attention wandered. Suddenly the wheezy pedal organ burst in to life. The bride had arrived!

Matt and Mike moved out to stand in front of the Minister, and Matt turned to see Lizzie walking down the aisle towards him on Bill's arm. She was a picture of loveliness.

The Reverend Anderson was unhurried and precise, and gave a short address as part of the service. Finally at the appointed moment, Matt slipped the ring on Lizzie's finger, and they were pronounced 'Man and Wife'.

At the church door the couple were deluged with confetti as the small crowd closed in on them. Everyone kissed the bride, and Matt's hand was shaken till it hurt. Finally they drove away in the shiny Ford sedan owned by the trucking company, and rented by Matt for the occasion.

A procession of cars headed for Spinifex Plains, strung out on the road to try to avoid the trail from the car in front, but even so, they all arrived at the station coated with red dust.

There was a marquee on the lawn in front of the house, with a huge buffet table at the end, laden with food. Cold turkey, legs of ham and bowls of salad were laid out. Bull Drummond had arranged the catering and organised staff from the hotel, and Dalgety's had provided the French champagne for the toasts. As usual, there was a keg of beer and jugs of fruit cup.

Apart from the official table, seating was informal, and once all were in their places with a plate of food and a drink in front of them, the feast began, preceded by 'Grace' from the Reverend Anderson.

At the end of the first course, the champagne was poured then Bill got to his feet and proposed the 'Loyal Toast'. Everyone stood and raised their glasses to 'The Queen!'

After a pause, Mike stood and made a pretty speech, ending in a toast to the bride and groom. Matt responded briefly but adequately, and the carousing continued.

By five o'clock, everyone felt replete, and they were ready for the drive home. On a side table was a pile of gifts, all beautifully wrapped. Joan would put them away for the time being.

Lizzie, with her mother and Anne, disappeared inside the house, and came out twenty minutes later with Lizzie dressed in 'going away clothes'. They crowded round as the couple stood by the car then Lizzie threw her bouquet, to be caught by none other than Mary!

'May it bring you good fortune my dear Mary,' Matt thought, as he helped Lizzie into the passenger seat, then climbed in behind the wheel.

They drove off with the horn tooting, and a clatter of tin cans tied to the back bumper. Bill stood with his arm around Joan, who dabbed the tears from her eyes as they waved them off.

The Victoria Hotel didn't have a bridal suite, but the best room had been decorated with flowers, and a bottle of champagne in an ice bucket to greet the weary couple as they opened the door. Matt picked up Lizzie, and carried her across the threshold, and sat her on the bed.

'Well, Mrs Harrison, would you care for a glass of champagne?' he asked.

She wrapped her arms around his neck and kissed him passionately.

'Later,' she replied, drawing him down on to the bed.

'I'm starving,' Matt announced looking at his watch as he sat up in bed. Lizzie stirred beside him.

'What time is it?' she asked sleepily.

'Time for breakfast,' Matt replied climbing out of bed. 'We have a long way to go today.'

He took his toilet bag and towel, and headed off to the showers.

At eight o'clock they were sitting down to breakfast, the only occupants in the dining room at that time.

All their bags were packed in advance and waiting for them in the hotel, so they needed only to be at the airstrip for the flight south, due at nine thirty. Mike had promised to pick them up a little after nine.

'Well good morning! And how are the lovebirds today?' Mike stood over them by the table. He was early.

'Worn out,' Lizzie replied. Mike grinned from ear to ear.

'We'll drive out in the Ford, and then I'll return it to the trucking people,' Mike said, accepting the offered cup of coffee as he sat down. 'We've got plenty of time.'

The DC3 was approaching the airstrip as they pulled up at the tin shed. Mike opened the boot and loaded the cases on to Johnny's trolley. The sleek silver plane taxied towards them then cut its engines. Johnny hurried out with the steps.

'Well, it's goodbye for now,' Mike said. 'Have a wonderful trip, and we look forward to seeing you soon.' He hugged and kissed Lizzie then shook Matt's hand.

At Perth airport, Matt opened the taxi door for Lizzie while the driver stowed the bags.

'Esplanade Hotel please,' he instructed the driver.

At the reception desk, they received a warm welcome, and were escorted to the honeymoon suite, where vases of flowers and a chilled bottle of champagne greeted them 'With the Management's compliments'.

'How about a glass of champagne?' Matt asked, hanging his jacket in the wardrobe.

'Don't be silly.'

He turned to see Lizzie standing naked by the bed.

They had two days to spend in Perth before the ship sailed. Matt phoned Peter at the Department, and invited him and Jenny to dine with them at the hotel that night. He then rang the rooms of Mr James Price, and arranged to meet him that afternoon, whilst Lizzie did some shopping and had her hair done.

That evening they sat in the cocktail bar, sipping their drinks as Matt told Peter about his meeting with Mr Price. It had gone well, and Matt was to start with him as soon as he returned form overseas. Lizzie and Jenny hit it off immediately, and were chatting together. The evening went well, and they parted, with Peter and Jenny promising to see them off on the ship.

Next morning Matt rang Dave Barlow and told him about the meting with the old surgeon, and in turn was told that Mr Price's position on the Honorary Staff would be vacant about the time they returned, and that Matt could take up the appointment immediately.

The final task was to find a place to live when they got back. They visited a prominent real estate agent and discussed the situation. He advised renting a fully furnished home in the short term whilst they looked around for something to buy, and assured them that he would have something suitable for them on their return.

At ten o'clock on Saturday morning, Matt and Lizzie stepped on board the SS *Oriana*, P&O's beautiful new 42,000 ton liner. A steward accompanied them to their cabin, and opened the door. They were greeted by vases of flowers and a champagne bottle in an ice bucket!

'With Compliments of the Company,' the steward said with a smile. 'My name is Andrew, and I will be your steward for the voyage. If you need anything before we sail, please call me.' He indicated a bell button on the wall, then retired, closing the door.

It was a beautiful deck cabin on the starboard side, and through the window they could see the sparkling ocean beyond the busy harbour.

Lizzie fell into his arms. 'Darling, its like a fairy tale come true,' she said, and they embraced passionately.

The jangle of the telephone interrupted them. It was Peter. 'All settled on board are you?' he asked. 'We thought we'd come down now to say goodbye as the ship sails at one o'clock.'

'Wow! This is some cabin!' Jenny said, as Matt ushered them in and showed them their home for the next twenty eight-days.

The door buzzer sounded, and Andrew entered with two extra glasses and a tray of canapés. 'Visitors must leave the ship at twelve forty-five,' he said quietly to Matt who nodded and thanked him.

They sat chatting with glasses of champagne, until ultimately a blast on the ship's horn interrupted, and a voice on the public address called 'All visitors ashore please! The ship is about to sail.'

Matt and Lizzie stood on the deck as streamers were thrown, and a brass band played on the dock. Peter and Jenny waved as the ropes were cast off, and the streamers gradually broke and drifted into the water as the ship edged away from the wharf, then slowly made its way towards the mouth of the harbour.

As they gained speed and sailed through Gage Roads past Rottnest

Island, Matt told Lizzie how he had stood on the bridge of the *Griffin* and surveyed the same scene long ago, in another life.

They stood arm in arm, watching as the coast of Western Australia gradually disappeared beyond the horizon, and then walked slowly to their cabin.